AN ODIOUS LITTLE MAN

by

Richard Ayres

Published by New Generation Publishing in 2019

Copyright © Richard Ayres 2019

First Edition

The author asserts the moral right under the Copyright, Designs and Patents Act 1988 to be identified as the author of this work.

All Rights reserved. No part of this publication may be reproduced, stored in a retrieval system or transmitted, in any form or by any means without the prior consent of the author, nor be otherwise circulated in any form of binding or cover other than that which it is published and without a similar condition being imposed on the subsequent purchaser.

www.newgeneration-publishing.com
New Generation Publishing

Acknowledgements

The author would like to thank Westlands Writers and Catherine MacDonald for their advice and constructive criticism made during the writing of this novel.

Chapter 1

Charles had been outside the building for fifteen minutes, pacing impatiently back and forth. There were many others standing there, but most seemed resigned to having to wait for taxis or lifts. When Charles's taxi finally arrived, the driver was Asian, of course: all cab-drivers were these days. He clambered into the back seat.

'Where you want to go, sir?'

'You must know that, for God's sake. I told your operator when I phoned to make the booking.'

'Always advisable to check, sir. Sometimes we are told wrong.'

'It's 58 Stannet Crescent. In Littleton Parva.'

The cab set off. Charles sank back in the seat and prepared himself for the onset of – what? Fear? Panic? Depression? They'd all been hovering, ready to assail him while waiting for the taxi, but they'd been held at bay by irritation and a desire to get home quickly. Now, with nothing to occupy him apart from the passing scenery, all too familiar to him from numerous previous journeys on the same route, he waited for the onslaught to begin.

But it didn't. He felt, not calm exactly, but resigned. And something more than that: what was it? It couldn't be relief, surely? But it was: relief, albeit tinged with anger. It was how he'd felt twenty years ago when Celia had told him she was leaving him. The marriage had been failing for years - her fault of course - and he'd dreaded the day when she might say she was ending it. But when she finally did, he found relief, and release.

It mirrored the situation in which he now found himself. The past year had been one of growing apprehension, punctuated by revelations which served only to heighten his angst. But today he'd been told the news he'd been anticipating, and it was almost welcome. He was reminded of stories he'd heard: how condemned men hurried to the gallows, desperate to put an end to weeks of fear.

'Very nice out here, sir.'

'Eh?'

'Very nice big houses out here.'

Charles managed to suppress the annoyance he usually felt when cabbies thought they were entitled to chat to their customers.

'Yes. It's very pleasant.'

'You live here long, sir?'

'Over thirty years. It's the next turning on the left.'

The taxi drew up.

'That £7.80, sir.'

Charles had only a £10 note. 'Make it £8,' he said as he handed it over.

'Thank you, sir.'

Was this said with a trace of sarcasm? Charles didn't care. He pocketed the two proffered pound coins and climbed out, aware that he'd broken one of his long-held principles: never to tip people for simply doing a job for which they were paid.

Keith Barker, his next-door neighbour, was clipping his hedge as Charles walked towards his front gate. Charles nodded to him and received a nod in return. The Barkers had been Charles's neighbours in the village for nearly thirty years, and for most of that time they went out of their way to avoid him. If they ran into him, they rarely spoke. *Damn them*, Charles thought. He had been to the Barkers' for dinner, just once, back when their kids were of primary school age. Bloody hell, their children must be in their mid-thirties now, with children of their own. Charles and Celia never had kids. It had been his decision that they should not. But now, at his time of life, and given the situation in which he now found himself, he realised it might be useful to have grown-up children.

He let himself in through the front door. From the hall he could hear Radio 4 in the kitchen. He always left the radio on when he went out so he wouldn't be faced on his return with the funereal hush of an empty house. Even worse was the sight of the house looking exactly as he'd left it. It would be comforting to see someone else's unwashed coffee cup on the draining board, a lipstick-covered cigarette-end in an ashtray in the lounge, maybe some discarded women's clothes in the bedroom. But any unwashed cup would be his, he knew no women who smoked, and it would just be his neatly folded pyjamas on the bed.

He'd have a coffee and think about where to go from here. And yes – a cigarette. He'd given up the habit years ago, but had started again six months back when bleakness had begun to descend on him. He tried to restrict himself to five a day, but now – what the hell? He'd have a cigarette whenever he felt like it.

He made a cup of instant coffee and was about to carry it into the lounge when he heard the front door opening and 'Mr Pettifer? Are yer in? It's me, Mrs Williams!' being shouted from the front porch. It was Tuesday: his cleaner's weekly visit.

'In the kitchen!'

She waddled in, encumbered by a bucket, a mop and a bag of assorted cleaning materials. She was in her late forties, he guessed, overweight but with the faint remnants of a former prettiness lurking in her bloated features. She'd been cleaning for him since Celia had left, and he'd continued to employ her even though he didn't care for her over-familiarity and her tendency to try and mother him, despite being years his junior. But recently, to his surprise, he realised he'd begun to find it comforting.

'How yer keeping, dear? Feeling a bit better, are yer?' He was always irritated by her Brummie accent. Many people of her class from the south of the county spoke that way.

'I'm not so bad, Mrs Williams. Will you be having a cup of coffee before you start?'

'No, dear, I'll get on, have it later.'

'Okay. I'll get out of your way, take my coffee out

on the patio.'

'You do that, dear. Yer can have a crafty fag out there, can't yer?'

As Charles picked up his coffee cup and cigarettes, he was struck by the thought that when he was Chief Planning Officer in Staffridgeshire he would never have tolerated such impudence from the lower orders in his department.

Despite it being October, it was hot out on the patio. The sun blazed from a deep azure sky, and the floating wisps of cirrus clouds gave only occasional relief. Charles was still wearing a collar and tie. He whipped off the tie and undid the collar, but that had little effect; his shirt was too tight and his trousers too thick. He thought of the outfit that Keith had been wearing while clipping his hedge - tee-shirt and jeans. Charles had never worn such items even as a young man, and he had no intention of starting now. If only old men realised how ridiculous they looked dressed in jeans! They all seemed to do it now. Charles had his standards, and he was determined not to let them slip.

He'd almost finished his coffee and had just lit a second cigarette. He'd tried reading the *Telegraph*, but the sun was too dazzling, and he couldn't be bothered to lug the heavy patio chair into the shade. He'd assumed that sitting here he'd start mulling over his 'new situation' – that was what he'd christened it, it was comfortingly anodyne – but instead, prompted by the lawn that needed cutting, he began to consider his garden. Why? He'd not given it a thought for God knows how many years.

The garden had been Celia's hobby. She'd planned it all and had spent much of her spare time working in it. Charles's contribution had been just to mow the lawn, trim the hedges and prune the trees. He'd resented the time it took up and hadn't touched it since Celia's departure, apart from occasional excursions with the lawnmower. The beds were covered in weeds, and the numerous pots and tubs, still with soil in them, were also weed infested. Those pots had been Celia's obsession. She'd planted them with annuals every spring and tended them as though they were her children. They hadn't interested him; he'd had more important things to occupy his mind: his job was very demanding. That's why he'd insisted that Celia give up her teaching career, so she could devote time to running the home.

Looking at the neglected tubs, a vision from the past startled him. It was Celia, a young Celia, bending over them. Why was this vision so vivid? He hadn't thought of Celia in that way for years. But he'd noticed recently that the events, sights and sounds of the past had begun to seem more immediate, more vibrant, than anything that occurred in the present.

He was still too hot. He'd have to change into a short-sleeved shirt and lighter trousers. He got up and carried his empty cup into the house. In the kitchen, pop music was on the radio and Mrs Williams was filling the kettle. She put down the kettle and hurried over to turn the radio off.

'Oh, 'ello, dear. I was just making meself a coffee. D'yer fancy a refill?'

'Why not? Thanks, Mrs Williams. I'm just going upstairs to change into something cooler.'

While he was upstairs, he was struck with an idea. A very strange idea, something he'd never considered before. All his professional life he'd made a point of avoiding prolonged contact with the working classes. He was not easy with them, and he supposed they felt the same way about him. But now, such was his new situation that he realised he needed the company of anyone, whatever his or her social background. Yes: he'd do it.

When he returned to the kitchen, Mrs Williams was pouring hot water into the coffee cups.

'Why don't you come and join me in the garden to have your break?' he said. 'It's too nice outside to be cooped up in here.'

She gave him a sideways glance. During their usual

brief exchanges they rarely made eye contact.

'Yer sure about that, Mr Pettifer? Only, the company says we mustn't take breaks with them what we clean for. Yer won't tell 'em, will yer?'

'Of course not! Come on, let's go outside.'

Chapter 2

Once on the patio, seated opposite each other, the first sips of coffee taken and cigarettes lit, there was silence. Mrs Williams seemed uneasy. She didn't look at him, just stared at the garden. Charles was equally discomforted; what could they talk about? They had nothing in common, not that he knew anything of her life or her interests. He didn't even know if she was married. Best to talk about her work.

'So, Mrs Williams, how many clients do you have?'

For the first time, she looked at him. 'What d'yer mean, clients?'

'Sorry. I mean, how many people do you clean for?'

'About twenty.'

'Are they all local? I mean, do they all live round here?'

'Some of 'em do.'

'Do you enjoy your work?'

'It's all right. Need the money, don't I?'

This was proving to be hard work. Charles began to wonder if his attempt to connect was such a good idea.

'How long have you been cleaning for people?'

'Over twenty years.'

'Do you get on with most of your cli … most of those you work for?'

'Most of 'em. Some of 'em are a bit snooty.'

'Oh, really?'

'It's mainly the women. Some of the men are all right.'

'Well, I'm glad to hear that. These days, according to the media, all males are beasts.'

She took a swig of coffee, lit another cigarette, rested her elbows on the cast-iron table and looked him full in the face, grinning at him.

'I could tell yer some tales about the men I've cleaned for.'

'Could you?' Charles wasn't sure he wished to hear what she might be about to say.

'Course, it don't happen now, not since I got old and fat. But when I started ... well, yer won't believe this, Mr Pettifer, but I was quite a looker. Had a good figure too. And some of the men, even the married ones, fancied their chances.'

'Oh, really? That's – '

'Never forget the first time, me. I were standing at his kitchen sink and this bloke came up behind me and grabbed me ... well, me tits. Then he turned me round and tried to snog me. He were an old man, dirty old bugger.'

'So what did you – '

'There were another time when it were a young 'un – he were the son of the woman I were cleaning for, toffee-nosed bitch, she were. He were a good looking young fella. He put his hand up me skirt. Don't mind tellin' you, Mr Pettifer, if I 'adn't been at work, I mighta let him have his way with me.'

Charles was unsure of an appropriate response to that. But it wasn't necessary because Mrs Williams was now in full flow. She became animated as she told her stories, and Charles found himself observing her closely. Her face, now enhanced by a permanent grin, took on the features of a younger woman. She waved her arms about as she spoke, and her large breasts bounced impressively. Charles wondered what she looked like when she was off duty and dressed up to go out. Then, for the first time, he noticed she wore a wedding ring. She was usually wearing rubber gloves.

He interrupted her. 'What does your husband do for a living, Mrs Williams?'

'Bert? He don't work. Had to retire years ago, didn't 'e? Bad back. No good for working on a building site.'

'Oh, I'm sorry to hear that. So are you the sole

breadwinner?'

'Bert does odd jobs on the side. We get by. The kids help us out sometimes. Our Kevin's an electrician, got his own business.'

'That's good. Tell me, what do you do in your spare time? Do you have any hobbies?'

She laughed. 'Hobbies? Boozin', mainly. Bert still sees his old mates and we go down the pub a lot. They all bring their wives. We have a right old laugh.'

'That's good.'

'Yeah. It's a great boozer, the *Flying Horse*. Yer ought to come down sometime. Some nights it's a pub quiz, sometimes it's bingo. We've made a lotta new friends. And quite often they have a rock band – they play all the old stuff. Don't like this modern stuff, me. D'yer like rock music, Mr Pettifer?'

'I'm afraid I haven't listened to it since I was a teenager.'

'What d'yer do in your spare time, Mr Pettifer? Got a lot o' friends round here, have yer?'

Charles baulked at the prospect of telling her that he had no friends. He just said that he enjoyed reading, listening to classical music, and watching TV documentaries.

She stared at him appraisingly. 'If you don't mind me sayin', dear, I think yer ought to try and get out a bit more.'

Should he tell her that he *did* go out: to the theatre, to concerts, to events in the library, to public lectures at the university? No. If she understood at all, she'd think he was trying to impress her with his lifestyle. That wasn't his intention, of course, but the class divide had opened up again.

They sat for a few minutes in silence; then she suddenly jumped to her feet.

'Oh Lord, I've been sat here for ages! The van'll be coming to collect me soon, and I ain't even started on yer upstairs!'

'Oh, don't worry about that, Mrs Williams. It'll keep till next week.'

'Yer sure about that, dear?

'Yes, absolutely.'

'I'll get on then. Reckon I've just got time to do yer bathroom.'

'If you insist, Mrs Williams, but there's no need to hurry. I've enjoyed our chat.'

'So've I, dear. And don't keep calling me Mrs Williams. We've known each other for ages. Me name's Annie. You're Charles, aren't yer? I'll call yer Charlie, if yer don't mind.'

She didn't wait for him to reply, but touched him briefly on the shoulder before walking into the house.

He was stunned by her touch. How many years had it been since he'd received a touch like that? The only physical contact he'd had recently was with nurses and doctors, all done in the course of duty during medical investigations. But from Mrs Williams – no, Annie, he supposed he must now think of her – it spoke of affection. Could that really be the case? What did she mean by it?

Probably nothing. He'd noticed the working classes were excessively tactile, even in public. It was all part of the maudlin sentimentality that now seemed to be a feature of their culture. He often had to turn off the TV news when bereaved parents were interviewed following some random stabbing or shooting – oh, he was our little angel! He was such a nice lad! Never had a bad word to say about anyone! – all these statements accompanied by sobs and tears over which the camera lingered. What tosh. What was their little angel, probably a member of a gang of hoodlums, doing out on the streets at midnight? Charles longed to hear a news report where the departed was referred to as a right little bastard who deserved everything he'd got.

'I'm off now, Charlie! See yer next week, dear!' came from the kitchen door.

'Oh, right. Goodbye!'

He couldn't bring himself to call her Annie. And he didn't really want to be called Charlie; nobody had called him that since his schooldays. At university, he referred to himself as Chas and continued to do so during his early years at work. But as he climbed the career ladder the name Charles seemed much more appropriate for someone in a responsible position, and woe betide any of his colleagues who tried to use a diminutive.

As he sat, another cigarette in hand, he became aware of the silence that had followed Mrs Williams's departure. He realised he'd enjoyed listening to her, the sort of half-ashamed enjoyment experienced when one stumbled on inane comedies on television. But more than that, he'd found himself envying the active social life she evidently had – not the boozing in a down-market pub, of course, but the fact that she and her husband enjoyed the company of Bert's former colleagues; no, 'workmates'. Charles had never socialised with his colleagues except at the annual Christmas office parties, and after his enforced early retirement eighteen years ago, he'd had no wish to see them again.

A wave of tiredness swept over him. The morning had been stressful, and then Mrs Williams's company hadn't been exactly relaxing. He decided to go to bed, have a nap. It was something he'd started doing quite frequently.

Once on the bed, he found he couldn't relax. It wasn't just the news he'd received that morning, but an awareness that he needed to do something to occupy himself before the time came when he'd be unable to do anything without assistance. At all costs he must beware of slipping into the situation where all he'd have to think about would be his past.

Mrs Williams's account of her active socialising continued to niggle at him. He'd had a social life, of sorts, for the first few years after he and Celia had moved here. Celia got to know a few other women in the locality who attended her fitness club, and invitations to dinner soon followed, to which he was of course invited. He'd felt uncomfortable at those soirees. All the other husbands there knew each other, and he'd found it hard to participate in the sort of meaningless chit-chat that they engaged in. It had soon got to the stage when he started to make excuses for not attending.

Then, when Celia left, he no longer had to give excuses because the invitations ceased. He didn't mind. He'd had his work to occupy him, and had all the social contact he needed at the local Rotary Club lunches, many of whose members he knew in a professional capacity, and there was also the opportunity to take local County Councillors to one side and discuss matters of mutual interest. He'd had some very useful conversations with Councillor Dobson, Chairman of the Planning Committee. They'd almost become friends.

But then he had to retire. Dobson had told him in no uncertain terms that it would be best for both of them if he ceased to attend the lunch meetings, in fact, any Rotary function. He had no alternative but to comply.

He'd managed to cope with solitude. But now, for the first time in his adult life, he was frightened. He needed contact with people, people with whom he had common interests. But who? He called to mind all those with whom he'd worked with in the planning office. They'd been his subordinates, of course, and most treated him with due deference. Which of them would he want to see? The Area Officers, perhaps? But three of them had been older than him, perhaps now dead, or if not, decrepit and possibly senile. There was one who'd been much younger, that bloody Beasley woman. The bitch. He wouldn't mind seeing her again, just to tell her what he thought of her.

But there was one, Gordon Tagg, who'd been the Traffic Management Officer, with whom he'd got on quite well, mainly because he was a fellow southerner. Yes, Gordon Tagg! Why not?

Energised, he climbed out of bed, and entered his

study. He was certain he still had Tagg's phone number. He'd phone him, suggest a get- together. Yes, his number was still on his list of contacts.

Why wait? He picked up his phone and tapped in Tagg's number.

Chapter 3

Since he'd retired, Keith spent a lot of time in his garden. He found it comforting, because gardening was done with the future in mind: in autumn and winter one laboured with thoughts of the following spring and summer, and one could forget the prospect of the ever-narrowing horizons that would come with old age. It also reminded him of his childhood when he'd helped his dad on the allotment.

He was in his garden now, and had been for much of the morning. He'd removed the summer growth from the astilbes, strimmed the heather, cut back the dead wood from the escallonia and forsythia, and removed the seed heads from the rhododendrons. He had yet to dig over the vegetable bed, but he'd leave that until the first frosts came. He'd given the lawn a final trim with the mower-blades set high to inhibit the growth of moss.

He had only one task left today, clearing up the few leaves that had fallen on the lawn. It had been a wet spring and a warm summer, and most trees were still in full leaf. Debbie always asked him why he didn't wait until they'd all blown down, but he knew that to leave them to accumulate and start to rot wouldn't be good for the grass.

He collected the leaf-blower from the shed and set about blowing the leaves off the lawn and into piles on the side beds, there to be hoovered up. As he did so, a familiar wave of annoyance swept over him because most of the leaves weren't his; they were from the overgrown trees and shrubs in the bloody garden next door. He knew that as late autumn drew on, *all* the leaves on his lawn would come from Pettifer's side. Pettifer's garden was a jungle. It hadn't been like that when his wife had lived there; indeed, she'd seemed to spend most of her time outside, probably trying to keep out of the bastard's way.

Keith had done all he could today: time for a coffee. He put the leaf-blower in the shed, took off his boots in the side passage and entered the kitchen. Debbie was standing over the cooker, preparing something for the evening meal.

'Fancy a coffee, Debs? I'm having one.'

'Yes, please. Finished for the day, have you?'

'Yes. All that's left now is clearing up leaves every week. And you know where most of those come from.'

'Yes. You keep telling me.'

'Y'know, Debs,' he said as he filled the kettle, 'I'm thinking I might go round and tell bloody Pettifer to do something about it. He could afford to get someone in to prune the trees, couldn't he?'

'He'd probably shut the door in your face. You've hardly spoken to him since that evening we had with him and Celia just after they moved here.'

'Fuckin' hell, Debs, that was over 30 years ago.'

'Well, I've never forgotten it. And I do wish you'd stop swearing.'

***

Keith and Debbie had been living in Stannet Crescent for five years when the Pettifers moved in next door. Debbie saw them the day the removal van arrived with their furniture. As she watched her new neighbours directing the removal men, she noticed that the male was very short; in fact, the female, presumably his wife, was about four inches taller, and she was wearing flat heels. She told Keith about what she'd seen, but he didn't seem very interested.

She gave them a few days to settle in, then decided to go round and make herself known. She walked up their drive and rang on the doorbell. The door opened, but only a fraction. It was the woman.

'Good morning! I hope I'm not disturbing you, but I thought I'd come and introduce myself. I'm your next-door neighbour, Debbie Barker. Welcome to Stannet Crescent!'

The door opened a little further, and Debbie's first impression was of a thin, plain woman wearing a pinafore over a dress that hung down to mid-calf. She looked at Debbie briefly, didn't speak, but turned and called up the stairs, 'Charles! It's our next-door neighbour!'

There was the sound of feet clattering down the stairs and 'Well, don't keep her standing on the doorstep, Celia,' was said by the short, sandy-haired man as he reached the hallway. He turned to Debbie.

'Well, hello! Come in! I'm Charles Pettifer. Lovely to meet you! Oh, this is Celia. Whom do I have the pleasure of addressing?'

Debbie was struck by his high-pitched voice. She introduced herself, and Pettifer grabbed her hand to shake it. He kept hold of her hand for slightly longer than was necessary, then stepped back and looked at her. He stared at her for some time, his gaze traversing her whole body. Debbie wasn't sure if she was discomforted or flattered.

'Would you care for a coffee? Celia was just about to make one, weren't you, Celia?'

Celia didn't reply, but turned and walked away, presumably towards her kitchen. She had yet to speak. Debbie wondered if perhaps she didn't welcome her visit.

'Oh, thanks very much, but I'm afraid I don't have time. I only called to introduce myself.'

'Oh, that's a pity. It's so nice to know we have such a friendly neighbour. It would be such a pleasure to get to know you better. I'm sure we'd have a lot to talk about.' He said this while gazing into her eyes, and he touched her hand briefly.

Well, there was no doubt that he was charming, Debbie thought, but charm could be deceptive, self-serving. She wondered what he was like when he turned it off.

'I'd like very much to invite you round for a meal,' he said, 'but it'll be a while before our kitchen's sorted out.'

Debbie thought for a moment. *Yes, why not? It*

would be good to have some visitors. 'Well, why don't you come round to us? How about Saturday? Say about seven?'

'That would be delightful! I'll look forward to that very much!'

'Good. Right, I must be off now.'

He escorted her to the front door and didn't close it after she turned to go. As she walked down the drive, she had the uncanny feeling he was staring at her backside.

Back in her house, she wondered what Keith's reaction might be to the invitation she'd made. Pettifer had sounded upper-class and that wouldn't endear him to Keith. But she was intrigued by him. Despite his being small and over-effusive, there was something beguiling about him. And he'd made it obvious that he found her attractive. It was a long time since she'd received the sort of looks and body language that he'd offered; she'd rather let herself go since raising the kids and being at home, and no longer dressed to display her assets.

Saturday evening. Keith was in the dining room laying the table; Sam and Paul were in their bedroom. Debbie was in the kitchen adding final touches to the meal. She was unused to preparing meals for visitors. They rarely entertained; Keith spent most evenings marking or doing lesson preparation and didn't welcome guests.

The doorbell rang.

'That'll be them, Keith! Can you let them in?'

She heard the front door being opened, and then immediately a loud, high pitched voice. 'Hello! You must be the man of the house! Pleased to meet you! I'm Charles Pettifer.'

Keith's reply was almost inaudible. From Celia, Debbie heard not a word. She hurriedly rinsed and dried her hands and went into the hall.

'Debbie! How wonderful to see you again! My, you look stunning!' He placed his hands on her shoulders, pulled her towards him and kissed her on both cheeks as though they were long-parted old friends. His aftershave reeked of expense. Debbie dared not look at Keith. She said, 'Keith, this is Celia.'

Keith shook Celia's hand. She said nothing.

Debbie noticed that Celia had put on make-up, but not with any great expertise; her lipstick was too red and served only to emphasise her pallid features. Her hair was scraped back into a French pleat from which wisps were escaping. She was wearing a cardigan which had seen better days and an ill-fitting loose skirt with an uneven hem.

'Come into the lounge,' she said. 'We've got time for a drink before the meal.'

Once settled in the lounge, Keith asked Pettifer whether they'd prefer red or white wine.

'I'd prefer a scotch, if you've got it. Celia will have tonic water. Well now, Keith, what's your job?'

Keith said he taught at the local comprehensive school.

'Teacher, eh? Not a bad number, all those long holidays, though I imagine it can be a bit tough having to deal with all those thickoes you get in comprehensives. If you ask me, it was a bad day when we got rid of grammar schools. This country needs a meritocracy.'

Keith began an outraged response, but Debbie interrupted him and hurriedly asked Pettifer what he did for a living.

'I'm Deputy Chief Planning Officer in the county; been here for a while before we bought next door. I don't reckon I'll be deputy for long, though. The chief is totally incompetent, a bit of a wanker in fact. I reckon I'll be asked to step into his shoes before too long.'

Debbie hoped he wouldn't use that sort of language in front of the boys - she'd told them to come and introduce themselves once the guests were in the lounge. As if on cue, the door opened, and they entered.

'Ah, this is Sam and David. Boys, say hello to Mr and Mrs Pettifer.'

Shyly, the boys obliged and received a 'Hello, you two' from Pettifer, who then ignored them and started telling Keith more about his career prospects. But Debbie had noticed Celia's eyes light up when the boys came in, and she was smiling at them. Then, for the first time that evening, she spoke.

'Hello David, hello Sam. How old are you?'

'I'm eight, and Sam's six,' said David.

'Oh. Do you go to the same school?'

'Yes. I'm in Year 4 and Sam's in Year 2.'

'And do you like school?'

'Yes. It's nice.'

'Oh, that's good. I used to teach boys of your age. I really enjoyed it. What I liked most was –'

'Oh, come on, Celia, they won't be interested in all that. Any chance of a refill, Keith?'

'Well, dinner will be ready now,' said Debbie, 'so if you'd like to follow Keith into the dining room? Boys, you can go back upstairs now; start getting ready for bed.'

Dinner was not a success. It wasn't four people all participating in a lively group conversation; Pettifer addressed his remarks exclusively to Debbie, while Keith tried to draw Celia out by asking her questions about her time as a schoolteacher, to which she gave mostly monosyllabic replies.

Pettifer complimented Debbie on the food and on her dress, asked her about her interests, quizzed her about her upbringing, all the while smiling at her and maintaining continuous eye contact. Debbie was suddenly aware that for the first time since she was a younger woman, she was being 'chatted up' – there were no other words for it. Not only that, she was beginning to respond in kind. *Good heavens we're flirting!* How could it be that such a disagreeable man was able to make her do this? She wished now that she wasn't wearing the rather revealing dress that she'd chosen: she hadn't worn it for years, but it still fitted her well.

At last the meal came to an end.

'I'll just clear the table,' she said, 'and make some coffee.'

'Here, let me give you a hand,' said Pettifer. 'I'll bring some of the plates and things out to you in the kitchen.'

It would have been impolite to refuse his offer. She picked up two plates, carried them to the kitchen, and placed them on the work-surface beside the dishwasher. She was standing facing it, wondering how long her guests would stay, when Pettifer entered, put his plates on the work-surface and stood beside her.

He put his arm round her waist and whispered, 'You are a lovely lady!'

She froze. His hand began caressing her back, then it moved to her front, then almost up her breast. 'I'd like to see more of you. A lot more.'

For just how long was it that she felt excited, turned on? A few seconds, was it, before she came to her senses? She jumped away from him.

'I don't think I need any more help, Charles. Go back to the dining room while I make the coffee. And after you've drunk it, I think it might be a good idea if you and Celia left.'

He grinned at her. 'Playing hard to get, are we? Well, I welcome a challenge. Till the next time, Debbie!'

Debbie never told Keith what had happened in the kitchen. She didn't need to: Keith had been outraged by the remarks that Pettifer had made about comprehensive schools, by his arrogance, and by the way he'd treated Celia. 'I don't want anything more to do with the man,' he'd said, 'and I assume you don't either.' Debbie had concurred, with perhaps slightly more enthusiasm than she'd felt.

She did, however, manage to speak a few words to Celia on the rare occasions when she left the house, always when Pettifer was at work. It was always just an exchange of pleasantries, nothing of any significance was ever discussed. Sometimes, when they were both in their gardens, 'hellos' were shouted over the hedge.

But some years later, the front doorbell rang, and when Debbie opened the door she was taken aback to find Celia standing there. She was wringing her hands together and looked as if she'd been crying.

'Celia! Are you all right? Would you like to come in?'

'No, I mustn't. I've come to say goodbye.'

'Goodbye? What do you mean?'

'I'm going to live with my sister in Leamington.'

'You mean …?'

'Yes. I'm leaving Charles.'

'Oh, Celia, I'm sorry … I mean I'm sorry I won't be seeing you anymore.'

'So am I. I would have loved to have got to know you better, but Charles … well, you see, our marriage has been failing for years. I can't take any more.'

Debbie resisted the temptation to say that she was surprised that Celia had put up with him for this long.

'Well, I hope things get better for you in Leamington. Is your sister married?'

'Oh, yes. She's got two children. I love having children around. Look, I've got to go. Charles might be home soon.'

'Well, goodbye then, Celia. I hope you'll be happy with your sister.'

'Just one thing, Debbie. I know Charles can seem … well, difficult. But please don't judge him too harshly. He's got problems. He needs help, but he won't do anything about it, he just loses his temper when I suggest it.'

'Oh, I'm sorry to hear that. A psychological problem, is it?'

'Sorry, I must go now.'

She almost ran down the garden path.

When Debbie had told Keith about this, he said that

Pettifer had it coming. 'Celia's probably got wind of the fact that that bastard's got a bit on the side.'

'Bit on the side, what d'you mean?'

'Oh, come on, I told you about it. That young woman who visits him occasionally when Celia's out. Remember, I caught her leaving once. She was carrying a briefcase, and when I said "Good morning," she said, quite unnecessarily, that she was Mr Pettifer's personal assistant.'

'Yes, and I told you there was no reason why that shouldn't be true.'

'Personal assistant!! Well, even if she is, I bet he's shagging her.'

'I do wish you wouldn't use that sort of language, Keith. You never used to.'

Chapter 4

'Aazat!' yelled Jamie.

'No way!' Tommy protested. 'It was way outside the off stump, wasn't it, Gramps?'

'It was a bit too close to call, fellas.' Gordon painfully pulled himself upright behind the makeshift stumps. 'And I'm afraid this poor old bugger needs a rest. My back's killing me. In any case, your mum and Gran will be home soon. I'd better go in and clear up the mess in the kitchen. You two carry on, do a bit of fielding practice.'

'No, like, we'll come in too. Let's finish the Superman Quest, Jamie.'

Gordon was about to say they shouldn't spend a lovely afternoon like this playing computer games but stopped himself in time. He had to be careful what he said; it wouldn't do to let them think their grandfather was just another boring old fart. He'd deliberately used the phrase 'poor old bugger' to show he was with it, but they probably heard much worse language at school. He'd overheard teenagers outside the local school gate, and their conversation, if such it could be called, was laced with profanities.

He pulled out the stumps and slowly made his way into the kitchen. He really must try to lose some weight, but Margaret produced dishes that were hard to resist. He'd thought about going to a gym, but he baulked at the thought of exposing his flabby 71-year-old body to the no doubt well-honed muscular young hunks who frequented those places.

He cleared the kitchen table of the remains of lunch, put the greasy plates in the dishwasher and put the cutlery in the bowl by the sink and turned on the tap. While he was waiting for the hot water to come through, he stared out at the garden.

You couldn't really call it a garden, despite its size;

just an expanse of scruffy grass. It had started out like that when Paul and Hilary, their twins, played in it, and it hadn't really recovered when Paul married early and produced children of his own who delighted in being given free rein to make as much mess as they liked, something they weren't allowed to do in their parents' garden. No sooner had they grown up than Hilary belatedly married – Gordon and Margaret had thought she was on the shelf – and produced Jamie and Tommy, who carried on the family tradition of botanical desecration

He mused over the sequence of children and young adolescents who, over the years, had been frequent visitors to his house, sometimes, as Jamie and Tommy had just done, stopping over for the night, and in whose company he delighted. He liked young people. They were open and tolerant towards old fogeys like him, far more so than his generation had been towards their parents and grandparents. He remembered his own youth, how he'd secretly rejoiced in Bob Dylan's *The Times They Are a' Changing*: how did it go? *Come mothers and fathers throughout the land, and don't criticise what you don't understand. Your old world is rapidly aging.* In many ways, he thought, his had been an arrogant generation. Jamie and Tommy often listened, without complaint, when he played them his old Beatles and Rolling Stones records.

Steam rose from the sink. Gordon let it fill the bowl and immersed the cutlery in it. Margaret couldn't understand why he didn't put these items in the dishwasher, but he didn't want to admit to her that the process of bending for the protracted period required to insert each knife, fork and spoon into the slots in the plastic container was excruciating. He was careful not to complain to Margaret about his back problem: there was nothing worse than a moaning husband, he'd once overheard a neighbour saying to her.

'Gordy, we're back!' was shouted from the hall. He'd been so immersed in his thoughts that he hadn't registered the front door being opened.

'I'm in the kitchen, love.'

Margaret entered, put down her shopping bags, and came over to him. They exchanged pecks on the cheek, for them an automatic 'hello' and 'goodbye' greeting, however brief their parting. Few of their married friends did that. Gordon still held Margaret's hand when they were out walking.

'Hi, Dad!' Hilary entered. She came over and kissed him. 'How's your back?'

'Mustn't grumble. You both had a good day?'

'Oh yes. I've bought a little black number for Giles's office do. Mum's bought some new cushion covers for your settee. We had lunch in Panaro's – it's getting quite trendy.'

'Fancy a coffee or tea before you go?

'Can't, I'm afraid, Dad. Got things to do before Giles gets home. Hope the boys behaved themselves. Where are they?'

'In the lounge.'

'Don't tell me – they're playing games on their laptops. Jamie! Tommy! We're leaving now. Come and say goodbye to Granny and Gramps.'

The next few minutes were taken up by hugs and kisses all round. Such demonstrations of affection extended across the three generations.

'Oh, look. There's a message on the answering machine,' said Margaret as they came into the hall after waving goodbye to the car. 'I bet you heard the phone ring and chose not answer, didn't you?'

'I was outside. Nobody ever rings on the landline now except junk callers. It would have been someone – '

'Someone asking if you'd been involved in an accident, or an Indian saying your computer had been compromised. I know, Gordy.'

Forty years of co-habitation had resulted in their often finishing each other's sentences, but Gordon never found it irritating.

Margaret picked up the phone and clicked the 'hear message' button. A distorted voice came through the speaker.

Hello Gordon! It's Charles here, Charles Pettifer.

Margaret and Gordon stared at each other, mouths agape.

Long time no see! Look, I wondered if you'd care for a get-together sometime. Catch up on old times. And if you're in contact with any of our old colleagues, why not ask them along as well? Give me a bell and let me know what you think. Cheers!

'I don't believe it!' said Margaret. 'The nerve of the man! Why on earth should he think you'd want to see him again!'

'I often wonder why I've never run into him in town,' said Gordon. 'As far as I know he still lives in Littleton Parva.'

'He's lying low, if he knows what's good for him. Horrible little man!'

Margaret had met Charles Pettifer only once, when Gordon had persuaded her to attend the planning department's Christmas get-together. She never went again. No doubt Pettifer's intention had been to be the life and soul of the party, but his domineering manner and his risqué jokes had come across to her as mere attention-seeking. As the evening wore on, he'd spent most of his time chatting to the junior female staff, some of whom seemed to be flattered by his attention. For Margaret, the tipping point had been when, at the end of the evening, he'd asked her to dance. He'd held her far tighter than was necessary, and began rubbing his hand up and down, but mainly down, her back. She'd had enough, walked off, and asked Gordon to take her home, she was tired.

She hadn't told Gordon about that incident, because he'd already come to a point where he said he found Pettifer's management style intolerable. She didn't want to risk Gordon jeopardising his career chances by confronting Pettifer about his behaviour that night. But soon after that,

Pettifer had unexpectedly taken early retirement. He was no longer part of their lives, and the incident at the Christmas party was almost forgotten. Gordon was still standing by the phone, looking thoughtful, rubbing his chin.

'You're not thinking of calling him back, surely?' said Margaret.

Gordon hesitated. 'No, I doubt it,' he said eventually.

'Anyway, he didn't leave his number, did he? So you don't have to make the decision. Here, let me show you the new cushion covers I've bought. Hope you'll like them.'

They went to bed early. Margaret was tired after her shopping expedition and cooking dinner; Charles was feeling the effect of his cricket game with the boys and had been longing to lie down all evening.

He sat on the bed, eased off each slipper by pushing it with the other foot, and turned to give Margaret her a goodnight kiss, but she was already sleeping soundly. He lowered himself onto his back and maneuvered a pillow under his knees. Had he remembered to take two paracetamol? Yes, he had.

As he waited for them to take effect he began thinking, as he knew he would, about the phone message from Charles Pettifer. He was baffled: Pettifer had spoken as though they were old friends, which they certainly were not. What had prompted his call? Had something significant happened to him? And why should he also want to see other former colleagues? Surely he must have known that most of them disliked him?

Gordon still couldn't understand why Pettifer was so keen to make contact. But he was curious to know what a man like him would be like now that he was old and without power or influence.

The paracetamol was beginning to work. As he began to doze, he came to a decision: he *would* contact Pettifer; there was something he'd always wanted to ask him. He hadn't left a number, but Margaret had evidently forgotten that it would be listed on 'received messages' on the handset.

Chapter 5

Charles hadn't wanted to meet Gordon Tagg in Staffridge. It was a place he rarely visited. For essential supplies he relied on Tesco deliveries and the small shop in his village. For other purchases and for entertainment he travelled to Birmingham.

But Gordon, when he'd returned Charles's phone call, had been insistent that they meet in Staffridge, saying he had arranged to go shopping there afterwards with his wife. Charles had resisted the temptation to comment about those whose wives were allowed to wear the trousers.

He wasn't finding it easy walking to the coffee shop where they were to meet. He'd left his car in the multi-storey, and when descending from the third level, he'd had to cling to the stair rails to avoid falling forward because he was wearing shoes with built-up heels, things he hadn't worn since retiring. Even now, in the pedestrian area, he was having to walk with a pronounced stoop which made it hard to see ahead, and none of the people he encountered made way for him.

It was a Saturday morning and the town centre was crowded, not just with shoppers but with children and teenagers. Charles had been Chief Planning Officer when the streets had been pedestrianised, indeed he'd been instrumental in pushing the scheme through. But it was no longer the place he'd envisaged. The term 'pedestrianised' seemed not to apply to the bands of young cyclists demonstrating their wheelie skills, nor to those of their seniors who drove motorised mobility scooters one-handed while simultaneously speaking into their mobile phones. Had Charles been more agile, he would have chased after them and given them a lecture about their behaviour. Not that it was his job to do so: why were there no police around to enforce order?

Something else began to annoy him: the number of

people around who seemed to think it was their right to ask for money. The beggars were bad enough, those squatting outside boarded-up shops, sleeping bags beside them, caps in front of them containing coins, coins which probably, Charles thought, would be used to buy drugs.

Even worse than the beggars were those who thought they were entertaining the public, like the man who was standing by the war memorial playing an amplified guitar and singing some pop song into a microphone. As far as Charles was concerned, it was noise pollution

One incident in particular outraged him. He was approached by a young man who asked him if he'd be interested in a leaflet which gave details of Oxfam's work in Yemen. 'Who the hell to you think you are, accosting me in the street?' was Charles's response. 'If I give to good causes, it's to those of my own choice. I don't need do-gooders like you telling me what I should do. Bloody charity-muggers!'

Consequently, he was in a foul temper when he arrived at Caffé Nero. He'd decided to get there early so he'd be seated when Gordon arrived. He didn't want Gordon to see him hobbling in, and he wanted to get the measure of his former colleague before greeting him. He was hoping he'd aged considerably, lost his hair, put on weight.

Inside the coffee shop, after a long wait in a short queue – he could scarcely hide his impatience at the inefficiency of the young women behind the counter – he managed to carry his latte and chocolate brownie over to a seat by the window. He sipped his coffee – God, it was insipid; he should have asked for a double shot – and stared out into the street.

After only a few minutes, he spotted him, walking purposefully towards the café. Christ, he'd had hardly changed at all! Yes, he'd put on weight, but he carried himself erect, and he still had all his hair, albeit it was greying.

Gordon entered and looked around. His eyes passed over Charles without recognition. Charles didn't want to stand up and draw attention to the difficulty he'd have in doing so. Why hadn't the idiot recognised him? Then he realised; he'd still had hair when Gordon had last seen him.

Gordon did another sweep of the room, and when he looked towards him, Charles waved. There were a few seconds when Gordon's face looked blank, then surprised, and then a smile spread across his features. 'Charlie!' he said and walked over. He extended his hand: Charles remained seated for the handshake. He was annoyed that he'd been called 'Charlie'. Was that the way his staff had referred to him behind his back?

'Good to see you again, Gordon.'

'And you, Charlie. How are you keeping?'

'Oh, I'm fine. And you?'

'Okay, apart from the usual niggles that come with old age.'

'Well, go and get yourself a coffee. And while you're up there, get me another latte. And I want a double shot.'

As he waited to be served, Gordon was glad of the chance to collect himself. He'd been shocked by Pettifer's appearance. The bald pate made him unrecognisable. His face was deeply lined, almost wizened. How old was he – 75 maybe? Only a few years older than himself.

But even in their short exchange, it was evident that one thing about him hadn't changed. Pettifer had *ordered* him get him another latte with a double shot. It wasn't a request; there hadn't even been a 'please'. This, Gordon realised, was why he was thinking of him as Pettifer, not Charles, not that he'd ever addressed him by his first name. The look on his face when he'd called him Charlie!

He carried the coffees back and winced as he bent to place the tray on the table.

'Got a bad back, have you, Gordon? Must be an

effort, having to hold yourself upright.'

'On the contrary, it's my most comfortable position.'

'I'll believe you. Thousands wouldn't.'

As Gordon sat down, the door opened, and a young woman entered with two children. They evidently recognised some friends sitting with another woman at a table nearby and ran towards them screaming with delight. The two women exchanged loud greetings and began an effusive conversation, conducted equally loudly, while the four children ran whooping round the tables.

'What in hell's name made you choose this place?' Pettifer asked. 'It's full of riff-raff. Couldn't you think of somewhere quieter?'

'I always come here for coffee. I like it here. It has such a varied clientele: all ages, all backgrounds. And I like seeing kids enjoying themselves.'

'Huh. No accounting for tastes, I suppose. Anyway, how are you enjoying your retirement? Keeping busy, are you?'

'Oh yes. Family, of course, but Margaret and I belong to lots of clubs and societies. We've made a lot of new friends. And you?'

'Don't have a minute to call my own: concerts, theatre, lecture courses. Anyway, are any of the others coming?'

'Others?'

'Yes. Other old colleagues.'

'But I told you when I phoned you: Fred, Max and Joe all retired long before I did. We met up for a few years, but that tailed off. Haven't been in contact with them for years. For all I know, they might be dead.'

Pettifer drained his coffee and peered round the room, still crowded and noisy. 'Bloody hoi polloi,' he muttered. 'Anyway,' he continued, 'what about that Beasley woman? She was a lot younger than the rest of you. What happened to her?'

'Jeanette? Didn't you know? A few months after

you left, she got the post of Deputy Chief Planning Officer down south. Remarkably young, she was, to get such a senior post.'

Pettifer stared at him. For once he seemed lost for words. But he wasn't silent for long.

'Well, we can all guess how she managed that. When she was an area officer up here, she was in cahoots with that Labour councillor, Jarvis, wasn't it? No doubt she got him to put in a good word for her with the comrades on the interview panel down there.'

'I think you'd find, Charles, that most councils down south are solidly Tory, certainly in the shires. And Jeanette was a very professional woman. She was probably no closer to Jarvis than you were to Councillor Dobson. You seemed to spend most of your –'

'Anyway, who took over from her as Area Officer in the north of the county?'

'I did, Charles.'

'*You* did? Good God, you were a traffic engineer! That hardly qualified you to deal with matters such as development control and land-use planning.'

'In case you've forgotten, I obtained a Planning Diploma after I qualified as a traffic engineer. Now if you'll excuse me, I need to visit the gents.'

Once in the toilet, Gordon fished out his mobile and texted Margaret. *Are you in town yet? Could you come to Café Nero asap? Don't think I can take much more of Pettifer. Say you've had a phone call from Hilary who needs us to go over there immediately. Invent some family crisis. xx*

The answer came almost immediately. *I'm in the library. Give me ten minutes or so. Didn't I say you made a mistake agreeing to meet him? xx*

Gordon had a pee, then took his time washing and drying his hands. What the hell could they talk about, other than their time at work? It had been common knowledge in the office that Pettifer's wife had left him and that they'd had no children, so to ask him about his family life was a non-starter. Then he remembered there *was* something he wanted to quiz him about: indeed, it was the main reason he'd agreed to this meeting. He'd been so angered by Pettifer's attitude that it had slipped his mind.

When he returned to their table, Pettifer was staring fixedly at the queue at the counter.

'What do you reckon to that, then?' he said.

Gordon turned to look. 'What d'you mean?'

'That black woman. She came in while you were having a piss. Wait till she turns round. She's a stunner.'

At that moment, the woman did turn, gazing round to seek a vacant table. For once, Gordon had to agree with Pettifer; she was indeed beautiful, with a lithe inviting figure.

'Lucky bastard who's with her,' said Pettifer. 'Have you ever had a bit of black, Gordon? Wish I had. If they all looked like that, I might not object so much to the way they're taking over the country.'

It was all Gordon could do not to smack him round the head and walk out. Was the bastard deliberately being provocative? He gritted his teeth and then took a sip of his coffee.

'Charles,' he said, 'one thing has always intrigued me. Why did you suddenly take early retirement?'

'What do you mean by that? I'd accumulated enough pension to get out while I was young enough to enjoy it.'

'But why so suddenly? You didn't tell any of us you were going. We didn't get a chance to organise a goodbye do for you. First we heard of it was when we were called to a meeting with the Deputy Chairman who told us you'd already gone. We all wondered if – '

'Jesus Christ!' This was shrieked. People at the nearby tables turned to look at them. 'Can't a fellow decide to retire without having to tell everyone and having to put up with hypocritical goodbye speeches and all that sentimental twaddle?'

'So there was no other reason – '

'No, there bloody wasn't!' Pettifer's face was puce. 'What a load of gossiping old women you lot were!'

Interesting, thought Gordon. He seemed to have touched a raw nerve. But he couldn't push it any further. He was saved from having to open a new conversational gambit by the arrival of Margaret.

She rushed over to him. 'Oh, Gordy, sorry to interrupt' – she nodded at Pettifer – 'but we've got a bit of an emergency. Hilary has just phoned: we need to go over and see her, now.'

Gordon stood up. 'Oh, what's happened? No, tell me about it while we're on our way. Oh, Margaret, you'll remember Charles, Charles Pettifer?'

'Yes, I think so. Hello.'

'Well, I certainly remember you, Margaret. I'll never forget that staff party when – '

'Sorry, we really have got to leave now. Come on, Gordy.'

'Just one thing before you go, Gordon. About Jeanette Beasley. Which county did you say she worked for?'

'I didn't. All I know is that it was somewhere down south. Sorry, Charles, we really must be off. Interesting to meet you again.'

'Indeed. We must do it again sometime.'

'Thanks for rescuing me, Margy,' said Gordon as they hurried away. 'God, that man's more insufferable than he was as my boss.'

'Well, I only glanced at him, but I thought he looked old and ill, pathetic almost. And why did you say you didn't know where Jeanette worked?'

'Because I don't want him to try and contact her, of course.'

In fact, Gordon had phoned Jeanette Beasley frequently in the months following her departure, mainly to ask for her advice on planning matters. But though he'd probed gently, she never revealed what had passed between her and Pettifer when she'd been summoned to see him after their disagreement at the area officers' meeting. She was, as always, the consummate professional. He hadn't spoken to her for years: their only contact now was the exchange of Christmas cards.

'Margy, what did Pettifer mean when he said he'd never forgotten you after the staff party?'

'Oh, probably because he asked me to dance, remember?'

Gordon didn't pursue the matter. He was now thinking about Pettifer's reaction to his question about his early retirement. He'd always thought there was something strange about his sudden departure. There was nobody left with whom he could discuss the matter, apart from Jeanette. Thanks to their exchange of Christmas cards, he had her address.

Chapter 6

Charles, still in his pyjamas at ten o'clock, stood at his bedroom window staring at the cheerless scene in front of him. In the space of five days, the Indian Summer had been eclipsed by a premature winter - cold, and permanently gloomy with a persistent drizzle that occasionally turned to bursts of heavy rain.

He hated winter; the endless murky days and the long evenings spent in the lounge trying first to read, then watching television in a fruitless attempt to entertain himself, finally giving up and resorting to porn on his computer. Another five months of this stretched before him. He'd be imprisoned in the house; long walks in the soggy countryside were now beyond him. There'd certainly be no more meetings with Gordon Tagg. Their encounter in Caffé Nero had been a disaster. He was beginning to regret some of the things he'd said to him.

He tried to comfort himself with the quotation, *If winter comes can spring be far behind?* but was immediately shattered by the realisation that for him, next spring might be beyond reach. This made him angry, an anger that energised him. He must get dressed; he'd forgotten that Mrs Williams would arrive in half an hour. He found himself almost looking forward to her visit, though today there'd be no sitting with her on the patio for their coffee.

He was sitting in the kitchen with a slice of burnt toast and a cup of tea when he heard the front door open and Mrs Williams's 'I'm here, Charlie!' He wished he'd told her not to call him that.

She entered the kitchen. 'Good morning, Mrs Williams,' he said.

'Now then, Charlie, I told yer to call me Annie, didn't I?'

'Oh, yes. Sorry.'

'That's okay, dear. Are yer all right? Yer look a bit

peaky, if yer don't mind me saying so.'

'Oh, I'm all right. The weather's getting me down a bit.'

'It's 'orrible, ain't it?' She seemed to be staring at him. 'Oh, Charlie, are yer growin' a beard?'

Charles was horrified. No, he wasn't growing a beard. It was just that he hadn't bothered shaving since Monday; there'd seemed little point to it, being confined to the house. He realised he hadn't washed this morning either.

'No, it's just … it's just that I have a skin irritation. It's getting better now.'

'It rather suits yer, Charlie. Well, I'd better get goin'. I'll start in the lounge.'

'Okay, Mrs … Annie. I'll go and read in my bedroom.'

As he passed her to get to the hall, he noticed there was something about her that was different. Then it came to him – she was wearing make-up. He didn't know whether he was amused or flattered.

Upstairs, he went first to the bathroom. Peering into the mirror he wondered if Mrs Williams was right – would a beard suit him? It would certainly disguise his wrinkles. But she was probably just being kind. In fact, an abundance of hair on his face would probably only serve to emphasise the lack of it on his head. He reached for his electric razor.

Then he entered his bedroom and from the bedside table picked up the novel he'd been trying to read. He'd never been much of a novel-reader and was now finding it increasingly hard to concentrate on them; he couldn't keep track of all the characters.

'Charlie! I've made us some coffee!' was shouted up the stairs. Charles started; he'd almost nodded off.

'Come and sit down, dear,' she said as he entered the kitchen. 'I've made it strong, just like yer like it. Are we gunna have a fag? D'yer mind us smokin' indoors?'

'No, not at all.' He gave her one. As she leaned forward to accept the light he offered, she looked up at him. She had impressively large brown eyes but had overdone the mascara.

'Well now, Charlie. Did yer manage to get out before the weather changed, like I told yer to?'

'Yes. On Saturday I met up with an old colleague for coffee.'

'Colleague?'

'Yes, someone who used to work for me.'

'What was yer job, Charlie? I dunno anything about yer, really.'

'I was Chief Planning Officer here in the county. I moved up here to be Deputy 38 years ago and was promoted several years later.'

'Blimey, yer was important, weren't yer? You're not from round these parts, are yer? Did yer come up here from down south?'

He decided to tell her about his career history. It was a long time since he'd had the chance to talk to anyone about his progress up the ladder. He spoke at some length. She didn't interrupt but stared at him unblinkingly between drags on her cigarette. She really did have beguiling eyes, her skin around them remarkably unwrinkled for a woman of her age.

'Sorry,' he said. 'I must have been boring you.'

She didn't contradict him, and it occurred to him that she probably had no idea what a planning officer did, even if she knew the species existed.

'But what about when yer was a kid?' she asked. '*Was* you born down south?'

'Yes. In the home counties. Berkingshire. Not far out of London.'

'One of them posh places, is it?'

'Well, I suppose it is quite a wealthy area.'

'So was yer mum and dad well off?'

'Not especially. My father worked in a bank.'

'Bloody rich in my book, Charlie! Bet you had a

nice time when yer was a kid, eh?'

Charles didn't reply, he was wondering whether to tell her, and if so, how much. He'd been thinking a lot about his childhood recently; somehow, as he aged, he found he was remembering things that had been long forgotten – or things that he'd subconsciously buried.

'I fancy a refill, Annie. How about you?'

'Go on, then.'

He busied himself making more coffee, then handed her a cup and sat down opposite her.

'Well, are yer gunna tell me about when yer was a kid, then?'

He'd already decided, while making the coffee, that he would. There was nobody else to whom he could talk about it, and to tell the story might be – what was the word? – ah yes, cathartic. But it would have to be a bowdlerised version.

'Okay, Annie. But stop me if I start boring you, won't you?'

'Get on with it, Charlie.'

'Well, I can't say it was a very happy childhood. For a start, I didn't get on well with my father.'

'Why was that, Charlie?'

'Well, you see, I was born during the war, and my father was called up soon after I was born. I didn't really meet him until he was demobbed – I'd have been about three then, and it was like meeting a stranger. I'd been brought up by my mother and grandmother and hadn't had much contact with men. I think I was a disappointment to him. He wanted me to do things like play football with him or go on long country walks. I was more interested in reading comics or playing in the recreation ground with my mother.'

'Bit of a mummy's boy, were yer?'

'I suppose I was. And I didn't really have many friends.'

Charles wondered about telling her that they lived close to a council estate and that his parents told him the children there were too rough to play with. But then he remembered that Annie lived in a council house – no, social housing it was called now – and to tell her this might offend her.

'Didn't yer make friends when yer went to primary school?'

Charles hesitated, and took several sips of coffee.

How much should he tell her? That though he'd liked a few of his fellow pupils, those who spoke as he'd been brought up to speak by his father, but that most of them, those with common accents, hadn't seemed to like him? That he'd hated times spent in the playground because as his classmates grew taller they started teasing him for being so small, that some bullied him, pushed him about, knocked him over?

He compromised by telling her about his first day at school.

***

He'd been crying when the infant teacher came to the school gate and took the children away from their mothers. They were led into what seemed to be a vast room which was filled with small square tables. He was told to sit at one of the tables already occupied by Robert Edwards and Richard Massey, boys from the council houses who'd pushed him around on the rare occasions when he'd left the house without his mother. When he sat down, his feet didn't reach the floor. Robert and Richard were grinning at him, and one of them kicked his ankle.

The teacher clapped her hands. 'Now, children. My name is Miss Daniels. I'm your teacher for the next year. When you wish to speak to me, you must put up your hand. And always address me as "Miss".'

Charles registered that she was tall and skinny and wore her hair in a bun. She didn't look very friendly.

'I hope you're all going to be good children, and I don't want to see anyone crying. You're not babies any more, and in any case you'll be seeing your mothers again at three o'clock. Now, look at the radiators under the window. See the bottles of milk on them? They're for you to drink at break time. Aren't you lucky to have milk to drink at school?'

There was a murmur of assent.

'Your mothers and fathers never had milk at school. You have Mr Attlee to thank for having it. Does anyone know who Mr Attlee is?'

Charles knew. He'd seen a large photo of a bald moustached man in his dad's newspaper, and had asked him who he was. 'The blighter's name's Attlee,' he'd said. 'God help us, he's our Prime Minister.'

He looked round at his classmates. All their faces were blank, so he shouted out, 'He's the Prime Minister!'

Miss Daniels strode over and stood in front of him. 'Stand up, boy!'

He obeyed. He noticed that she had a large mole on her chin from which ginger hairs were sprouting.

'What's your name? Well, Charles Pettifer, what did I say about how you should behave when you wish to speak to me? Well?'

Charles remembered. 'We have to put up our hand.'

'We have to put up our hand *what*?'

Charles didn't know what she meant.

'*Miss*!' Miss Daniels shouted. 'You must always address me as *Miss*! I will let you off this time, but if you do it again I'll send you to the headmaster, and he'll show you what happens to disobedient children, and that will apply to the girls as well as the boys. Now sit down.'

Charles was crying again. Snot began running down from his nostril, but he hadn't got a hankie.

'Right, children. In a few minutes, the headmaster will come in. You must stand up when he enters and listen carefully to what he says.'

Almost immediately, a door opened and a man walked in. He was short and stout, with a red face and ginger hair, and was carrying a stick. Miss Daniels made a beckoning gesture to the class, and they stood up.

'Have they settled down, Miss Daniels?'

'Yes, Mr Harley.'

'Good. Now, children, listen carefully. My name is Mr Harley, and I'm your headmaster. You will have six years at this school, and I expect you all to obey your teachers and work hard. And you must never, ever, misbehave, otherwise you'll be sent to my office and I'll punish you.'

As he said this he tapped his stick against his leg.

'When you get to Junior Four, I will be your class teacher. But you'll see a lot of me before that, because once a week I will be taking you for religious instruction. Do any of you know what that means? No? Well, I'll be telling you about Jesus Christ our Saviour, and how you should follow His teaching.'

Charles had not the slightest idea what he was talking about.

'Very well, Miss Daniels. Carry on with your lesson.'

***

'Blimey, Charlie, was all schools like that, back then?'

'Well, quite a few, I think.'

'I thought yer'd have gone to posh school, like, bein' as how it was down south.'

'It was far from posh, Annie. The buildings were Victorian and in a bad state of repair: it was just after the war. The toilets were in outside huts.'

'Girls' lavvies as well as boys'?'

'Oh yes; separate huts, of course.'

Should he tell her about his experiences in the toilets? Why not? It might amuse her.

'The toilets were disgusting, Annie. The urinal was just a wall with a drain under it, and it was all covered in green slime. The smell was appalling. I'll never forget the first time I went in there. I was shocked that I had to … well, had to expose myself in front of other boys.'

'Get yer willie out, yer mean?'

'Yes. Not only that. The boys all competed to see how high up the wall they could urinate.'

'Pee, yer mean?'

'Yes, I tried to join in, but I was hopeless. Then Robert Edwards uri … peed all over me.'

Annie sniggered. 'That Robert Edwards kid seemed it have it in for yer, Charlie.'

It was time to admit it. God knows why he was still ashamed of it after all these years.

'Yes. And it wasn't just him. He had a gang, and they all bullied me.'

'Didn't they get the cane?'

'Yes, but the headmaster used the cane on most of us, even some of the girls.'

'Did you get the cane?'

'Yes. I'll tell you about it, if you've got time.'

'So long as yer don't mind me givin' the upstairs cleaning a miss. I like hearing about all these things that 'appened to yer, Charlie.'

And Charles was finding he was enjoying telling her.

***

He hadn't minded being in the classroom. He'd been able to please his teachers by being attentive and working hard. But one subject he hadn't liked: religious instruction, taught by Mr Harley.

Mr Harley often spoke of gentle Jesus meek and mild, but he didn't emulate him. Once the class had reached Junior One, the cane made its appearance. The class had been told to learn the Lord's Prayer, and each pupil had to stand and recite it. Three of them failed in their attempts.

'Edwards, come out to the front! Hold out your

hand!' Three swipes of the cane. 'Now the other hand!' Three more swipes.

'Sit down, boy, and stop snuffling. Now you, Massey.'

Massey received the same. Silence had fallen over the class. Charles was feeling sick.

'Now you, Daphne Barnard; yes, you! Don't think because you're a girl you can get away with it.'

Daphne was a tall girl, very thin, quite pretty, but she was shabbily dressed and had dirty hair. When the nit-nurse paid her weekly visits, it was always Daphne who received the closest attention from her. She lived in one of the concrete huts in nearby Bakers Wood. Charles had been told by his father that the huts were built to house American soldiers during the war, but were now occupied by Poles, and by a few English who were too idle to try and find work. He'd told Charles to have nothing to do with the likes of those people. That was a pity; Charles liked Daphne. She sometimes spoke to him after he'd been bullied.

She came to the front, held out her hand, and received the same punishment as the boys. She didn't cry but smiled at Charles as she returned to her desk.

Charles managed to avoid Harley's cane until he reached Junior Four where Harley was the form teacher. He taught them for every subject, including arithmetic, not Charles's favourite, and it was his failed attempts at long division which resulted in a caning on both hands. It was more painful than he'd believed possible, but he managed not to cry. When he took his seat, he felt his hair being ruffled by Daphne, who sat behind him.

***

'Did yer fancy that girl Daphne, then, Charlie?'

Charles realised that in his enthusiasm to entertain Annie, he'd probably said too much. He didn't want her to know about Daphne Barnard.

'Do you mean, did I find her attractive? We were only children, Annie. We didn't think about the opposite sex in that way. It was just that she was friendly, and it was good to have a friend.'

'That ain't how it is these days, dear. Ain't yer seen how some older primary schoolgirls dress? And I've seen some of 'em snoggin' with lads.'

'Well, that wasn't how it was then,' Charles said emphatically. He was beginning to think it might be time to terminate this conversation.

But Annie obviously had other ideas. She lit another cigarette and settled back in her chair. 'Go on, Charlie. Tell us some more.'

'That's all, really. I managed to pass the Eleven Plus and went to Grammar School.'

'Was you the only one who passed?'

'No, there were two of us. The headmaster announced it to the whole class, and of course as soon as break-time came I was set by Robert Edwards and his gang.'

'Just you? What about the other kid who passed?'

'Oh. She was a girl. Girls weren't really bullied.'

'Was she that Daphne friend of yours?'

I'll have to lie, thought Charles. He wanted to tell her about the bullying and how at last he'd triumphed over it, but not what had happened afterwards.

'No, not Daphne. It was a girl called Carol. She was very quiet. I hardly ever spoke to her.'

He took a surreptitious glance at his watch. Only about five minutes to go before the van came to collect Annie. He'd just got time to tell her about his triumph.

'When the headmaster announced that we'd passed, he told the class to give us a round of applause. Robert Edwards and his gang didn't join in, and Edwards was glowering at me. After that, I couldn't concentrate on the lesson. I knew they'd be gunning for me in the playground at break. Sure enough, as soon as we were outside, Edwards and his gang surrounded me. They were shouting

49

things like 'Bloody Grammar bugger! Snobby little swot!' Then Edwards moved towards me. He was obviously going to punch me.'

'Did yer run away?'

'I couldn't. His gang was surrounding me. But something really weird happened. A sort of mist seemed to blur my vision. I scrunched my hand into a fist, pulled back my arm, and punched Edwards on the chin. I didn't think about doing that, I just did it. Hard to explain, really.'

'Blimey, Charlie! Did he hit yer back?'

'No, he just stood there. His mouth was wide open – I can remember that clearly because he had rotten teeth. So I stepped forward, and I think I probably raised my arm – I certainly intended to hit him again. But he suddenly turned and ran off. Then all his gang shuffled off.'

'Good for you, Charlie! Bet yer had no more trouble from that lot, eh?'

'No, but I only had a few months there, and – '

He was interrupted by the persistent ringing of his front doorbell. Annie looked at her watch and jumped up.

'Oh, that'll be the bloody van come to collect me! I should be outside waitin' for it.'

Saved by the bell, thought Charles. He'd been shaken when she'd said to him 'Good for you, Charlie'. It was almost as though she was playing a part scripted by a malevolent demon from his past. He had to get her out of the house so he could recover.

'Let me help you collect up your things,' he said, eager to undertake some displacement activity. The affection for her that had been growing as he'd told her his story had evaporated when she uttered that single sentence, *good for you, Charlie*, but he didn't want her to be aware of this. Fortunately, she was intent on collecting up her gear and the flurry of activity obviated the need for further exchanges.

He watched her from the kitchen as she went into the hall to answer the front door. She opened it and told the van driver to hang on a minute. Then she turned, walked back into the kitchen, said, 'I enjoyed our chat, Charlie,' and flung her arms round him. Charles didn't return the hug and backed away. The demon from his past was scripting events again.

With a 'Seeya next week, dear,' she turned and left.

Charles staggered into the lounge and collapsed onto the settee. All thoughts of Mrs Williams evaporated. He was back in the playground, having just punched Robert Edwards.

***

'Good for you, Charlie! That showed the sod!'

It was Daphne Barnard.

A great change had come over Daphne in the past year. She was even taller, but she was somehow plumper. Her dress clung tightly to her. Her clothes were still shabby, but her blonde hair was no longer dirty, was longer and tied back in a ponytail. Charles still liked her, but she was somehow different: she looked and acted older than the other girls in his class. Sometimes she said things to him that he didn't understand.

'Innit good we'll be goin' to Grammar together, Charlie?'

'Yes.'

'Ere, Charlie, come with me. Wanna show you something.'

She took his hand and led him towards the back of the girls' toilets. Charles looked round, but the playground was now almost empty. Break-time was over. Once behind the toilet, Daphne turned to face him, then pulled him towards her. She held him tightly, pressing her body against him. His eyes were level with her neck. She bent down and kissed him on the lips. It was a sloppy kiss and went on for a long time: Charles didn't like it.

Then she whispered in his ear: 'Yer can touch me titties if yer like.'

Charles, terrified, broke away and ran as fast as he could back into the classroom. Mr Harley gave him three strokes of the cane for being late. Daphne did not return to the classroom for the rest of the day.

Chapter 7

Gordon and Margaret had their division of pre-Christmas duties honed to near perfection. It was easier for them, and certainly for Margaret, now they spent Christmas and Boxing Day at Hilary and Giles's house.

So they shared the Christmas shopping, then Margaret wrapped the presents while Gordon attended to the Christmas cards. They sent over 100 cards, many of them to friends they'd accumulated over a lifetime. Some friends now sent them long Christmas messages by email, or even worse, e-cards, but Gordon was determined not to resort to this. If everyone started doing that, there'd no longer be a display of cards on various surfaces around the house, part of Christmas ever since his childhood.

It was nearly nine o'clock and he'd been at his task, sitting at the dinner table, for nearly an hour. Margaret was wrapping presents in the lounge. He still had a few cards to write but decided to give it a rest for a while. Looking at his list where he ticked off 'cards sent' and 'cards received' every year, he'd realised that over the past three years he'd lost six old friends, something that was now likely to happen with increasing frequency. He still sent cards to their widows or widowers, even though some of them he'd never met. It was a gesture of generational solidarity.

He got up and went into the lounge. Margaret was sitting on the floor amidst a sea of wrapping paper and coloured ribbons.

'I've had enough for tonight, Margy. There's a play on ITV that's had a good preview in the *Guardian*. Shall we watch it?'

'Yes, let's. I've had enough too. Just let me clear this stuff away.'

'Oh, leave it till tomorrow, love. Nobody's going to see it except us.'

They settled down on the settee and started

watching the TV drama. For Gordon it was spoiled by the lengthy advertisement breaks, all promoting products for Christmas. It had been like that since early November. There was one pleasing thing about them, though – the way the people in them reflected the country's racial diversity. But he hated the way the Christmas season now began even before Halloween, and he hated Halloween as well - bloody American import. And what had happened to Guy Fawkes Night? When was the last time he'd seen kids asking for a penny for the guy?

When the drama ended, Margaret said, 'Shall I turn over to BBC1 for the ten o'clock news?'

'I don't think I can stand it, Margy. It'll be all about Brexit. I'll go and finish writing the cards; I've only got a few more to do.'

'Well, I'll get on with my parcels.'

Back in the dining room, Gordon had only four more cards to write. He dealt with the first three in just a few minutes. He'd been putting off writing the last card, because he was still undecided about whether to write a message in it. Would she appreciate it? Or would she hate being reminded about something she'd probably long forgotten?

He opened the card. The first bit was easy: above 'Season's Greetings' he wrote *To Jeanette*, and underneath, *With very best wishes from Gordon. Hope all's well with you.*

He came to a decision. She'd probably just read it with mild curiosity, so on the other side of the card he wrote *Thought you might be interested to know that a couple of weeks ago I met Charles Pettifer in town. It was his idea we met. Haven't seen him since he retired. He's aged a great deal, but still behaves in much the same way. He asked about you but I told him we were no longer in contact.*

He shoved the card in the envelope and was about to seal it when something occurred to him. He extracted the card and added his email address. She probably wouldn't reply, but he hoped she would. It would be fascinating to know what she'd have to say.

***

Gordon had met Jeanette when he moved to Staffridge with Margaret on taking up the post of Traffic Control Adviser. He was based in the County Office and reported directly to Pettifer's deputy. Pettifer seemed to spend much of his time liaising with county councillors. He took little notice of Gordon.

Pettifer was a strange fellow. Diminutive in stature, he wore a sharp, almost spiv-like brown pinstripe suit, brightly covered shirts and garish ties. His voice was high pitched. Some of the staff with whom Gordon became friendly told him that when he lost his temper his voice became even more shrill.

This didn't bother Gordon too much: he managed to keep out of Pettifer's way. He even began to find him a derisory character. Although Pettifer was short, when he walked he didn't hold himself erect. His shoulders hunched forward and his arms dangled in front of him so his hands almost touched his knees. Gordon privately christened him 'Piltdown Man'. Then one day he realised why Pettifer's stance was so hunched; he wore two-inch high stacked heels and obviously found it hard to balance on them.

Gordon enjoyed his job, and got on well with Sam Griffiths, Pettifer's deputy. But after a few years, Sam was forced to take extended sick leave. The day after his departure, Gordon was called into Pettifer's office.

He was sitting at his vast expanse of desk, on the telephone to someone. He beckoned Gordon to sit down on the chair in front of the desk. The phone call went on for a long time.

'Right, Mr Tagg,' he said after replacing the receiver. 'We're in a new situation now old Griifiths is no longer with us. I don't reckon he'll be returning, his health's been poor for some time.'

'Oh, I'm sorry to hear that. I assumed – '

'It'll be some time before I can appoint a new deputy. That's where you come in. Griffiths always attended the monthly meetings I have with the area officers – just to take the minutes of course. You'll be doing that from now on. The next meeting's in a fortnight. Make sure you show me the minutes before you give them to Gillian to type up. Okay?'

'Well, yes, but couldn't Gillian take the minutes, then – '

'Good God, man! My secretary's got better things to do with her time! Right. A week on Friday then.'

He reached for a file on his desk and began perusing the contents. The meeting was obviously over. Gordon got up and left. He had to go through Gillian Tebbit's adjacent office – the door to the corridor from Pettifer's room was permanently locked. Gillian ignored him as he passed through. She was holding a mirror to her face and adjusting her make-up.

Gordon wasn't given any further briefing for the meeting, just told to be there at 10am with notebook and pen. He arrived five minutes early and found the four area planning officers already seated round the table. Pettifer wasn't present.

Gordon was acquainted with all four of them; he occasionally visited their offices to explain new aspects of county policy on traffic management. Three of them were men in late middle age, mild mannered and conservatively dressed, whom Gordon thought of as archetypal public servants. The fourth, Jeanette Beasley, was much younger than her colleagues and recently appointed. She was very tall, dressed smartly but unostentatiously, had frizzy hair, severe features half-disguised by large black-rimmed spectacles, and spoke softly but articulately. Gordon rather liked her.

He sat down amongst them.

'To what do we owe the pleasure, Gordon?' asked Jeanette. 'What's happened to Sam Griffiths?'

'Oh, haven't you been told? He's on sick leave, and it seems – '

He was interrupted by the door to Gillian's office being opened and the entry of Pettifer who marched to the head of the table and slammed down a sheaf of documents.

'Mr Tagg will be taking minutes from now on. For the foreseeable future, anyway. Why are you sitting down there, Gordon? You're no use to me there. Up here, next to me. Right. Down to business. I have here a list of policy decisions taken by me in consultation with the Planning Committee.' He thrust a bundle of papers in front of Gordon. 'Well, pass them round, man!'

'Right,' he said. 'While you're reading those, Gordon will make us some coffee. The machine's on the bench over there. I hope you make a better brew than Griffiths did.'

As Gordon bent to the task assigned to him, he wondered if this a deliberate attempt to humiliate him. Or was it just in the nature of the man? There was silence in the room while the officers perused the papers. Was he supposed to carry the coffee cups over to the table? It seemed that he was. The officers all thanked him when he placed the cups in front of them. Pettifer didn't. He said 'Well, bring the sugar over, then,' and then, 'Time's up! Right. Any questions or comments?'

There were a few questions from Joe, Fred and Max, seeking clarification, to which Pettifer gave impatient replies. Gordon minuted these exchanges. There were no comments. Gordon wondered if there ever were.

'Very well, then. Let's get on with the next item: your reports. I've read them all carefully. Joe, it took me far too long to read yours. For God's sake, man, why can't you use bullet points and plain English? Anyone would think you're trying to impress us with your literary talents. Well, it doesn't impress me.'

The next ten minutes passed with Pettifer

commenting on the reports from Fred and Max. He was critical of many of the decisions they'd taken. There was no praise for anyone, beyond a statement at the end to the effect that most of the other things done or proposed were reasonably acceptable, he supposed.

It was Jeanette Beasley's turn to be interrogated. Gordon noticed she was biting her lower lip. Pettifer seemed to be taking his time before starting the procedure.

'So, *Ms* Beasley, would you care to elaborate on what you're recommending regarding the planning application for a housing development in Little Drayton?'

'I think that's clear in my report.'

'Oh yes, it's clear what you *intend* recommending. What I don't understand is, *why*?'

'Because a development of 100 houses would be far too large for a community like Little Drayton, and – '

'So you don't think we should meet the community's housing needs?'

'But the application is for four-bedroomed houses. Nobody in Little Drayton would be able to – '

'So we shouldn't give consideration to people who want to move into the locality? Is that what you're saying, *Ms* Beasley? If we followed your line of reasoning no one would be able move anywhere.'

'But it's not just that. The village can't provide for an influx of newcomers. The primary school is very small, there's only one small village store, there isn't a – '

'Then that'll give some budding entrepreneur an opportunity to open a new shop, won't it? And as for the school, what makes you think the owners of four-bedroomed houses would want their kids to mix with the locals?'

Pettifer's voice was growing shriller and Gordon noticed that Jeanette's hand was trembling slightly. She inhaled deeply before saying –

'And then there's the matter of the Green Belt. The proposed development will encroach on it. It will – '

'Green Belt? *Green Belt*?' His voice was now

almost a screech. 'For God's sake, what's that got to do with it? I know what this is all about. This sort of development is against your lefty principles, isn't it?'

'I can assure you, Mr Pettifer, that – '

'Oh, be quiet, woman! I've heard enough. Make an appointment with my secretary to see me next week. This meeting is over. Stay behind, Mr Tagg. We need to discuss your minutes.'

The area officers shuffled out.

Gordon could hardly believe what he'd just witnessed. He looked at Pettifer, who was still sitting at the table. Could it be a slight smile that flickered across his features?

Gordon's mood changed abruptly. He was usually a mild-mannered man, but on occasions when he witnessed injustice he became angry, and indifferent to any consequence that might arise from that.

He stood up and remained standing next to Pettifer, who looked up at him.

'Mr. Pettifer, that was the most appalling display of bullying I've ever seen in all my years in town planning. Not only are you extremely rude, constantly interrupting your colleagues when they try to speak, but you also denigrate them, and in front of each other. Quite frankly, you are a disgrace to your position.'

Pettifer stood up, no doubt with the intention of confronting Gordon face-to-face. But he couldn't; his eyes came up only to Gordon's chin. Abruptly, he sat down again, and Gordon had the satisfaction of noticing that his sandy hair was carefully combed over in an unsuccessful attempt to disguise a bald spot.

Pettifer remained seated and addressed his next remarks to the chair that Gordon had recently vacated.

'You've got a lot to learn about management, Tagg; you need to show subordinates who's boss. But it isn't just that that's bugging you, is it? You didn't like the way I spoke to our Ms Beasley, did you? I noticed the way you were looking at her. Fancy your chances, do you? You're on a loser there, matey. She's one of those feminists. They need keeping in their place.'

Gordon bent over so they were face to face. 'Mr. Pettifer,' he said quietly, 'I can understand you must find it demeaning to work with a woman who towers over you, both literally and metaphorically. But notwithstanding that, just let me say you are without doubt the most odious little shit I've ever had the misfortune to work for.'

As soon as he finished speaking, he knew he'd probably burned his boats. Instant suspension would result, followed by dismissal, and the probability of never being employed in planning again. How on earth could he explain this to Margy?

He was expecting Pettifer to explode, but he didn't. He stood up, a grin on his face and clapped his hand on Gordon's shoulder.

'You're a man after my own heart, Gordon! You've got all the makings of a Chief, in a few years, maybe. So let's forget all this. I think it might be an idea if you no longer attended these meetings; you've got enough to get on with. Oh, on your way out, tell Gillian to come in and clear up the coffee things.'

Gordon was amused by the look of amazement on Gillian's face when he told her this.

For the next few weeks, Gordon had little contact with Pettifer beyond occasionally bumping into him in the corridor, when Pettifer treated him to a knowing grin. Gordon had no opportunity to visit the area offices, so had no means of discovering what had resulted from the summons Pettifer had issued to Jeanette Beasley. But as far as he knew, the result of the planning application for the proposed development at Little Drayton still hadn't been decided.

In subsequent weeks, he noticed a change in Pettifer. There was no longer a grin when they encountered each other in the corridor; indeed, the man seemed unaware of Gordon's presence. From some of the junior staff, Gordon learned that he'd become quieter, almost withdrawn, though there were still the occasional outbursts of temper.

Then, all the senior staff were called to a meeting in his office. But Pettifer wasn't there: his seat was occupied by a county councillor, the Deputy Chairman of the planning committee.

'Gentlemen and Lady,' he said. 'Thank you for attending at such short notice. I have a brief announcement to make. Mr Pettifer has decided to take early retirement, with immediate effect. The post of chief planning officer will be advertised, and we hope to have a replacement in post within two months. In the meantime, please carry on your normal duties.'

They all left through the door to the corridor, no longer locked. As they walked off, Gillian Tebbit came towards them. She averted her eyes, but Gordon noticed she was crying.

***

Although Gordon and Jeanette had been friendly, she'd never confided in him the reason why she'd suddenly taken up a new post in the south of England. Perhaps it might have had something to do with Pettifer's unexplained early retirement? Gordon hoped she'd email him: it would be good to have more contact with her other than just the exchange of Christmas cards, and perhaps she could be persuaded to tell him more of what had happened.

Chapter 8

It was nearly eleven o'clock, and Charles was still in bed. He'd slept badly and was trying to doze, but was in discomfort. His limbs felt weak, his head ached, the thought of breakfast nauseated him. And even if he'd felt well, he'd have nothing to get up for. Another solitary day stretched before him.

Apart from all this, it was the so-called festive season that was bringing him down. He'd never liked Christmas Day, a joyless 24 hours spent in the company of first his parents, then his wife.

A packet of painkillers was on the bedside table. He'd taken two on going to bed to help him sleep. They'd worked for about two hours, but he'd woken at midnight, wanting to piss. On returning to his bed, wide awake, he'd known he'd need to take two more, and in any case a headache had started to develop. He'd woken yet again at three o'clock, his headache worse and with a dull pain in his limbs. He hadn't dared take any more pills and had just laid there, horribly alert, trying to breathe deeply in an attempt to relax, but breathing itself had become an effort. He'd tried to remember happy times in his past – there had been a few - but that had resulted in making the present even bleaker, and the future didn't bear thinking about. He'd caught himself wondering if the packet of painkillers might be the ultimate remedy for his woes – the Final Solution to the Pettifer problem. But no, that was the coward's way out. In any case, he'd paid taxes all his life and the bloody NHS should take responsibility for him instead of wasting time and money on the obese and undeserving drug addicts and alcoholics.

He turned himself over, wincing with pain. Perhaps he might nod off if he tried sleeping on his back? He was adjusting his position when the front doorbell rang. Who the hell would be calling on him? Nobody ever did apart from Mrs Williams and occasional door-step vendors whom he always treated to a tirade of abuse. He decided to ignore it. But it didn't stop, and became more persistent.

Muttering all the foul language he knew, he pulled his legs over the side of the bed and sat, still swearing, until he felt strong enough to stand up. He had to lever himself against the bed head to do this. It was bloody freezing. He reached for his dressing gown and pulled it on with some difficulty because he was tottering. He had the same problem putting on his slippers. His head was thumping. And all the time that fucking doorbell continued to ring.

He stumbled over to the window and pulled open the curtains. Outside it was raining, of course. His front door wasn't visible from the bedroom, but a car was parked on the road outside his house. He didn't recognise it.

It was an effort to get down the stairs; his legs felt like jelly. Once in the hallway, he peered at the frosted glass of the front door but could make out only a distorted shape. It was tall, and still pressing on the doorbell. Outraged, he yanked open the door, shouting as he did so, 'Whatever it is you're selling, I don't want it!'

He was confronted by someone muffled against the cold; the shape was female and carrying a briefcase. The top of her head was covered by a hood. But one thing immediately stood out: the face was black. Such was his surprise that he stopped shouting and stared at her, open-mouthed.

'Mr Pettifer?'

'Yes.'

'My name's Katia Whittaker. I'm your Macmillan Nurse.'

Macmillan Nurse? What the hell ...? Then he remembered: mention had been made of the service when he was attending the hospital. That was months ago, and back then he was still in denial.

'You should have received a letter informing you of my visit. Didn't you get it?'

He could only shake his head.

'Well, are you going to let me in, Mr Pettifer?'

He fully opened the door and beckoned her to enter. It occurred to him that the cliché *speechless* was entirely appropriate to his condition, not just because he was surprised but because he had no idea how to address her, let alone engage in conversation.

'Is there somewhere I can hang my coat, Mr Pettifer?' she said as she stood in the hallway.

Words came to him. 'Oh. Yes. Hooks are in that cupboard.' She divested herself, hung up her coat, and turned to face him. He noticed that under a blue uniform she was slim and shapely. Her hair was straightened and hung down to touch her shoulders.

She picked up her briefcase. 'Shall we sit down, Mr Pettifer? We have a lot to talk about.'

'Do we? You'd better come in here, then.'

He led her into the kitchen. The lounge would be inappropriate for a serious discussion, which her demeanour pointed to it probably being. She sat down at the table, rummaged in her briefcase and extracted a file.

'Please sit down, Mr Pettifer. Before we go any further, I need to check that these case-notes are accurate.'

He obeyed. She had an air of authority about her and spoke firmly in the accent of an educated woman, quite unlike most of the nurses he'd encountered in Staffridge hospital. He didn't want to get on the wrong side of her, not this early in the proceedings.

'Right. I have here a summary of your case history. I'll read it out to you, and you'll confirm by saying "yes", if what is written is accurate. If not, just say "no", and we'll discuss the matter further.'

She began reading, starting with his early symptoms which he'd reported to his G.P. followed by the various investigations he'd had at the hospital, then the diagnosis and finally the prognosis. He was able to confirm that the notes were accurate. He watched her as she concentrated on ticking the boxes. She was a striking woman, but he found it hard to gauge her age. Was this because she was black? He hadn't been this close to a black person before. She could be anything from 25 to 40, though her figure was that of a young woman.

'Right!' she said. 'Now, how are you feeling since your prognosis? Any pain, discomfort, weakness, nausea? Are the symptoms getting worse? Is the medication you were prescribed effective?'

There was no point in dissembling. It was, in any case, a relief to tell someone exactly how he felt. She listened attentively, made the odd note.

'Okay,' she said when he'd finished. 'I'll now run through all the ways I can help you.'

Charles decided it was time he asserted himself. Thus far he'd felt as though he were a student sitting in a tutorial.

'Look, Mrs …'

'It's Ms Whittaker.'

'Right. Well, I was wondering, would you like a cup of tea or coffee? I'm dying for one myself.'

She seemed to be giving the question serious consideration.

'Thank you very much, Mr Pettifer. I'd like a coffee. Milk, no sugar, please.'

As he busied himself making the coffee, he decided it was time to see if the old Pettifer charm still worked, even though he was still in his dressing gown. When he returned to the table with the mugs, he leapt straight in.

'Will I get frequent visits from you? It will be you, I assume?'

'Visits will be as often as you need them, Mr Pettifer. And yes, it will be me, unless you have any objection.'

'No. Why should I?'

She hadn't yet tasted her coffee; she stared at him, then said, slowly and deliberately, 'Some patients seem not to like having a member of an ethnic minority visiting them in their houses.'

'More fools them!' he said, and as he was saying this he realised, to his surprise, he meant it. 'Look, what I wanted to say was this. If you're going to be seeing me regularly, please don't keep calling me Mr Pettifer. My name's Charles.'

'Oh, very well, I'll call you 'Charles'.'

'And may I call you by your first name? Did you say it was Katia?'

'Yes, it is. And yes, you can.'

For the first time since she'd been in the house, she smiled. It was a dazzling smile. She was not just attractive, but beautiful. Good God, wasn't she the woman in the coffee house where he'd met Gordon?

'Do you by any chance visit the Caffé Nero in Staffridge?' he asked.

'Yes, quite often. Why?'

'I think I saw you in there a few weeks ago. You were with – 'he was about to say 'a white man' but stopped just in time – 'with a young man.'

'That would have been my fiancé.'

'Lucky fellow!'

She treated him again to her smile. 'Now, Mr … sorry, Charles; I think it's time we got down to business. We can do that over coffee, okay?'

Charles concurred. He realised his head was no longer aching, there was less pain in his limbs, his breathing was easier. Was it possible in the space of fifteen minutes for a dying man to feel about 20 years younger? It seemed to be so.

She launched into an account of the services her organisation could provide or arrange for other services to provide. Charles couldn't take it all in – palliative care, pain management, self-administered morphine, help in the home, possibly short periods of respite care in a hospice.

'Do you have relatives who visit you, Charles? No? Friends or neighbours perhaps? Nobody? Are you totally by yourself?'

He answered these questions by shaking or nodding

his head. For the first time since his retirement, he allowed himself self-pity.

'I can provide emotional support if you think you need it, Charles. It's my specialism.'

'I didn't know Macmillan nurses specialised. How do you do that?'

'By taking a further qualification. I did an M.Sc. in Health Psychology.'

Charles was humbled. It was rare for him to experience humility, and he didn't know how to express it. He just watched her as she drained her coffee and got to her feet.

'Well, Charles, you've got a lot to think about. I'll phone you after Christmas to arrange another time to come and see you. But if you feel down and need to talk, phone me. Here's my card.'

'Thank you, Katia. I'm very grateful.'

'It's my job, Charles.'

He followed her into the hallway and extracted her coat from the cupboard. As he handed it to her, he was seized by a desire to hug her. But she was already walking towards the front door.

'Oh, there's a letter for you.' She picked it up and handed it to him. 'Looks like a Christmas card. Goodbye, Charles.'

Chapter 9

After Katia had left, Charles walked back into the kitchen, a smile on his face. It seemed he might have something to look forward to, however short the time to enjoy it might be.

He opened the Christmas card. He only ever received four cards, and he knew who this one was from: Bonzo Barnes, the friend he'd made at Grammar School. He read Bonzo's greeting and laughed out loud. Bonzo had made his time there almost tolerable.

***

It was a mile from Charles's house to the new town, up a steep hill. He was running, because he was late. Late for his first day at the Grammar School. It was his father who'd delayed him by giving him a lecture on how he should conduct himself.

He was feeling self-conscious and nervous. Self-conscious because he was in his new school uniform which didn't fit him well. His navy-blue blazer was too large because his mother told him he'd have to grow into it; she couldn't afford to buy a new one every year. For the same reason, his grey flannel shorts extended to just below his knees. Only his cap was the right size.

He was nervous because he had no idea what awaited him. Nobody in his extended family had ever been to grammar school. Would he be given much homework? Were the pupils caned? And what would his classmates be like? Might they tease him because he was so small and because his uniform was too big for him? And what about the older pupils: would they bully him, hit him? They'd be far too big to confront like he had Robert Edwards.

Breathless, he reached a gate at the end of a long drive leading to the school. Standing beside it was a man, but he was wearing the school blazer.

'You a new boy?' he demanded.

'Yes.'

'I'm a prefect. You're late. Follow me.'

He led Charles up the drive to the school buildings and pointed to a door in one of them.

'That's the library. Get in there.'

Charles pushed open the door and was confronted by a man wearing a black gown.

'What's your name, boy?'

Charles told him, and was instructed to go and stand in the back row of a roomful of pupils. They were all taller than him, and the boy in front of him was so tall that he wasn't aware that a man was standing at the front of the room until he spoke.

'Good morning, First Year Pupils. My name is Mr Harrow, and I am your headmaster. Firstly, I have one thing to say to the boy who has just arrived, and that is this. *Punctuality is the politeness of princes.* You will do well to remember that, boy, during your time at this school.'

The boys and girls standing nearby turned to stare at him. Charles felt himself blushing.

'The purpose of this short assembly is to tell you which of the two first year classes you'll be in,' the headmaster continued. 'I shall now read out a list of names. Pay attention. Those of you who scored the highest marks in the Eleven Plus examination will be in Class 1A. The remainder will be in Class 1B.'

Charles was to be in 1A. To his relief, Daphne Barnard was to be in 1B.

'Now,' the headmaster concluded, 'your form mistresses will introduce themselves.'

Two women sitting either side of him stood up. One introduced herself as Miss Crowe, form teacher of Class 1A, who asked her class members to follow her out of the hall.

Nobody spoke as she led the pupils out into a corridor. She stopped outside a classroom, told them each to enter and to search for the desk with his or her name on it, and then to sit down.

'Good,' she said when they were all settled. 'Now, when I point to you, I want you to stand up, call out your name, and then say which primary school you attended, and the town or village in which it's located. I shall do this in alphabetical order.'

There were about 30 in the class, and the procedure took some time. With a surname beginning with 'P', Charles had a long wait before it was his turn. He noticed that many of his classmates had very posh accents: only a few spoke like those at his primary school. When Miss Crowe eventually pointed to him, he was so nervous that his voice came out as a squeak. Some of his classmates giggled.

By the time his first year neared its end, Charles still wasn't sure if he was happy or not. At least there was no bullying, apart from on the first day when all the new boys were dragged to the toilets by fourth formers, there to have their heads thrust down the pans and the toilets flushed. Apparently, it was an initiation ceremony, and there seemed to be no malice in it. After that he was left alone by the older boys.

There was no caning either – at least not in front of the class. At the end of assembly the headmaster sometimes read out a list of names, mostly boys in the fourth and fifth year, who were told to report to his study where they received four or six of the best, but so far that fate hadn't befallen anyone in Charles's class, though it had to two boys in class 1B.

But Charles felt he didn't really belong. The posh boys and girls made it clear he wasn't one of them by mocking his accent whenever he tried to chat to them. The pupils from the nearby manufacturing town of Chessenden, mainly the boys in class 1B, were much more direct in their assertions, often employing foul language: apparently he was a fuckin' jumped-up little swot.

He was resigned to things being the same in his second year, but there began to be changes. Most of the boys, but not him, now wore long trousers, and he noticed some had started doing strange things to their uniforms. They rolled their school ties into a narrow pencil shape and folded back their collars. A few had evidently persuaded their mothers to tailor their trousers to be much narrower. The most dramatic change was to their hair; they started greasing it up into a quiff at the front, and combing it round from the sides so that it met at the back. He'd heard one of them referring to this as a 'duck's arse'.

Charles couldn't understand all this, until one day at the end of assembly the headmaster railed against those boys.

'I will not have Teddy Boys in this school!' he shouted. 'From next week, any boy wearing narrow trousers or altering his uniform in any other way, or growing his hair in a ridiculous style, will be called into my office and be caned!'

Charles had read about Teddy Boys in his father's newspaper. 'Scum of the earth', he'd called them. But Charles had never seen one in either the old or new towns. It seemed that most of them came from, or gathered in, Chessenden.

The girls couldn't, of course, adopt a similar style, but Charles noticed subtle changes in some of them, those whose uniforms began to fit more tightly round their hips and who suddenly seemed to acquire pointed breasts. It was these girls who spent much of their break time with the boys who aped the Teds, and, most surprisingly, singing with them. They sang songs that Charles had never heard before, songs with strange words like 'be bop a lula' and 'all shook up'. He plucked up courage and asked one of the Teds what it was all about. 'It's rock'n'roll, kiddo! You just ain't with it!' was the response.

In fact, Charles had heard the term: it had been used by his father. Charles used to listen to *Two Way Family Favourites* on the wireless while his parents were preparing Sunday lunch, and on one occasion, several listeners requested a record sung by someone with a peculiar name – Elvis, was it? Immediately, his father had jumped up and turned off the wireless, shouting, 'What's the BBC thinking of, exposing us to that rock'n'roll rubbish? It's jungle music!'

Charles asked the Ted where he could hear rock'n'roll.

'On Radio Luxembourg.'

'What's that?'

'A music station on the wireless. It's 208 meters on the medium wave.'

Charles managed to tune into Radio Luxembourg one evening when his parents were out. What he then heard was nothing like the music he'd been brought up with, the stuff his parents listened to. He didn't like it. It was noisy, wasn't tuneful, there was too much drumming, and everything seemed to be sung in an American accent. He couldn't understand why his classmates raved about it. He came to the end of his second year feeling even more alienated from his peers, and apprehensive about what might await him in the following year.

But things began to change for him in the third form. He'd grown a few inches and managed to persuade his mother to buy him a pair of long trousers when he told her he'd be the only boy in the class still wearing shorts. Even more significant, he began to sprout hair on his face. He could hardly believe it, and occasionally had to sneak into the bathroom to use his father's razor.

It seemed he was one of the first in his class to have to shave. His long trousers and the hint of stubble on his upper lip resulted in some of his classmates, especially the girls, starting to treat him differently. Daphne Barnard, still in the B stream, but to whom he sometimes spoke at break time when she was not surrounded by fifth form boys, came up close to him one day. 'Hey, Charlie, you're turning into a bit of all right,' she said. 'Why don't you come up to the top of the playing field with me in the lunch hour?'

Charles had heard of the things that went on at the top of the playing field, notwithstanding the patrols mounted by teachers attempting to enforce gender segregation. After a biology lesson in which the boys and girls had been taught separately, girls had begun to intrigue him, but he hadn't the confidence to explore further, and certainly not with Daphne Barnard. 'Bit of all right', she'd said. Did that mean he was handsome? He began to examine himself in the mirror; well, he certainly wasn't ugly. If only he was taller, and if only his voice would break properly. It wasn't just high-pitched; now it sometimes broke into squeaks.

Bonzo Barnes joined the school at the start of the fourth year when his parents moved to the area. Charles could still clearly remember the day he made his appearance. He was told to stand at the front of the class and introduce himself.

'I'm Rodney Barnes,' he said, 'but my friends call me Bonzo.'

He was tall, well-built, with jet-black hair swept back in a quiff, and his voice was that of a man. He was very good-looking. Charles heard Liz Deacon, who sat behind him, say, 'Woooh, dig that!' In the one short sentence that Barnes had uttered, Charles noticed his strange accent. It became more noticeable as the English lesson progressed, because Barnes answered many of the questions put to the class, the answers to which other pupils didn't know.

Come break-time, Bonzo was rounded on by the boys, mocked for his accent, accused of being a bloody know-all. But he didn't slink away, he stood upright, shouted that he'd take on any of them who cared to challenge him to a fight. The gang surrounding him gradually fell silent. Then he said, 'I talk the way I do because I'm from Cornwall. If you don't like it, then tough. I don't like the way most of you lot speak, but you can't help it, can you? So piss off!'

Muttering, the boys sidled away. Charles was impressed by the way Bonzo had stood up to them. If only he could do that! He approached him.

'Hello, my name's Charlie.'

'Hello, Charlie.'

'I'll show you round the school at lunchtime, if you like.'

'Yes, I'd like that. I'm glad not everyone at this school's a tosser.'

The tour round the school only lasted half an hour, but when it ended, Charles thought he may at last have found someone who might become his friend. They were both outsiders. Then he discovered that Bonzo lived in the old town in a street very close to his. When four o'clock came, they walked home together.

But Bonzo's isolation didn't last long. He was good at football and was selected for the school's junior team. He was witty and used his wit to good effect in the classroom, his asides often reduced his classmates to helpless laughter. His mature good looks made him a magnet for the girls, including the posh ones, and he became one of those noted for frequent illicit excursions to the top of the playing field, on one memorable occasion with a girl in the Lower Sixth.

But he remained friendly with Charles: in fact Charles was taken under his wing. As a result, he began to be accepted by many in the class who'd previously mocked or ignored him. At weekends Bonzo got Charles to listen to pop music which he played on his Dansette. It was less raucous, more tuneful, than the early rock'n'roll, and Charles found he quite liked some of it; he was even able to join in the class singalongs.

It was when they reached the fifth form that Bonzo led Charles into pastures new. He persuaded Charles to attend form parties held in the local community centre. They played games to the accompaniment of pop music, played louder than Charles had ever heard. One game was a variant of musical chairs played with the lights off; the girls pranced round the seated boys and sat on the laps of the boys closest to them when the music stopped. Charles quite enjoyed this; when a girl was on his lap it didn't matter that he was short. Some of the girls wriggled about when he kissed them, he didn't know why, and Liz Deacon put her tongue in his mouth. He wasn't sure he liked that. After that party ended, Bonzo asked Charles: 'Did you give Liz Deacon a feel?' Charles thought he knew what Bonzo meant, but no, he hadn't dared do that; in any case he wasn't sure he wanted to.

Then, the GCE 'O' Level exams began, and after they'd ended the pupils were allowed to start their summer holiday early. Charles thought he'd done well enough to enter the sixth form, but he was sad that Bonzo wouldn't be joining him, because his parents were moving back to Cornwall. Even so, Charles found himself, for the first time, looking forward to the start of a new term.

In the sixth form, it was like being in a completely different institution. All the Teds and their female hangers-on had left; Charles was in the company of the serious and the studious. He emulated them, adopted their speech patterns, became an avid reader, participated in class discussions and was listened to. Most of the girls in his class were frumpish, and he was glad of that because he wanted no distractions from his studies.

When he reached the upper sixth, he was made a Prefect. He relished his new role. He loved striding round the school, ejecting pupils from classrooms, ordering them to clear rubbish from the playground, shouting at those whom he heard using bad language. He got great satisfaction from asking a pupil a question, then shouting an interruption before the question was fully answered. His power lay in his ability to give a detention, which, for the boys, could result in a caning from the headmaster. For the girls, it meant an interview with the senior mistress, which, if it occurred more than twice, resulted in suspension.

There was one occasion when he was challenged, and in such a way that destroyed his new-found sense of security. The patrolling of the upper playing fields had been relinquished by the teachers, and that duty had passed to prefects. Usually, when Charles marched towards a boy and girl engaged in illicit activities, they scrambled to their feet and hurried away before he could speak to them.

But in the final week of Charles's last term he encountered two fifth-form boys grappling with just one girl. The girl was Desiree Statham, also a fifth-former, who had the reputation of being a bit of a goer: some lads claimed to have gone all the way with her.

They didn't get up when Charles approached them, just sat staring at him.

'Get up, and get back down to the quadrangle!' he shouted. 'It's a detention for all of you, and you know what that means!'

Very slowly, the boys got to their feet. One of them gave Charles the 'V' sign.

'You heard me! Get going!'

'Oh, fuck off,' said one of them, and the two began to amble away from him.

Charles was enraged. He wished to God he was bigger so he could thump them, even though prefects weren't allowed to do that. But he would probably have come off worse.

Then he realised that Desiree Statham hadn't got up. She was still lying on her back, squinting at him. Her skirt was pulled up to mid-thigh. It was summer, she was wearing ankle socks and her bare legs were deeply tanned.

'Get up, girl!'

'What you gonna do if I don't, Charlie-boy?'

Charles felt a cold draught of uncertainty wash over him. He'd never had to deal with flagrant disobedience. He had to think before replying.

'I'll report you directly to Miss Able, and you'll probably be sent straight home.'

'Think I'll care about that? I've only got one more week in this dump anyway.'

'Suit yourself.' Charles turned, ready to walk away.

'Hang on, Charlie! Why don't you come and sit down here beside me?'

'Why on earth d'you think I'd want to do that?'

''Cos you fancy me, don't you, Charlie? I've seen the way you look at me, staring at me tits. D'you want to see 'em properly?'

She began to unbutton her blouse. Charles was seized with something approaching panic. He turned away, but at the same time he knew he had to assert himself.

'I've always thought it unfair,' he said, not looking at her, 'that girls can get away with all sorts of bad behaviour because they're never caned. I think you deserve six of the best, just like the boys get.'

She let out a scream of laughter. 'D'you want to cane me, then, Charlie? Would you like that? Bet you would! Blokes say I've got a nice bum.'

Charles turned, to find she was lying on her stomach. She hoisted up her skirt. Charles gasped at what she revealed, turned away and almost ran back down the playing field.

Once he'd calmed down, he decided not to report the incident; it would make him look a fool. But he made himself a resolution. He would never again put himself in a position where he'd be demeaned by a female. He'd put a stop to any potential insolence before it started by making it clear, right from the start, who was boss. At least he probably wouldn't have that sort of trouble from the bluestockings at university.

By the time he got home, he'd managed to regain his equilibrium. But when he went to bed, he couldn't get to sleep. He kept thinking about what Desiree Statham had revealed. Charles allowed himself to wonder, not for the first time, if his life might have been different had he left school after the fifth form while he'd still had the confidence that Bonzo had helped him achieve. But would it have been a more satisfying life? That was something he dare not analyse; he'd never allowed himself to wallow in morbid introspection.

Chapter 10

Keith was sipping his coffee in his favourite café in Staffridge. He didn't frequent the coffee chains; he much preferred this small establishment where most of the clientele were elderly and where the coffee was better, and much cheaper. He'd been making a belated start on the Christmas shopping, armed with a list of items provided by Debbie, and had decided to take a break because the town centre was profoundly depressing on a cold, wet and almost dark winter day. All the shoppers looked miserable, hunched against the elements in their cheap hooded anoraks as they grappled with loaded shopping bags, and they seemed no happier when they entered the crowded, over-heated and garishly decorated shops. It being a weekday, there were few teenagers about, nor any buskers. Even the charity-collectors were subdued and stood silently, collecting tins in hand, perhaps aware that, in this weather, to dance enthusiastically towards potential donors would be counterproductive.

But despite the uninspiring scene, Keith always felt comfortable in Staffridge, because the shoppers were mostly working-class. Okay, they weren't Yorkshire people, but at a pinch Staffridge could be considered to be in the north. One of the things that he enjoyed about being retired was that he no longer had to adopt the sort of accent that seemed to be required for someone holding the post of deputy headmaster. He was reverting to the accent and speech patterns of his youth in Sheffield. Debbie didn't like it, he knew.

There were still numerous beggars about. Most of them weren't actively seeking alms; they were encased in sleeping bags. There was one pathetic creature to whom Keith sometimes chatted before giving her his spare change. It was hard to determine her age because, although her eyes and hair were those of a youngish woman, she was entirely toothless and her skin was scabrous. He'd come across her this morning in her usual position in the underpass. At least, he'd assumed it was her, but no part of her was visible, wrapped as she was from head to toe in her sleeping bag. He'd bent over and asked how she was, but there was no response, no movement. He'd decided it was best to let her sleep, but after he'd left her he'd been struck by the thought that she may have been unconscious, or even worse. He was feeling guilty because he hadn't returned to check. He didn't have time now.

As he drained his coffee cup and put on his coat, he was suddenly gripped by anger. Staffridge today had encapsulated all that was wrong with society. The Welfare State he'd grown up with was dying.

But as he drove out towards Littleton Parva his anger was replaced by something like guilt because he knew how privileged he was, owning a large home, and having a sizeable index-linked occupational pension. He had grown up in a back-to-back terraced house in Barnsley. When, thanks to Debbie's inheritance, they'd purchased a house with large garden, he'd felt ambivalent about it. Part of him felt ashamed; owning such a thing seemed to be a betrayal of his working-class roots. Debbie, on one of the occasions she'd challenged him - something she was now doing increasingly frequently - said she couldn't understand this obsession he had with working-class lifestyles: he'd been a deputy headmaster for heaven's sake; what could be more middle-class than that? He couldn't be bothered to explain that it was precisely people like them who should be paying more taxes. To atone for his sins he'd re-joined the Labour party when Jeremy Corbyn had been elected leader, and had started attending local party meetings.

Debbie was happy enough to lend a helping hand to friends in need, but uninterested in the wider ills of society. She came from a comfortable background, took little interest in politics, and had taken some persuading to vote in the referendum. On his recommendation she had, he hoped, voted 'Remain'. But he'd begun to notice that she was increasingly adopting the attitudes that had been held by her wealthy parents, attitudes he despised. He was beginning to have doubts about their future together.

He parked the car in his drive and entered the house. The downstairs lights were already turned on, though it was only three o'clock.

'Hello, I'm back!' he shouted.

There was an almost inaudible reply from the lounge.

'Can't hear you! I'll be with you in a minute. Got to unload the car!'

When he finally made it into the lounge, he found her kneeling in front of the Christmas tree surrounded by coloured lights and baubles. She got to her feet.

'Did you manage to get everything?' she asked.

'Mostly. I'll go through the list with you once I've had a cuppa.'

'How was Staffridge, then?'

'Depressing. D'you want a cup of anything?'

'Not yet. I want to finish this tree, and then make a start on the mince pies.'

He made a cup of tea and carried it into the lounge.

'Any news? Any phone calls while I was out?'

She turned away from the Christmas tree and faced him. 'No phone calls; not for you anyway. But something interesting happened.'

'What was that, then?'

'Charles next door had a visitor. I was upstairs changing the bedding, and I noticed a car draw up outside his house. I couldn't resist watching. A woman got out. She was wrapped up against the cold, but she looked quite young. And she was black.'

'What?'

'You heard. A youngish, black woman.'

'Bloody hell. D'you reckon he's got a new cleaner?'

'She wasn't carrying any cleaning equipment, and anyway, his Mrs Williams was only there yesterday. And this woman was there for well over an hour. I saw her drive off.'

'So, what d'you think that was all about?'

'I've thought about it, and I reckon she might have been a social worker.'

'How come?'

'You must have noticed how he is recently. He must be finding it hard to cope, not having a family to help him.'

'Suppose so. Well, if he's managed to get a social worker, he should count himself lucky. There are folk far worse off than him who don't seem able to get one.' Just in time, Keith stopped himself from launching into a lecture about the scenes he'd witnessed in town.

'Y'know, Keith, I reckon the poor man must be lonely now he doesn't seem able to get out. He never has any visitors apart from his cleaner. Christmas must be an awful time for him. I've been thinking …'

'Yes? What have you been thinking?'

'I might just call round on him sometime, ask him if he's okay, ask if there's anything we can do for him.'

'Bloody hell, Debbie, we haven't spoken to him for God knows how many years!'

'I know, and I feel a bit guilty about that now. I reckon that's what's probably worse for him, not having anyone to talk to. You never know, he might even ask me in for coffee. I'd like to see inside his house.'

'Well, that's up to you. But just promise me one thing – that you won't invite that bugger round here.'

She didn't reply. Keith assumed that, as usual, he'd annoyed her with his language. Well, tough. She'd have to learn to put up with it.

Chapter 11

Jeanette was looking forward to having her son and daughter-in-law come for Christmas with their baby. There had been a time earlier in her life when she'd resigned herself to never having a family of her own.

She was enjoying being in her 60s because she'd never really liked being young. She'd known she wasn't the most attractive of girls and had taken refuge in books and in her studies. At the time she'd told herself this would bring her benefits in later life and that she didn't need the company of those who seemed determined to fritter away their youth on frivolities.

She'd made a few friends at university, all women. They'd told her that town planning seemed a strange career objective, all dry-as-dust statistics and reports and dreary policy meetings; nothing creative about it. But by then, she'd become a socialist and environmentalist, and planning seemed to offer an opportunity to change society for the better without having to engage in campaigning or demonstrating, the sort of activities that would bring attention to herself. Jeanette had never liked being the centre of attention. She was essentially a back-room girl.

And as a back-room girl, she'd had no need to worry about how she looked. She was tall and had dressed demurely so as not to draw attention to herself; flat shoes, of course. She also had poor sight, but the fancy specs the optician tried to sell her served only to emphasise her strong features – she had a hooked nose – so she'd chosen black horn-rims, large enough to accommodate varifocal lenses and hide the bushy eyebrows which, as a matter of principle, she never plucked. Nothing, however, could disguise her frizzy hair. No one, she'd hoped, would look at her twice.

'Post's come, darling,' announced Andrew as he entered the room. 'Just Christmas cards and junk-mail by the look of it.'

'Can you open it, Andy? I want to finish getting up these fairy lights.'

'Sure.'

He rifled through the envelopes. 'There's a few just addressed to you. D'you want to open them?'

'Yes. Leave them on the sideboard, please. I'll look at them later.'

'Right. I'm off to do the shopping then: be back in about an hour. Give us a kiss.'

They embraced.

After Andy had left, Jeanette thought, as she often did, how lucky she was to have met him when she'd reconciled herself to lifetime of lonely spinsterhood. Andy had been a lecturer at the University of Sussex, and she'd met him while attending an extra-mural course on challenges to the environment. Serious discussions between them in the university coffee bar were soon followed by meetings in town, where the conversations began to become more personal. Gradually, they became an item, and Jeanette discovered that under the rather reserved exterior, Andy was an amusing, affectionate man.

They'd married in haste, and she'd never regretted it. Their son was born when she was 42. Their joint income meant she could abandon the need to seek career progression, and she retired early and then gave all her energy to enjoying her marriage and raising her son.

She completed the decorations and went to the kitchen to wash her hands and make a cup of tea. She carried the cup back into the lounge and noticed, on the sideboard, the Christmas cards that Andy had left unopened.

They never had many cards. She knew without looking at them whom one would be from – Gordon Tagg. She picked up the cards, and yes, on one of the envelopes was his unmistakable scrawl.

Gordon Tagg. One of the few people she'd warmed to during her time working in Staffridgeshire. Perhaps that was because as traffic control advisor he'd stood outside the hierarchy and hadn't felt the need to assert any authority. Consequently, every officer treated him as an equal; all except one, of course: that loathsome Charles Pettifer.

She opened the envelope and extracted his card, expecting to see just the usual *with best wishes, Gordon* written in it: but there was something else. She read it and nearly spilled her tea. Just seeing the name Charles Pettifer written down was enough to shake her, but not so much as the fact that Gordon had actually met him, and that they'd evidently discussed her.

***

Jeanette knew she'd been lucky to have been appointed as an area planning officer in Staffridgeshire at such a young age. But although the title sounded impressive, it didn't come with much power. On major issues she could only make recommendations to Pettifer, and the final decision was his.

When she first took up her post, he spoke to her with the sort of scrupulous politeness that disguises contempt. She noticed this wasn't the way he addressed other female members of staff, so she assumed the way he spoke to her was not only because he didn't want her in the job, but because she was unattractive. It was the way quite a few men had treated her in her previous positions.

But the politeness didn't last long. Pettifer found fault with many of her planning recommendations and voiced these in front of her fellow area officers in the monthly meetings held in his office, meetings seemingly designed to demean and denigrate. It culminated on the occasion when he told her to *be quiet, woman* when she tried to explain her reasons for recommending the rejection of an application for housing development. To add to her humiliation, he told her, in front of the others, to report to his office the following week.

There was no one in whom she could confide. She

spent the next week torn between anger at the way Pettifer had behaved and worry about what he intended to say to her. What might he have in mind to do; maybe make life so uncomfortable for her that she'd have no alternative but to resign?

On the day of the interview, she wondered how to present herself. She was damned if she was going to make a special effort for the occasion, but then an idea came to her – why not wear trousers? Trousers suited her, her university friends had told her; they certainly disguised her thin legs, went well with flat shoes, and suited what she knew was her only redeeming features, her trim waist and neat backside. Not that she wanted to impress Pettifer, far from it. Wearing trousers would be a gesture of defiance; it was an unspoken rule that they were inappropriate attire for women in local government offices.

She stood outside his secretary's office. Access to Pettifer was always only via Gillian Tebbit's office, and entry to his domain was achieved only after she had alerted him. Debbie was about to knock, but then thought, *No, damn it, why should I?* She entered. Gillian was bending over a filing cabinet; her short dress had ridden up to mid-thigh. Gillian always dressed to flaunt her assets.

'Yes?'

'I've an appointment with Mr Pettifer.' She was tempted to add *As well you know.* But it wasn't just her physical assets that Gillian flaunted; she obviously relished her role as gatekeeper to the Almighty. Gillian's gaze lingered over Jeanette's trousers, and there was a distinct raising of her eyebrows, no doubt a gesture of disapproval that Jeanette was intended to see. Gillian sat down behind her desk and picked up the telephone.

'Miss Beasley is here to see you.'

There followed a silence. Evidently Pettifer was talking to her; she smiled at whatever he was saying, but when she put down the phone the smile was abruptly extinguished.

'You can go in now.'

Pettifer's desk was placed so that he faced those who entered. He remained seated behind it, something Jeanette had noticed he always did when addressing staff who were standing.

'Ah, Ms Beasley. Come in. Sit down.' He indicated the chair placed at the opposite side of his desk. It seemed the meeting was to be confrontational.

'Now, Ms Beasley, I want to discuss further the planning application for housing development in Little Drayton. Firstly, who in your office knows of your recommendation that the application be rejected?'

'Only my deputy, at present.'

'Are you sure about that?'

'Of course. I follow the standard procedure; not to inform junior staff of my planning recommendations until they've been agreed by you.'

'And can your deputy be trusted not to have divulged this information to anyone else in your office?'

'Absolutely. Frank Lappin is highly professional.'

'Might he have told people outside your office? Friends or family, perhaps?'

'Mr Pettifer, I don't make it my business to ask my staff what they talk about outside working hours. But I can only repeat what I said; Frank Lappin is highly professional and I'm certain he would never divulge confidential work information to family or friends.'

'Not even to his wife?' He smirked. 'Pillow talk, perhaps? A lot of things can be said in the afterglow.'

Jeanette was outraged. She couldn't trust herself to reply politely, so remained silent.

'And what about *you*, Ms Beasley? Are you as professional in your private life as you claim your Mr Lappin is?'

'Mr Pettifer, I regard that suggestion as highly insulting.'

'Okay, okay; no need to get on your high horse. What about your other outside contacts?'

'What exactly do you mean by that?'

'Your comrades in the Labour party.'

Suddenly, she felt less self-assured. How much did Pettifer know?

'Mr Pettifer, I am not a member of the Labour party. I gave up my membership when I moved here.'

'But you've got a pal in the local party, haven't you? You're quite matey with Jeremy Jarvis, I believe. You've been seen a few times having coffee with him over in Congleton.'

Jeanette was taken aback. She did meet up with Jeremy Jarvis occasionally. She'd first met him when she'd just moved to the area; he came to her door, canvassing for Labour. He was a county councillor for the ward in which she lived and was seeking re-election.

'Well, Ms Beasley? Are you going to deny it?'

'Mr Jarvis is an acquaintance. He lives a few doors away from me. Sometimes we run into each other when we're out shopping, and yes, occasionally we have a coffee together.'

'Congleton seems a fair distance away for you to go shopping. What's wrong with Staffridge? Might it be that Jarvis doesn't want his wife to know he meets you?' This was said with another smirk.

Jeanette had had enough. She stood up, ready to leave.

'Hang on, Jeanette; you don't mind if I call you Jeanette, I hope? Sorry, we seem to have got off on the wrong foot. Don't go, let's have a coffee and talk about this sensibly. You have milk and no sugar, don't you?'

He rose and walked over to the percolator on the other side of his office. Jeanette felt at a disadvantage: to walk out now might be seen as an admission of guilt.

'Let's go and sit on the easy chairs over there,'' he said as he busied himself with the percolator. 'We may as well be comfortable.'

He seemed to be implying that they were to have a cosy chat, something Jeanette didn't relish. But she didn't want to receive another accusation that she was on her high horse. She crossed the room and sat down at the coffee table. There was one other chair beside it.

Pettifer carried over the coffee, then pulled over the chair and sat down close to her.

'Now, Jeanette. Let me tell you what all this is about. It might surprise you to know that Counsellor Dobson is a keen environmentalist; yes, some Tories are. But he has to balance this with the need to provide much-needed housing in the area. He regards it as the utmost importance that the application for housing development in Little Drayton is approved.'

'But if you're going to overrule my recommendation that it's rejected then he'll get his way, won't he?'

'Ah, but Jeanette,' - she was conscious of him staring at her, but she was determined not to meet his eye – 'we don't want evidence of discord in the planning department to become public. That would give ammunition to opponents like Jarvis.'

'I don't see how I can help.'

'Ah, but you can. I'm suggesting you change your mind about recommending rejection, and bring your deputy Lappin on board. Then, call a meeting of your team in the area office to explain what the policy is.'

Jeanette was so stunned by what he'd suggested that she was lost for words.

'If you can do that, Jeanette, I'll make it worth your while.' And with that, he leaned forward and put his hand on her knee.

Stay calm, Jeanette told herself. She took a sip of coffee then rose slowly to her feet, his hand slipping from her knee as she did so.

'I'd like a week to consider what you've asked. Is that acceptable?'

'Yes, but no longer. Time is of the essence.'

She turned to leave. Pettifer remained seated, but said, as she walked towards the door – 'I like your trousers, Jeanette. They fit you very well, if I may say so.'

It took Jeanette a long time to get to sleep that night. Anger was still there, of course, but also self-doubt. Had she revealed too much to Jeremy Jarvis at their meetings? Usually, by mutual agreement, their conversations were limited to national and international political and environmental issues, but at one meeting Jeremy had mentioned the planning application in Little Drayton, saying that Counsellor Dobson was all in favour of it being approved. She remembered blurting out, 'Not if I have my way, it won't,' and immediately regretting it, especially when Jeremy had grinned at her and said, 'I'm glad we see eye-to-eye about that.'

When she woke up after about two hours of intermittent sleep, she knew she'd have to meet him again. The first thing she did after breakfast was to phone him.

They met in their usual café. They always met in Congleton because it was across the county boundary, and there was little chance of any Staffridge counsellors or local government officers seeing them together – not that they had anything to hide, of course.

'What's this all about then, Jeanette?' said Jeremy when they were seated with their drinks. 'Sorry, I can't stay long, but you sounded a bit stressed when you phoned.'

'Jeremy, I shouldn't be telling you this, but – '

She gave him an account of her interview with Pettifer.

'And you're sure he said he'd make it worth your while if you changed your recommendation?' Jeremy asked. 'Did he say how?'

'No. And I didn't ask.'

'Interesting,' said Jeremy. 'Very interesting.' He looked at his watch. 'Sorry, Jeanette, I've got an appointment coming up. I'll have to leave you. See you again soon, I hope.'

'But Jeremy, what do you intend doing about all this?'

'Not sure yet. But whatever I decide to do, you can rest assured your name will be kept out of it.'

After a week had passed, Jeanette walked into Gillian's office.

'I want to see Mr Pettifer. Now, please.'

'I don't have an appointment for you.'

'Oh, he'll see me.'

'Not without an appointment he won't.'

Jeanette marched straight over to Pettifer's door and opened it. He was sitting at his desk.

'What the hell …?'

'I've just come to tell you that I've decided not to change my recommendation about the Little Drayton planning application. That's all I want to say.'

Before he could reply, Gillian entered. 'I'm sorry Charles, she just barged in.'

Jeanette turned. 'Don't worry, Gillian, I'm just about to barge out.'

As she left, she heard Gillian say to Pettifer, 'What a bitch that woman is.'

A few months later, Pettifer had taken early retirement, and the planning application had been rejected. Jeanette had left to take up her new position in the Havant. And subsequently she discovered that Counsellor Dobson had provided a glowing reference for her when she'd applied for the post.

***

Despite the initial shock of reading Gordon's card, Jeanette found she was, in fact, quite calm. In the past, before she married Andy, whenever the events in Staffridgeshire had surfaced in her thoughts she'd become emotional, before trying to expunge the memory by hurriedly thinking about something else or engaging in frantic activity.

But that was the old Jeanette. For the new, married

Jeanette, the one with straightened hair, plucked eyebrows, discreet make-up, contact lenses and wearing fashionable clothes, the memory evoked little emotion, except perhaps a trace of guilt. She was still uncertain whether she'd been complicit in the events that had led to Pettifer's early retirement. Although still on the left and voting Labour (though with less enthusiasm than she had once done), she had come to realise that nefarious activities could take place across the entire political spectrum.

She was still holding Gordon Tagg's Christmas card. At the end of his short message, he'd written his email address. Was this an invitation to contact him? Did she want to? What would they have to say to each other after all these years?

Quite a lot, she imagined. No doubt there were things that each of them knew that the other didn't. She wondered if he knew what had happened to Jeremy Jarvis: she'd had no contact with him since their final meeting. She knew Jeremy liked her, very much. Was that the reason why …? No, that was one thing she still didn't want to think about.

Chapter 12

Debbie decided that on reaching a certain age, the day following Boxing Day was one of the most profoundly dispiriting of the year. Once the joy of hosting the children and grandchildren was over, there was little to look forward to. Keith was all for taking the decorations down immediately – 'Christ, we only put them up for the kids and grandkids' – but Debbie refused to countenance this; it would be an admission of their advancing years. But she did agree to the disposal of the Christmas tree: its needles had begun to litter the carpet. In any case, the tree was Keith's responsibility; it was he who purchased it, erected it in its holder, and strung the lights over it, a job which involved the use of the sort of language which upset Debbie. He used it ever more frequently these days and always exaggerated his Yorkshire accent when doing so. Somehow the 'f' and 'c' words sounded more obscene when their vowels were pronounced the Yorkshire way.

They were discussing the season as they ate their breakfast.

'The trouble with this time of year,' said Keith, 'is because we don't even have New Year's Eve to look forward to. It's just weeks more of bloody winter.'

'Well, New Year's Eve is for young people, isn't it? And face it, Keith: we're not the age to go clubbing, not that we ever did. And you don't even stay up till midnight and watch TV with me, do you? I'm by myself when Big Ben chimes.'

'I find all that crap on TV depressing. And why do we always have to see what's going on in bloody London? What's wrong with Sheffield, or Manchester? Anyway, this whole time of year brings me down.'

'Oh, come on. Count your blessings. Think how awful Christmas and New Year must be for those who're on their own, no family, no friends.'

'Even worse for those who're homeless, out on the

streets. This fuckin' government …'

He launched into his by now familiar diatribe against the Tories, then extended it to include Brexit and populism, culminating in a verbal assault on Donald Trump. Debbie knew better than to interrupt him. She waited until he'd finished and then said, 'But we could do something to cheer up someone who must be lonely.'

'What are you on about?'

'I'm thinking about Charles Pettifer next door. Just think, his cleaner won't have come over the Christmas period, and I haven't seen that social worker calling again. He must have spent the whole time just sitting by himself, poor old man, and – '

'Poor? That's one thing he isn't. Why d'you waste your time worrying about him? You know he's a bastard.'

Debbie got up and started clearing the breakfast table. She couldn't trust herself to reply. It would only bring on a lecture about how she ought to be thinking about the wider ills of society rather than worrying about an over-privileged sexist sod like Pettifer.

'What have you got on today?' she asked.

'Not a lot. I'm going down town to get some printing ink. A pack of cartridges is almost as bloody expensive as the printer was.'

Great, thought Debbie. She knew he'd also go and have a coffee in town like he always did. That would give her about an hour to do what she'd been intending to do for months.

Charles Pettifer's front garden was just as overgrown as the back, but at least, thought Debbie as she walked up the path, there weren't any large trees to shed leaves and further enrage Keith.

She rang on Pettifer's doorbell. No response. She waited for a minute, then rang again. 'Hold on, can't you!' was just audible from inside. She had to wait a further minute before the door was opened. She was confronted by a very old man leaning on a walking frame.

'What is it? If you're selling something, I'm not interested.' The formerly high-pitched voice was now almost a croak.

'It's me, Charles; Debbie Barker from next door.'

Rheumy eyes peered at her. 'Good God, what do *you* want? Come to complain about something, have you?'

'No, of course not, Charles. I've just come to see how you are.'

'Sure about that, are you? You and your husband haven't spoken to me for years. Why the sudden concern?'

'Aren't you going to invite me in, Charles? It's cold out here. I can explain when we're in the warm.'

He looked her up and down. The last time he'd done that, thought Debbie, it was with a lascivious smile on his face. Now, it was done with suspicion written all over it, rather as if he were checking to see if she were carrying an offensive weapon.

'You'd better come in, I suppose.'

He shuffled down the hall, and Debbie followed. He'd always been stooped, but now he was bent almost double.

'Now, what's all this about?' he said when they entered the kitchen. There was no offer of any refreshment, nor even an invitation to sit down.

Debbie, with many false starts and hesitations, tried to explain that she was concerned about him given that he'd probably been on his own over Christmas, with no visitors, and asked if there was anything she could do to help. He didn't interrupt but just stared at her while she spoke. Her speech tailed off.

'I reckon you've just come to satisfy your curiosity, haven't you? Well, I am as you see. I'm old and unwell. And yes, I have been on my own over Christmas, but that's nothing new – ' he started coughing, and this went on for some time before he continued – 'so you can report that back to your husband.'

'You usually have a cleaner come in, though?' Debbie ventured.

'Isn't it obvious? You don't think *I'm* responsible for keeping the place clean and tidy, do you?'

In fact, Debbie had already registered the cleanliness of the place – work-surfaces pristine, the Welsh dresser polished, no unwashed dishes in the sink, no clutter anywhere, though there was an array of what looked like medicines on one of the kitchen cabinets. And the place smelled clean; there wasn't the odour of solitary old age about the house that she'd anticipated.

'Are you eating properly?' she asked, 'I've noticed you have a Tesco delivery. Can you manage the cooking?'

'Frozen ready-meals. Don't have much of an appetite anyway.'

'D'you mind me asking, Charles, do you have a social worker visiting you? I saw a woman call before Christmas – '

'She's not a social worker!' This was shouted with almost his old screech, but then his face crumpled. Tears appeared at the corner of his eyes, and he gave what sounded like a sob. He turned away from her, and she thought he heard him croak, 'I'm sorry.'

Debbie touched him briefly on the shoulder. 'Charles, I'm sorry if I've upset you. I'll leave now, if you want.'

'No! Don't go!' This was almost shouted. He turned to face her. 'Stay for a coffee, or tea if you prefer.'

'If you're sure. I'd prefer tea. Would you like me to get it?'

'No! I'm not that incapable! You go and sit in the lounge – it's across the hall.'

'Will you manage to carry it in?'

'I use a trolley.'

Debbie walked across the hall, entered the lounge, and was immediately aware of the deep-pile carpet. The room was spacious with windows at both ends and furnished with leather sofas and what looked like antique coffee tables set against them. Under the front window was an office desk, on top of which sat a computer. One side of the room was taken up by a large bookcase, on which the books seemed to have been meticulously arranged according to their height. There was enough space between the bookcase and one of the sofas for a television, which was set at an angle so it faced the centre of the room. Despite the luxury of its accoutrements, the room gave off an aura of unused bleakness; the creaseless cushions on the sofas challenged anyone to dare lean against them. There were no Christmas cards on the mantelpiece. The place resembled an estate agent's showroom.

But one feature was at odds with its surroundings. In the centre of the room, facing the television, was a shabby reclining armchair, one of those which, at the press of a button, can tip the occupant forward to help him stand up. On the seat of the chair was a TV remote control.

This chair, set in a room which obviously never hosted other people, spoke of Charles's isolation and desolation. Here, she assumed, he'd sit alone, flicking from channel to channel. If he were amused or irritated by what he saw, there was no one with whom he could share his feelings. Then he'd retire to bed, probably more depressed than he'd been all evening. Debbie was awash with pity for him.

Should she sit on one of the sofas? There wasn't any alternative. She removed one of the cushions and perched on the edge. Then she noticed, on the coffee-table in front of her, a few Christmas cards. They were lying flat.

Should she? Why not? She'd probably be warned of Charles's approach by the trundling of the trolley. She picked up and opened one of the cards. In it was written, *To Charlie: see you in the New Year, Annie xx.*

Annie? See you in the New Year? Oh, it could be his cleaner. Surprising she should sign off with kisses.

She picked up another card. *With best wishes from Bonzo. No fun getting old, is it? Can't pull the birds like we used to! Hope you're well.*

Pull the birds? Must be an old school friend: Debbie's elder brother used to refer to 'birds'.

She picked up the third card and was staggered to read, *With all the best from Celia. I do hope you're well and happy.*

So they'd remained in contact! Or maybe it was just she who sent a card, and he never reciprocated? That would be just like him – or like the man he used to be.

She read the final card. *Dear Charles, I still think of you a lot. Hope you think of me. It would be so nice if you'd let me call in on you sometime like I used to. Love, Gillian xxx*

Gillian? Who the hell was she? She must be someone local, to have mentioned calling in on him. And love and kisses?

Debbie had left the door ajar, and it was opened, pushed by a trolley behind which followed Charles. She hurriedly put the card back on the table. Charles manoeuvred the trolley over to her and began trying to lift the teapot and cups on it onto the table in front of her, but he staggered, nearly lost his balance. She caught the look of despair on his face.

'Here, let me do that, Charles.'

'Thanks.' Then he muttered to himself '*Useless! Useless!*'

Debbie poured the tea and sat back on the sofa. She'd placed his cup next to hers.

'You don't mind me sitting next to you, then?' he asked.

'Of course not. Why should I?'

He grasped the arm of the sofa and slowly lowered himself so he was next to her. Despite the length of the three-seater sofa, he had to sit close to her so he could reach his cup. Their shoulders were touching. It occurred to Debbie that the last time they'd had physical contact was decades ago when he'd propositioned her in her kitchen. She felt a twinge of regret for the passing of the years. They simultaneously reached for their cups, sipped from them, and replaced them. Then there was silence. It occurred to Debbie what a bizarre scene this would appear to an onlooker; two elderly people sitting very close to each other, staring into space and not conversing. She wanted to ask him about the nature of his illness, but would he want to talk about it? Her mother had always shied away from discussing the prospect of her imminent death. And from the look of him, she reckoned Charles didn't have long.

She peered round the room, seeking inspiration from her surroundings.

'What a wonderful collection of books you have, Charles. Almost a library. Do you do a lot of reading?'

'Used to. Find it hard to concentrate these days.'

'Watch a lot of television, do you?'

'A bit. Most of it's rubbish. Can't stand watching the news; it's nothing but Brexit. So I go to bed at ten.' His voice had begun to quaver.

'I see you've got a computer. D'you spend much time online?'

'A bit.'

'Do you use email?'

'Used to, when … when ...'

He slumped forward, put his head in his hands and his shoulders began heaving. She couldn't reach for a hand to squeeze; there was no alternative but to put her arm round his shoulders.

Gradually, the heaving of his shoulders subsided. He pulled himself back. She removed her arm, but didn't know what to say to comfort him, so she reached for his hand. He grasped it as though it were a lifeline.

They sat, hand in hand, for several minutes: there was nothing they could talk about. Debbie recalled meetings with old friends, those whom she'd not seen for years and with whom she found she now had little in common, but nevertheless their conversation had been animated because they'd spoken of old times in their youth. But despite having been neighbours for decades, she and Charles had no old times to talk about.

Charles slowly disentangled his hand from hers and turned to face her for the first time since they'd been in the lounge.

'Debbie, I'm grateful for you to for coming to see me, but I think you ought to leave now.'

'Why, Charles?'

'Because I'm an old man, with all that implies.'

'Well, that doesn't matter; I'm an old woman now, aren't I?'

He touched her knee briefly, then edged across the sofa, reached for its arm and heaved himself to his feet. He pushed the trolley out of the room and stood in the hallway, having left the door open. The signal was obvious: he really did want her to leave.

On her way to the front door she stopped and turned to face him.

'Charles, I hate to think of you here alone. I can come and see you again, if only for a few minutes, if you'd like.'

'No. It's bad enough you're seeing me as I am now. I don't want you to see what I'm going to become.'

He pushed the trolley forward and opened the front door. As Debbie moved to leave, he kept the trolley between them. Outside, she turned to wave goodbye, but the door was already closing. Before it shut, she heard him start to cough.

As she walked down his path, sadness overwhelmed her. She was sad not just for him, but for herself. And at least he had women who sent him affectionate cards.

Chapter 13

Debbie was annoyed, as she often was when she and Keith went to Staffridge film theatre in winter. The argument started once they were in the car.

'Turn the heating down, can't you, Keith? I'm sweating already. It's nonsense having to wear all these layers when we have to strip off as soon as we get in the auditorium.'

'But for God's sake, Debbie, it's bloody freezing in the foyer, isn't it?'

'So why do we have to sit there for fifteen minutes waiting for the film to start? Oh, I know you want to be first into the auditorium so we can get a seat in the back row. But I've never understood why. The view of the screen's no better there than anywhere else. And it's probably hottest up there at the back. I have to spend the first fifteen minutes peeling of all these layers.'

'Well, you wouldn't be able to do that if you had people sitting behind you, would you?'

'And it's not as if the coffee they serve in the foyer's any good. Why don't we have coffee at home before we leave?'

'You know bloody well I like to time my coffee so I'm ready for a pee just before the film starts, so I can go for another hour or so without having to have another one.'

Debbie was on the verge of telling him that she was getting tired of having her life dictated by his bladder, but decided not to because these visits to the film theatre were almost the only activities in which they took part as a couple. The film showing that night was 'Saturday Night and Sunday Morning' which Keith wanted to see again because, he said, it had been ground-breaking in its portrayal of working-class life in the provinces. Debbie was less enthusiastic about it. She'd never cared for Albert Finney anyway.

Keith found a parking space some way from the

film theatre. He told Debbie, as he always did, that it was another good reason for arriving early. She gave her usual reply – that they weren't paupers and could well afford to pay the charge in the theatre car park.

After that exchange, they no longer walked side-by-side. Keith reached the entrance first, pushed at the revolving door and entered without waiting to see if Debbie was close behind him. When she reached the door, she was so annoyed that she shoved it harder than was necessary. It continued to revolve after she was inside, sending blasts of cold air into the foyer. She was then ashamed; she was usually assiduous in her respect for the comfort of others. She told herself it was living with Keith that was making her anti-social.

The stackable plastic chairs in the foyer were almost all occupied, despite their early arrival. This was often the case when the film to be shown was an old one and the patrons were elderly. Grey hair and bald heads abounded. The only thing that made the wait in the foyer tolerable for Debbie was watching and overhearing the conversations of her fellow patrons. Many of them she now knew by sight, and nods of recognition were sometimes exchanged, though she'd never spoken to any of them.

'Look, there are two chairs over there,' said Keith. 'Go and grab 'em while I get the coffee.'

She sat down on one of the vacant chairs, placed her handbag on the other, then looked up to find that the couple sitting opposite her were regulars with whom she was on nodding terms. The man was probably in his late 60s, overweight with a head of thick grey hair. His wife was of similar age, still attractive and probably slim, though this was hard to judge given the voluminous clothes in which she was wrapped.

She'd never been close to them before, and decided it was time to greet them.

'Hello. Chilly in here as usual, isn't it?'

'Isn't it?' said the woman. 'We were wondering

whether to come, but this film's special for us. It was the one we saw on our first date. It was just as cold then.'

'We didn't mind that, did we, Margy? When you're 18, any excuse to have a cuddle in the back row, eh?'

He reached for her hand and continued to hold it. Debbie felt a frisson of envy.

'I don't think today's youngsters would need that sort of excuse,' the woman said, 'not that you ever see anyone under 40 in here.'

'Oh, but you do on occasions,' said the man, 'when it's a film that's obviously on the syllabus on the Media Studies course at the university. Then you get gaggles of students. Not that they pay much attention to the film; they're either chatting to each other or playing with their mobiles.'

'Oh, come on, Gordy: they're not that bad.'

Debbie was about to continue the conversation when she spotted Keith negotiating his way towards them through the crush of people, a cup of coffee in each hand. When he reached her, he thrust a cup at her, and sat down beside her.

'Those bloody women behind the bar get slower each time we come here,' he said. Without waiting for an answer, he began telling Debbie about how he'd been gripped by Sillitoe's 'Saturday Night and Sunday Morning' when it was first published. He didn't acknowledge the couple sitting opposite them, and Debbie heard them start talking to each other about what their children had been like when at university. It seemed the limited interchange between them and Debbie was now over.

Debbie's attention to Keith's lecture began to wander; she'd heard it all before. She began to catch snatches of the conversation between the couple opposite: the man was saying he hadn't yet received an email from someone, and his wife was saying that she – presumably the 'someone' – might not wish to reply.

She tried to drag her attention back to what Keith

was saying but was startled to hear the woman say the name 'Charles Pettifer'. Surely not? Had she heard right? Keith was still in full flow, but she was no longer listening to him. Then the man said, 'But there's no chance of her running into Pettifer, is there? I went for years without seeing him until that time we met for coffee. And I haven't heard from him since.'

'Excuse me,' said Debbie, 'sorry to interrupt, but did I hear you mention the name Charles Pettifer?'

The man looked startled. 'Yes, you did,' he said. 'Why?'

'It's just that our next-door neighbour is called that. It's an unusual name, so I thought … '

'May I ask where you live?'

'In Littleton Parva.'

'That's him! My God, that's the sort of coincidence that only happens in badly plotted novels! How long have you been neighbours?'

Keith intervened. 'Too bloody long. The man's an arrogant - '

He was interrupted by an announcement asking people to take their seats in the auditorium. 'Come on, Debs, let's get in before the rush starts.'

'Hang on, Keith.' She turned to the man. 'I'd like to talk more about Charles Pettifer if that's okay by you. Shall we meet up here after the film?'

'Yes, why not? Maybe go on somewhere for a drink. My name's Gordon, by the way, and this is Margy.'

'I'm Debbie, and this is Keith. See you later, then.'

As they all joined the queue for the auditorium, Keith muttered to Debbie, 'Why the hell did you ask them to meet up? The last thing I want is to spend what's left of the evening talking about fuckin' Pettifer.'

'Hadn't you better visit the toilet before you go in? I'll save a seat for you at the back.'

After the film, they went to the bar of a hotel near the film theatre. That had been Gordon's choice; Keith would have much rather gone to a pub. There'd been a getting-to-know-you session, a brief exchange of past histories during which Keith and Debbie had learned that Pettifer had been Gordon's boss in the county planning office.

Keith was finding that, contrary to his expectations, he was quite enjoying listening to Gordon telling them about Pettifer at work; it seemed he was just as much a bastard as a boss as he was as a neighbour.

'Didn't anyone like him at work?' Debbie asked. 'Didn't he have any redeeming features?'

'All the senior staff loathed him,' said Gordon. 'He really seemed to enjoy undermining them and belittling them in front of their colleagues. But some of the junior staff thought he was okay, mostly the younger women. He could turn on the charm when he wanted to.'

'Charm!' interjected Margaret. 'That's not what I'd call it. Gordon took me to one of the planning office's Christmas dos. Pettifer asked me to dance and he ... well, he came on to me, and not very nicely. That was the last time I saw him.'

'Margy!' said Gordon, 'You never told me about that! Why not?'

'I didn't want to upset you, Gordy. You were already having problems with Pettifer at work.'

'How long ago was that, Margaret?' Debbie asked.

'Oh, way back. Do you have much contact with him?' Margaret asked her.

'Not really. It used to be just the occasional 'hello' if I saw him when he was setting off for work. Since he retired, we've hardly seen him. But just after Christmas I called on him because I reckoned he must be lonely. He is. He's a pathetic old man, and I think he's seriously ill. He's not the arrogant man he once was.'

'Will you be visiting him again?'

'No. He made it clear he didn't want me to see him getting worse.'

'He's got his come-uppance, eh, Gordon?' said Keith.

'Seems like it, but I wouldn't wish his fate on anyone,' said Gordon. 'By the way, I've just remembered; there was someone in the office who seemed fond of him; his secretary, Gillian Tebbit was her name, and – '

'Gillian?' Debbie couldn't keep the surprise from her voice.

'There you are, Debs,' said Keith, 'I told you he was shagging his secretary!'

Gordon drained his drink.

'Well, I think it's time we went, Margy.'

'Yes, we must be off too,' said Debbie.

The two women visited the Ladies before leaving.

'Margaret, I must apologise for Keith's language.'

'Oh, don't worry, I've heard far worse. Debbie, I'd like to carry on our conversation sometime. How d'you fancy meeting up in town for a coffee?'

'Without the men, you mean? Yes, good idea.'

They exchanged phone numbers and agreed to text each other to arrange a meeting.

Chapter 14

'Charlie! It's me, Annie!'

There was no reply. She carried her equipment into the kitchen: he wasn't there. And he wasn't on the landing either.

She wondered if he might have been taken to hospital. He'd been going downhill ever since Christmas. Last time she came, he'd been standing at the top of the stairs and had asked her to help him down. He was embarrassed, poor old bugger. Once she'd got him into the kitchen she'd kissed his cheek, and he hadn't backed away; in fact, he'd grabbed her hand and held it for a few minutes.

Maybe he was at the top of the stairs now? But he would have heard her call, wouldn't he? *Better check.* She went out into the hall, peered up the stairs. There was no sign of him.

'Charlie, it's me, Annie! Are yer in? Are yer all right, dear?'

There was a muffled, feeble call from upstairs. She couldn't make out what was said.

She lumbered up to the landing. The doors to the four bedrooms were closed, as usual. She was never allowed to enter them; he'd told her that three of them were never used, so weren't dirty. *Just like a man*, she'd thought; *twenty years of dust in 'em, I bet.* He didn't let her clean his bedroom either. He said he was capable of doing that. She wondered how often he changed his sheets. He certainly couldn't do that now, the state he was in.

'Which room yer in, Charlie?'

'In here.'

'Can I come in, dear?'

'Yes.'

She pushed open the door, not knowing what to expect. It was a large bedroom, but her practiced cleaner's eye immediately noticed it was a shambles, clothes strewn over chairs and on the floor, dust on the windowsills and there was a smell of – could it be? – yes, it was. Piss.

Charlie was sitting up in a large double bed, still in his pyjamas. He looked awful; deathly pale, eyes half closed.

'Sorry you have to see me like this Mrs … Annie.'

'Don't be daft, dear. Not feelin' too good, aren't yer?'

'It's just that … just that I need you to help me get out of bed. Legs not working too well. I'm sorry; it's not your job to – '

'What are friends for, dear? How long 'ave yer been like this? Did yer manage to get up yesterday?'

'No.'

'Yer mean yer spent the day in bed? What did yer eat?'

'I didn't.'

She noticed a large jug on the bedside table. It was almost empty, just a little water left, so at least he'd had something to drink. That probably accounted for the smell of piss.

'Come on then, Charlie. Let's get yer up.'

'Could you pass me my dressing gown? It's on the floor.'

She watched him struggle his arms into it and then gave thought to the next move. She'd have to pull his legs over the side of the bed so his feet touched the floor, and then try and heave him up. But what then? There was no way she could get him downstairs if he couldn't stand.

'Right, Charlie, I'm gunna get yer feet on the floor. I'll pull off the duvet.'

As she did, she noticed his pyjama bottoms were soaked. They'd slipped down his thighs and she caught sight of an old man's shrivelled willie. She didn't look him in the face; she wasn't embarrassed, but she bet he was.

She wrapped the dressing gown over his loins and began to pull his legs towards the edge of the bed. But when his feet were dangling over the edge, she could go no further without his help.

'Can yer try to lift yer bum off the mattress a bit, Charlie? Gotta try and get you sitting on the edge.'

He tried his best, but his efforts were feeble. He needed her help, and for her to give it meant she had to clamber onto the bed. The resulting manoeuvres resulted in their having intimate physical contact; at one point, she had an arm round his waist and a hand under his buttocks. *Blimey, I ain't touched a man like this fer years,* she thought. But it was like handling an infant; she was shocked by how thin and light he was.

Eventually, she got him sitting on the edge of the bed. His feet only just reached the floor. He hadn't spoken at all during the time they'd been grappling together. His eyes were closed, and he was breathing heavily.

'Right, Charlie. I'm gunna drag that chair over to yer and we'll try to get yer sittin' in it.'

As she started to move the chair his front doorbell rang.

'Looks like yer've got a visitor, Charlie.'

'Oh. Oh God. It's Katia.' His voice was shaky.

'Who's Katia?'

'I'd forgotten she was coming. Would you let her in, please, Annie?'

As she went down the stairs, Annie wondered who this Katia woman was, and why Charlie hadn't replied when she'd asked him. She felt rather offended. But at least maybe she'd now have some help getting him on his chair.

She opened the door and was confronted by a black woman. *Who the hell?*

'Good morning. I've called to see Mr Pettifer.' The voice was posh. Quite a few black folk spoke posh these days.

'Who are yer?'

'My name's Ms Whittaker. I'm Mr Pettifer's nurse. He's expecting me.'

Nurse? How long had Charlie had a nurse? And

why hadn't he told her?

'Yer'd better come in then.'

'Who am I talking to?'

'Eh? Oh, I'm Annie Williams, his cleaner.'

'Is he in the kitchen?' said the woman as she took off her coat.

'No, he ain't. He's in his bedroom. It's a good job yer've come. I need a hand to get 'im downstairs.'

The woman raised her eyebrows at this, so Annie told her how she'd found him and had to help him get out of bed, and how he hadn't eaten all yesterday and how he'd pissed himself.

'Right,' she said. 'I'll attend to him in his bedroom. There's no need to try and get him downstairs, not yet anyway. You can get on with your cleaning down here while I see him. If I require your assistance, I'll call you.'

Snotty-nosed bitch, thought Annie. But she wasn't going to let it go at that.

'Charlie's very ill, ain't he? What's wrong with him? It's serious, innit? How long's 'e got?'

'Mrs Williams, haven't you heard of patient confidentiality? If Mr Pettifer hasn't divulged the nature of his illness to you, that must be because he doesn't wish you to know. It would be most unprofessional of me to tell you. Now, I'll get on with my duties, and I suggest you attend to yours.'

She turned and started climbing the stairs.

Annie was outraged. Who the bloody hell did the cow think she was? She was only a nurse, for Christ's sake, though she didn't speak like any nurse that Annie had ever met. Annie bet she gave Charlie far more comfort than hoity-toity Ms fuckin' Whittaker ever did. Charlie was her mate now, wasn't he? They had cuddles, and she'd kissed him once, hadn't she?

She carried the hoover into the lounge and began furiously running it over the carpet, in her rage banging it against the furniture. What was going on upstairs, she wondered? Was that bitch examining him? Was he naked?

Then she remembered that under her blue uniform Ms bloody Whittaker was slim and shapely. And young. Did Charlie fancy her, maybe? Did he get excited when she examined him? Then she remembered his shrivelled willie. No, the poor old bugger was well past it.

She dusted the windowsills and bookcases, then went into the kitchen. It was a mess – dirty dishes in the sink, and on the table an overflowing ashtray, spilt tea, and a carton of milk which she sniffed. It was off.

She immersed the dirty dishes in bowl of hot water, and while doing so, she was struck by a thought. Okay, Charlie might not fancy Ms Whittaker, but suppose he was getting fond of her? Might she be fond of him? Were they getting matey? Would they talk about the sort of things that she wouldn't understand? They were both posh – educated, she supposed you'd call it. Would they become close friends? Would he get to prefer Ms Whittaker's company to hers?

She left the dishes in the bowl and slumped down at the kitchen table. Things had gone wrong, suddenly. Yes, she was fond of Charlie after a fashion, but she'd hoped something might come of their friendship. It was Bert who'd put the idea into her head. 'That Pettifer bloke's well off, ain't he?' he'd said. 'And he ain't got no relatives, has he? If yer plays yer cards right, Annie, I reckon he might leave yer some money in his will. He ain't got long, has he?'

It ain't bloody fair, she thought. She and Bert had been struggling to get by ever since he'd been forced to retire: no fat pension for the likes of building workers, not like Charlie probably had. And they were living in a council house and would have to pay rent till the day they died. And that bloody Whittaker woman: she'd get a nurse's pension when she retired, one of those that went up with the cost of living – index-linked, was it called? The thought of Whittaker being left money by Charles filled her with renewed rage.

She heard steps descending the stairs, and then the

kitchen door opened.

'Ah, Mrs Williams. Mr Pettifer is now up and dressed. I can manage to get him downstairs. I want to get him down so he can start using his walking frame. And he needs to get some food inside him. He tells me he has some frozen ready-meals.'

Annie couldn't bring herself to speak to the woman. She got up and marched towards the stairs, determined to get to Charles before that bloody nurse, just to give him a few words of comfort to remind him what old friends they were.

'Just a minute, Mrs Williams. There's something you ought to know. I've been talking to Mr Pettifer about how we might get him help with his personal needs. It's possible that he might agree to having regular visits from a care worker. If he does, this might impact on the service that you provide for him. I'll leave him to discuss that with you. But not today, I need to spend some more time with him.'

'Let's get 'im shifted downstairs. Then I'll be off.'

'I don't need your help, Mrs Williams. And you've still got the bathroom to clean, haven't you?'

''That's between me and Charlie, innit? I'm off now.'

Chapter 15

Charles, now dressed thanks to Katia's help, was still waiting for her and Annie to come and help him downstairs when he heard the front door slam, which was strange. Had somebody else arrived? Then the sound of feet ascending the stairs. Katia entered; she was alone.

'Where's Annie?' he asked. 'I thought you said you were going to ask her to help you.'

'She had to leave. Apparently the van arrived early to collect her.'

'But she didn't come to say goodbye.'

'She was in a rush. She asked me to say goodbye to you. Right, Charles, let's get you downstairs. I can manage on my own. I'll go down backwards in front of you and support you while you hold onto the bannisters.'

The operation took some time, but at last Charles was in the hall and clinging onto his walking frame. He managed to walk to the kitchen without Katia's help. He sat down at the table and noticed it was still covered in the mess he'd left there two days ago. Why hadn't Annie cleared it up?

Katia made short work of it, and then bustled about trying to find something he could eat and drink. There was no bread, nor fresh milk, so he had to make do with black coffee, a banana, and ginger biscuits.

'Now, Charles,' she said. 'I hope you've decided to agree to the suggestions I put to you upstairs. The mess in here just shows you need care workers to visit you at least three times a day, to get you up, get your meals, and put you to bed. I'll contact Social Services as soon as I get back to the office.'

'No! Not yet. I'd like time to think about it."

'Well, in the meantime, I think you should go into respite care. There's a good care home in Staffridge. It'll only be for a few weeks while we – '

'No! Please! Just give me a week to consider it.'

'Okay, just a week, then.'

There was no way Charles was going to agree to her suggestions. If care workers came in, they'd be sure to find his stash of paracetamol, and probably confiscate them. He'd be unlikely to have access to painkillers in a care home, would he? And there certainly wouldn't be any booze to drink with them. Over the past few days he'd become determined to put an end to all this once he'd decided he could take no more, and to do it in his own house at a time of his own choosing.

Katia was still going on about how much easier he'd find life if he did as she'd suggested. He'd heard enough. How could he stop her? He didn't want to offend her. What else might they talk about? He interrupted her.

'Katia, I've been meaning to ask you. Where did you study for your M.Sc?'

'Eh? Oh, I did it part-time at Leeds.'

'But I went to Leeds! Did you enjoy it there?'

'Well, as a postgraduate I never led what you'd call a student life. It was a part time course. Were you an undergraduate there?'

'Yes, I studied geography. Then I did a post-graduate course in town planning.'

'When was that?'

'In the early 1960s. Leeds was probably a very different city to how it was when you were there.'

Katia looked at her watch, then pulled a chair over to the table and sat opposite him. 'Tell me about your time there, Charles.'

'Why?'

'I'd be interested to hear about it. And it will do you good to talk about it.'

'Is this therapy?'

Katia smiled. 'Well, let's just say it might be cathartic for you.'

Charles doubted that this would be the case. But it would be good to have somebody to talk to who knew Leeds University; it was something that would be of no interest to Annie.

'Well, it was 1961 when I went up. I was shaken when I first arrived; the university accommodation office had put me in digs in a place called Armley. It was like being in a foreign country, rows of back-to-back terraced houses, washing lines festooned across the streets. And I felt even more alien when the driver of the taxi that took me there from the station kept calling me "love".'

'What were your digs like?'

'Not so bad, I suppose. The landlady was okay, but the meals she served up were terrible. You can only have so much sausage and mash. I had to share a bedroom with another first year student, but I got on well with him. He was studying sociology. The first evening we were there, he persuaded me to visit the local pub. That really was a novel experience, not at all what I expected.'

***

Ken Gubbins, Charles's digs mate, had a cockney accent and wore jeans and a baggy sweater. Charles had on a collar and tie and flannel trousers and was worried that Ken's attire might be de-rigueur for undergraduates. He'd set himself the goal of fitting in with his fellow-students right from the start.

Charles was apprehensive visiting the local pub. Those streets around it looked almost slum-like, and the pub was probably the same. He wasn't sure that two students would be welcomed by the locals.

But he was surprised by the pub's interior. Adjacent to the small bar, empty at this time of the evening, were several small rooms, all carpeted and with upholstered benches and chairs. The man behind the bar told them to take a seat in one of the rooms: Fred would be along in a minute to take their orders. The last thing Charles had expected was waiter service.

They entered the nearest room and sat at a table nearest the door. There was one other occupant seated across the room from them, an old man smoking a pipe. He nodded at them. They'd been sitting for perhaps a minute when a white-coated youngish man, presumably Fred, entered.

'Hey up, lads,' he said. 'What can I get tha?'

Ken asked for a pint of bitter. Charles didn't really care for beer, and would have preferred just a half pint, but didn't want to appear soft, so he ordered the same.

'Two sleevers o' bitter!' Fred shouted out towards the bar, and then left them.

'What the fuck's a sleever, I wonder?' Ken said to Charles.

The old man removed his pipe from his mouth and addressed them. 'Happen tha's not from round these parts, eh, lads? A sleever's a straight glass.'

'Oh, right,' said Ken. 'Thanks.'

'And by the way, lads. Best not use bad language. Albert – he's the landlord - don't like it. We get womenfolk in 'ere.'

Charles thanked him for telling them that. Fred arrived with their beer. Ken took a deep draught from his and lit a cigarette. They started talking about the relative merits of their subjects; they became engrossed in their discussion and forgot about the presence of the elderly man.

Then four people entered the room, two men and two women, all middle-aged. The men were wearing jackets with collars and ties, and the women were – well, dolled up to the nines was the phrase that came to Charles's mind. Was this a special occasion, maybe? They wouldn't dress like that just for an evening down the pub, surely?

The couples greeted the elderly man and crossed the room to sit. One of the men pressed a button on the wall behind him. The faint ringing of a bell came from the bar, and was immediately followed by the entry of Fred, who took their order. Charles looked round the room and noticed there were buttons on the walls behind every table.

'Want another couple of pints, lads, while I'm here?' said Fred.

'Yes please,' said Ken 'What about you Charles?' Charles still had most of his pint still to drink, but said, 'Oh,yes. I will, please.'

One of the women turned to look at them when she heard them speak. 'Eh, I've not seen you lads in here before. New students, are tha?'

Ken assented.

'Let me guess. I bet tha's lodging at Mrs Chambers's place, eh?'

'Yes, that's right.'

'Poor young buggers!' This from the man sitting beside her. 'The two lads who were wi' 'er last year only stayed six months. Couldn't stand the cold, or her cooking. Tha's best start looking for another digs straight away.'

Ken told her it was his intention to look for a flat as soon as possible.

'Tha's both from down south, aren't tha?'

Charles and Ken concurred.

'What football teams does tha support?'

Ken said he was a Chelsea supporter. The man and Ken began an animated discussion about the relative merits of northern and London teams. The other man joined in. They introduced themselves as Bert and Tom.

The women began talking to Charles. They told him their names, Daisy and Ethel. Daisy said they'd been born in Armley, as had their husbands who worked in the local mill, and that they'd lived here all their lives. Charles said, 'Oh, really?', then resorted to drinking his beer. As they were talking, more people had entered the room and greetings were exchanged. Everyone seemed to know everyone else.

'What's tha name, love?' Ethel asked him. Charles told her.

'I bet tha calls thaself Charlie, eh? Or 'appen Chas? I've gotta nephew who started calling himself Chas when he were teased at school for 'aving a posh name.'

Charles was seized by an idea. Chas! Yes! That was what he'd call himself! He'd never liked being Charlie, but had been worried that Charles was too formal a name for an undergraduate, and he didn't want to be mocked by his peers. In celebration of his new identity he drained his glass, and realised he'd drunk two pints.

More customers entered: the room soon became full of people and tobacco smoke, cheerful remarks were shouted across the tables, some of the women began to shriek with laughter. Charles and Ken were included in the jollity. Despite the novelty of his surroundings, Charles began to feel at home.

After two more pints, Charles, assisted by Ken, staggered up the street towards their digs. He was, he supposed, drunk. He rather liked the feeling.

'Not a bad evening, eh, Charles?'

'Bloody good. Oh, I'm called Chas, by the way.'

That night as he lay in bed, the ceiling spinning slightly, Charles found himself happy. The north was all right. Northerners were friendly. He was going to enjoy his time up here, he was sure.

***

'I didn't expect your story of life at university to begin with an account of an evening in a working-class pub,' said Katia, 'but evidently your time in Leeds started well. Did it continue that way?'

'Well, Freshers' Week was a complete waste of time. Induction in the Geography Department only lasted a few hours. After that, two 2nd year students, a man and a woman, showed us round the student union. That only lasted for the afternoon. After the tour of the union we had coffee with them in the cafeteria, where the men and the women sat at separate tables.'

'Why was that?'

Charles hesitated. Should he tell her, he wondered? It would involve using the sort of language employed by the 2nd year students, and he didn't want to offend her.

'Well, the 2nd year fellow asked us if we'd be attending the fresher's dance – he called it a 'hop' – at the end of the week. Most of the fellows said they would be. He then told us we shouldn't expect to … to *get off with* … any of the women because we'd be competing with 2nd and 3rd year students who knew the score. He said that was why it was called Fuck a Fresher Week.'

Charles had been avoiding Katia's gaze when he told her this, but when he glanced at her she was smiling. Encouraged, he continued.

'He went on to say we'd be better waiting for a week or so before going to the dances because then girls from the town started coming and they were often, well, "up for it" was the expression he used.'

Another smile from Katia. 'Did you go to any of the dances?' she asked.

'No. I hadn't come to university to participate in those sorts of activities. I spent the rest of Fresher's Week in the library.'

'What about your digs-mate Ken? Did you spend any time with him?'

'No. I was hoping we might pay another visit to the pub, but throughout that week he didn't come back to the digs until late. He'd spent every evening with his fellow sociologists in the union bar. And on the evening of the fresher's dance he didn't return until midnight. Apparently, he'd met a girl. I remember him saying she was "gagging for I", but because she was in digs, there was nowhere they could go to … well, to consummate the relationship. He said it was his intention to find a flat as soon as possible.'

'And did he?'

'Yes. At the end of the first term he moved in with some of his sociologist friends. I ran into him occasionally in the student union, but we seemed to have little in common. I felt inhibited about visiting the local pub by myself. To be honest, my evenings were lonely. I wanted to find a flat in Headingley where I'd be nearer to the university, hadn't I made any friends with any of my fellow geographers, so there was nobody with whom I could share.'

Katia got up. 'I fancy another coffee. How about you?'

'Yes, please. But are you sure you've got time?'

'Yes. I'm enjoying hearing about your experiences.'

As Katia busied herself making fresh coffee Charles became aware that he was feeling much better. If she'd intended this as therapy, it was working. But it then occurred to him - perhaps her interest in his history might be part of some research project she was engaged in – the thought processes of a dying man, perhaps? If so, did he mind? No. It was a pleasure to talk to someone intelligent. And attractive. As he watched her, her back to him as she attended to the kettle, he admired again her shapely figure; she had an invitingly trim backside. When she turned to face him, he was surprised to realise that it was a long time since he'd thought of her as a black woman. And the fact that she was didn't matter in the slightest.

She brought over the coffee and sat down.

'You haven't said anything about your course or your fellow students,' she said.

***

As term got underway, Charles began to find that some things were closer to how he'd thought a university environment would be. He liked the way the lecturers addressed the students as 'Mr' or 'Miss', the formal way in which tutorials were conducted, the guidance given about reading matter, the hush of the departmental library.

It was of course inevitable, in a cohort of nearly 30 first-year students in the Geography Department, that as the year progressed sub-groups began to emerge. Some of them soon adopted the uniform of sweater-and-jeans and spent much of their time when not in lectures in 'Caff', as the cafeteria was called. But Charles gravitated towards those who dressed as he did. When not in the library, he spent time with them in the union's lounge with its carpet and easy chairs. They discussed their lectures, the essays they'd been set, and then drifted on to wider topics such as their backgrounds - most were from the north - and their interests, including current events and politics. It intrigued him that the northern students were sometimes disparaging about his being a southerner, something the people in the Armley pub never had been.

One of the women in the group stood out as being different. Jenny Hearne was not much taller than he was, was plump, plain and wore glasses. She was a Londoner who spoke rather like Ken. She joined in the group discussions, but was less serious than the others, and began to address whispered asides to Charles, asides in which she mocked some of their companions. Charles had begun to find some of them a bit self-opinionated, and he developed a growing affinity with her. They began to sit next to each other in lectures.

'Hey, Chas,' she said at the end of one lecture, 'Let's go to Caff for coffee for once.'

'What, you mean not go to the lounge with the others?'

'That's right. I think Caff's more my scene. I've started going there quite a bit. Haven't you ever been in there?'

'Not since Freshers' Week.'

'Well, come on, try it. Time you met some people other than bloody geographers.'

Charles, when he wasn't in the library, got to spend time with Jenny in the noisy smoke-filled Caff. She introduced him to people, mainly 2nd and 3rd years, with whom she evidently had a closer affinity than the geographers. Many of the men were bearded and long-haired. When not engaged in ribaldry, they spoke earnestly about politics, and Charles began to see that Jenny had a serious side to her. Most of the other women in the group didn't participate. Much of what was discussed went over his head: they were left-wing but seemed to despise the Labour Party even more than the Tories. He didn't want to reveal his naivety by asking them questions: in any case, many of them, after their initial conversations with him, chose to ignore him.

One day when they were alone together in Caff, he asked Jenny to explain. 'I suppose your friends are Communists?'

She chortled. 'No way! They're in the Labour Soc and Marxist Soc.'

'But they deride the Labour Party! And they seem to loathe Hugh Gaitskell.'

'Of course they do. They're Trots.'

'What's a Trot when it's at home?'

'Chas, d'you really not know?'

He admitted that he didn't. She proceeded to give him a brief lecture about Leon Trotsky and the Fourth International. Why, he wondered, hadn't he known about it before? It hadn't been on his 'A' Level history syllabus. Then she told him the Trots were members of the Socialist Labour League, and that its objective was to have a socialist revolution.

'How come you know all this, Jenny?'

'Just by being with the Trots in Caff, and going to the union debates. I find it more bloody interesting than talking about the aerial differentiation of phenomena.' She was quoting a phrase used frequently by their geography professor.

'Are you a Trot, then?'

She looked him in the eye. It was rare for her to make eye contact.

'Not really, Chas. I pretend I am, so they accept me as one of their crowd. When they're not talking politics, they know how to enjoy themselves. They go to the Saturday hops, and they throw good parties. Why don't you come to one of the hops? You need to lighten up.'

'I can't dance, Jenny.'

'Neither can I, I just stand and shake about. That's all you need to do, and when they start playing that ballroom stuff, I go to the bar.'

'Jenny, another thing I wanted to ask you. The women in the group. They never join in the discussions. Are they Trots?'

'Of course not,' she was said scornfully. 'They're just dolly birds – don't you get that from the way they dress? They just like to be seen with blokes who're well known in the student union. And they like the parties.'

'Do you go to their parties, Jenny?'

'I used to. Not now, though.'

Charles thought he detected a note of sadness in her voice. It emboldened him to ask the question that he hadn't so far dared to ask.

'Jenny, are you … are you …'

'Spit it out, Chas.'

'Are you … attached to one of the fellows in that crowd?'

'Are you joking? A fat, ugly, short-sighted bat like me? When they've got all those dolly birds to choose from?' She rose to her feet. 'Come on, Chas. That bloody historical geography lecture starts in 10 minutes.'

She started hurrying off. Charles rose and hurried after her. When he caught up with her, he said, 'I'd like to go the hop with you next Saturday, Jenny, if that's okay by you.'

***

'So, you found yourself a girlfriend, then?'

'No! Jenny Hearne was just a friend! '

'But you wanted to go to the hop with her. Did she agree?'

'Yes, but we were just mates. Is that so hard to understand? There was never any hint of sexual feeling between us.'

'*Did* you go to the hop with her? Did you enjoy it?'

'Yes, I did, but no, I didn't. I felt totally out of place – deafening music, people gyrating about. I couldn't even gyrate: I've got no co-ordination, all I could do was shuffle my feet. And I felt a fool in my tailored trousers amongst all the jeans. After a few numbers some fellow came and tapped Jenny's shoulder and started dancing with her. I escaped to the side of the room and resigned myself to spending the rest of the evening as a wallflower.'

'What was Jenny's reaction to that?'

'She came and rescued me, told me she could see I wasn't enjoying myself, and suggested we leave. She asked me to take her back to her digs. On the bus ride there, she just chatted to me in her usual self-disparaging manner. In fact, it was then it occurred to me that she was the closest thing to a friend I'd got, and that was it. Just a friend, no hint of anything more, no suggestive remarks, no physical contact. When we got to her digs, she just thanked me and said she'd see me on Monday. Sorry to disappoint, Katia, but there wasn't even a goodnight kiss.'

'But were *you* disappointed?'

'No.'

'And you remained good friends?'

'For the remainder of the academic year, yes.'

'You seem to be suggesting that things weren't quite the same in your second year.'

'To start with they were, up until the Cuban missile crisis.'

'That sounds intriguing, Charles.' She glanced at her watch. 'I've got about half an hour before I must leave. Time for another coffee if you want one, and you can tell me all about it.'

Chapter 16

Charles hadn't really wanted another coffee, but Katia obviously did, and he thought it would help retain the easy informality of their chat if they had cups on the table between them.

'Come on then, Charles. The Cuban missile crisis. I'm all ears.'

'Well, I had a dreary summer vacation working in the Post Office, and I was really relieved to get back to Leeds. I still spent long periods in the library, but still had coffee-breaks with Jenny in Caff, and sometimes we went to the cinema. She persuaded me to start attending debates in the student union, but I wasn't impressed. Most of those who attended seized every opportunity to rant about their political beliefs. There was one fellow who – '

'Come on, Charles! The Cuban missile crisis! I haven't got all day!'

'Oh, sorry. Right.'

***

Charles had been back in Leeds for only a few weeks when his attention was diverted, as was that of every student, to events across the Atlantic. When he heard Kennedy's address to his nation about Soviet missiles being housed in Cuba, he assumed that like most crises it would soon be resolved. But it wasn't. Then when news came of the American blockade of Cuba and the approach of Soviet warships, he began to be worried. The worry turned to fear, fuelled by the near hysteria of students belonging to the union's political societies. As the warships sailed ever closer to Cuba, the talk was of World War 3 and nuclear oblivion.

Jenny provided no comfort. She was pessimistic and seemed to take the likelihood of war as a personal affront.

'It's not bloody fair, Chas,' she said. 'I'm only 19, and I haven't started my life yet. There's so much I still haven't done.'

'It's the same for me, Jenny.'

She glanced at him briefly. 'Then perhaps we ought to do something about it while there's still time.'

Charles was uncertain what she meant by that and didn't like to ask.

'Anyway,' she said, 'I hope you're coming on the demo in the city centre tomorrow?'

'Oh yes. I'll be there.'

It was mainly students in the large crowd assembled outside the soot-blackened Leeds town hall the following afternoon. Many of them Charles recognized from the debates in the student union. They were all lefties, of course – but then he spotted Malcolm Haynes. Haynes was president of the Liberal Soc.

Banners proclaiming 'No War Over Cuba' were held aloft, and the slogan was also being chanted. The crowd grew larger and began to spill across the road onto the pavement on the other side. Charles was close enough to hear altercations between the demonstrators and the shoppers trying to get past them. It gave the impression of being a generational conflict because the shoppers were all middle aged. He felt a sneaking sympathy for them, ordinary folk, probably like those in the pub in Armley, being challenged none too politely by arrogant youngsters.

'Ah, found you, Chas!' Jenny had come up behind him. 'Good turnout, isn't it?'

'Yes, it is, but they all seem to be students. I thought there'd be all ages attending.'

'But there are a few oldies; look, over there, those blokes holding their trade union banner. Oh! Looks as though things are about to start.' Two men had mounted the steps to the town hall, but they weren't standing together. One was Malcolm Haynes. The other, whom Charles recognized as president of the Marxist Soc, was carrying a megaphone which he raised to his lips.

'Comrades!' he blared. 'Our march will be along The Headrow, down Briggate, then along to City Square before returning here. Be disciplined. We must show that that only those in the forefront of the fight against capitalism can stop the Yanks from starting a war. Follow me.'

He descended the stairs and set off along The Headrow, followed by a cohort of those whom Charles identified as Trots.

Malcolm Haynes, still standing on the town hall steps, began shouting. He needed to, not having the benefit of a megaphone. 'Don't join that crowd of loonies! Give them a headstart before following. This demonstration's about peace, not about politics.'

'I'm surprised to see Haynes here, Jen.'

'I'm not. There are even a few Tories here.'

After a few minutes, Haynes gave a beckoning gesture to the crowd that remained, descended, and began leading them along The Headrow. Charles and Jenny followed. They could hear slogans being shouted by the Trotskyites ahead of them, but they were among an almost silent cohort. They were marching in the road with a police escort, and were largely ignored by the shoppers on the pavements.

The march ended back at the town hall. Jenny and Charles were near the rear of the procession and found that a dispute was taking place on the steps. The Trots were shouting at a group of people and began shoving them. Then one of those being shoved retaliated by punching one of the Trots.

'What the hell's going on, Jen?'

'I thought this might happen. It's the Commies. They hate the Trots even more than they hate Tories. Come on, Chas, let's get out of here before it turns into a riot.'

And a riot it began to be. They hurried away, but not before policemen charged up the town hall steps, truncheons drawn.

Charles was silent as they walked back towards the university. He was dismayed by what he had witnessed, a demonstration ostensibly in favour of peace degenerating into a brawl between those who no doubt saw themselves as the intellectual elite. He came to a decision: he would concentrate on his studies, ignore the political activities in the student union, and go out of his way to have no further contact with any of the Trots even if that meant seeing less of Jenny.

***

'Why have you stopped, Charles? All this is extremely interesting. The Cuban missile crisis occurred nearly thirty years before I was born.'

Charles had been so engaged in telling Katia about the political events of 1962, that it had only just hit him that his story was now leading him to a place where he didn't want her to follow. He wanted more than anything to retain the respect that she seemed to have for him. Christ, he'd only got a few months left, if that. It was bad enough having to rely on her for his relatively pain-free existence; the last thing he needed was her pity. But there seemed no polite way to end the discussion.

'Well, we were still walking back to the university and Jenny asked me to go to an end of the world party that she and her flat-mates were holding that night.'

'End of the world party? Are you serious?'

'Yes. We really did think our time was up. For years the government had been issuing notices advising people what to do in the event of a nuclear detonation – utterly pointless of course. My generation lived with that all through our teens. So we'd come to accept that the end of the world was a distinct possibility.'

'So, did you go to the party?'

'I took a bit of persuading. Parties weren't my thing. But Jenny begged me to go, she said it might be the last time we'd see each other. And when I thought about it, did I really want to spend what might be my last night on earth alone in my digs? Wouldn't it be better to be in the company of the only friend I'd made?'

'So you went.'

'Yes.'

'Go on then, Charles, tell me about it.'

How to start? Did he want to start? He hadn't intended telling Katia about it, and certainly not how it ended. He thought she might be interested in the concerns of young people back in the days of the cold war, which was why he'd mentioned the end of the world party. He'd become so immersed in recounting this that he now found himself in a situation where he might reveal something which he'd never told anyone and which he'd tried all his life to forget. No. He couldn't do it. Why should he? He was under no obligation to do so, confession wasn't part of his treatment, was it? Despite her M.Sc. she was only a nurse, after all. No, he'd go no further. He realised he'd begun to perspire.

'Are you all right, Charles?'

'No. Sorry, not feeling so good, suddenly. Think I need a rest.'

She reached over, grasped his wrist and held it.

'Your pulse rate's certainly a bit high. Would you like me to help you get upstairs?'

'No. I'll go into the lounge. Don't let me keep you. You must have other clients to see.'

'One thing I must do is go to the local shop and get you some fresh milk and some bread. Is there anything else you need?'

'No. Tesco delivery tomorrow.'

'Okay. I'll only be a few minutes. See you soon.'

'No, Katia, I'll probably be dozing off. Don't disturb me, just leave the stuff in the kitchen.'

She looked at him appraisingly. 'If you're sure, Charles. I'll see you next week then. And if you're no better I'll definitely be contacting Social Services about you having care workers visit you.'

She was still holding his wrist. She squeezed his hand and left.

Charles made it into the lounge and collapsed onto the settee. The animation he'd felt in the early stages of his conversation with Katia had evaporated. He felt drained, physically and mentally. Sleep would have been welcome, but he dare not lest he be haunted by vivid dreams of the events that were now in the forefront of his mind.

***

'Barbara, this is Chas,' said Jenny, 'the bloke on my course.'

'Hello, Chas! I've heard a lot about you. Glad you could come. Oh, thanks for the booze. Take it through to the kitchen, if you can manage to get there. You have to go through the living room.'

The living room was almost dark, the only light coming from a reading lamp, and so crammed with people that it was hard to negotiate a way through. Deafening rock music was blaring from a record player in the corner. No one was dancing; there was room only to stand. Jenny pushed her way through the crush, and Charles followed her into the kitchen.

It was just as crowded. There was much guffawing and giggling: the people there were obviously already well-oiled.

'Who are you hoping to make it with tonight, then?' Charles heard one fellow say.

'Don't know yet,' his companion replied. 'I reckon most of 'em are up for it. The virgins'll probably be the most desperate.'

'Come on, Chas,' said Jenny. 'Open your bottle and let's get back in the living room.'

Charles complied. As he followed Jenny out of the kitchen, he was wondering about what the two fellows had said.

The scene in the living room was demonic; dark, sweltering, smoke-filled, rowdy. The occupants were crammed close together shouting in an attempt to make themselves heard over the music, but this only increased the noise level.

'This isn't what I expected,' Charles shouted in Jenny's ear, 'How are we supposed to get to know other people?'

'It won't be like this for long,' Jenny shouted back. 'We want people to get properly sozzled before we quieten things down.'

There was another ten minutes of mayhem before the music suddenly stopped, and the shouting petered out.

'Okay, fellas and gals!' said Barbara, standing by the record player. 'I reckon we're all here now. Even if we're not all blown to pieces by bloody Kennedy and Khrushchev, let's make this a night to remember for however long we've got.' She held up her hand to silence the cheering. 'Those of you who want to dance can stay in here, but it'll be quieter music, just right for getting you in the mood. But if you want to get on with it, well, there are rooms upstairs. But be prepared for multi-occupation.' Laughter was the response to that.

The music started again, a gentle ballad. Jenny turned to face him and put her arms round his shoulders.

'Don't worry about your poor co-ordination,' she said, 'We just shuffle about. Put your arms round me, Chas.'

Tentatively, he did so. She took off her glasses and thrust them into his jacket top pocket, then put her cheek against his. His first thought was that he was glad she was short, before he became aware that her breasts were rubbing against his chest. What the hell was happening? Had she planned all this? But they were close friends, and it was acceptable for friends to embrace, wasn't it? She moved her feet from side to side in time with the music.

'You'll have to get closer to me so you can follow my lead,' she whispered, and moved her hands from his shoulders and placed them on his backside, pulling him towards her so his loins and thighs were pressed against hers. Her scent surprised him; he'd never known her to use perfume before. After his initial shock at this contact, Charles found he was able to respond to her movements back and forth. So this was dancing cheek-to-cheek! He'd heard that phrase many times but had never thought he'd do it, nor that it would be the pleasurable experience he was finding it to be. He began to lose himself in the music, the sensation of intimacy, and the feeling of accord with those dancing around them.

He became unaware of the passage of time, and it wasn't until the long-playing record finished that he noticed there were fewer people in the room. He looked around and saw for the first time that there were two settees pushed back against the wall. They were each occupied by a couple, laying along them full-length. One of the women was moaning loudly. Embarrassed, Charles waited for another record to start playing. But it didn't. Barbara, who'd been changing the records, was no longer in the room.

Although the dancing had ceased, Jenny remained pressed against him. She put a hand behind his head, pulled his face towards hers and kissed him. It was a long kiss. Charles found himself responding; his body was reacting in a way he'd never experienced before.

'Let's go somewhere more comfortable,' Jenny whispered. She took his hand and led him out of the room into the hallway, then up the stairs. She stopped outside a door and turned to him.

'Chas, I share this bedroom with Barbara. She's probably in there now with the fella she picked up. Don't worry, it'll be dark, and we've put up a sort of screen between the beds.'

If asked, Charles would have been unable to explain his feelings. His mind was a maelstrom of conflicting emotions; excitement yes, arousal perhaps, but also inhibition, apprehension, fear of the unknown. Jenny opened the door and led him into the room. He could make out the shape of a single bed in front of them. By the side of the bed there was what seemed to be a blanket suspended from the ceiling, and from behind the blanket came the sound of laboured breathing. Charles's inhibitions intensified; his arousal evaporated.

'Jenny, I'm not sure I can …'

'Don't worry about them. They're concentrating on each other. Come on.'

It took less than a minute for her to disrobe, and she climbed onto the bed. Charles remained standing, not liking to stare at her naked body.

'For God's sake, Chas! Come here! She dragged him onto the bed and began tugging at his shirt. When it was off, she began unzipping his flies.

Surely, it was the man who should take the lead in such a situation? 'No! Let me!' He pulled off his shoes, socks and trousers, hesitated before removing his underpants, then lay down beside her. Immediately, she clambered over him, rubbing herself against him, all the while kissing his face, then his neck. He lay there, tense, unsure what his role should be. After a few minutes, she climbed off him.

'Want to take it slowly, do you? Well, you're probably right. We've got all night.'

She laid beside him, gently caressing his chest, her hand slowly moving down his body. Her touch became intimate. Charles tensed. Things he knew should be happening to him were not. She grabbed his hand, placed it on her breast. He let it lie there: what was he supposed to do? She pulled his hand down to her stomach; he did what he supposed she wanted, and she began moaning. He was pleased to be pleasing her.

But after only a few minutes he leapt up, scrambled into his clothes, staggered out of the room, ran down the stairs and out of the front door. He kept on running, but with no idea where he was heading.

The world didn't end that night, of course.

Kennedy and Khrushchev came to an accommodation. But Charles and Jenny didn't; they no longer sat together in lectures, no longer had coffee together in Caff. Charles dreaded what had happened that night becoming common knowledge, but time passed, and nobody spoke of it. In any case he'd decided to limit contacts with his fellow students, to concentrate on his studies and abandon the fruitless attempt to have a social life.

This was made easier because he found he was increasingly having even less in common with his peers. The culture of undergraduate life had started to change. Many of the men, including some of those who went to the union lounge, started to grow their hair in a strange fashion, combed in a fringe over their foreheads, and to wear jackets that buttoned up to the collar. Eventually, he became aware of a phenomenon called the Liverpool Sound. It seemed to dominate every conversation.

It reminded Charles of how rock'n'roll and the Teddy Boy style had been an obsession among his classmates at school. But at least they'd had had the excuse of being impressionable adolescents. He couldn't understand how intellectuals, the elite 5% who'd made it to university, could demean themselves by being in thrall to something that was obviously designed to appeal to working class teenagers.

He spent the remainder of his time at university alone, working to obtain a first-class degree. He'd set himself an objective – to follow a career in town planning, and to rapidly climb the ladder to the top where he would set the agenda for those who worked for him. And as for women – well, damn them. Woe betide any female who tried to use her wiles to subvert his objective.

Chapter 17

Debbie, sitting in Caffé Nero, was looking forward to her meeting with Margaret Tagg. It was rare for her to meet up with anyone, because she had no female friends in the area. She had acquaintances, of course, but these were mainly the wives of Keith's former colleagues, women with whom she had little in common, and in any case, when she met them, it was in the company of the husbands, and the men dominated the conversation. Recently these gatherings had begun to be less frequent, and she'd noticed that some of the men had begun to look askance whenever Keith launched into one of his diatribes. At the last meeting, when he'd been heaping praise on Jeremy Corbyn, one of them had said, 'What's with the Yorkshire accent, Keith? What are you trying to prove?' and to her shame, Keith had rounded on the fellow and ended his verbal assault by telling him to fuck off. In fact, since that occasion there hadn't been another gathering – or maybe there had, and Keith hadn't been invited?

She'd begun to resign herself to social isolation and was increasingly reliant on email and WhatsApp for contact with her old school and university friends, exchanging news about their children and memories of old times. If only some of them lived closer to Staffridge. If only Keith would let her borrow the car so she could tour round and visit them. She'd suggested that she buy a car of her own - they could afford to - but Keith had climbed onto his latest hobbyhorse, concern for the environment, and had accused her of wanting to contribute to global warming and thus endanger their children's future. At that, Debbie had lost her temper – a rare occurrence – and they'd had a heated argument. She still felt unable to forgive him for some of the things he'd said.

Meeting Margaret and Gordon Tagg at the film theatre and going for a drink with them afterwards had been like experiencing the first day of spring after months of bleakness, though their obvious fondness for each other brought home to her the failings in her own marriage. Of course, Keith had to spoil the occasion by using foul language, but maybe it was that which had prompted Margaret to suggest they meet up without the men present. Debbie was struck by the irony of Charles Pettifer being the only mutual acquaintance they had. Margaret obviously had little time for him, and Debbie was looking forward to discussing him further. It would be a good starting point for a conversation from which she hoped a friendship would develop.

It was crowded in the café and rather noisy, but Debbie had secured a seat to the side of the serving area with just one chair opposite her. Margaret entered and Debbie waved to her, receiving a beaming smile in return. They exchanged hellos, and Margaret went to be served, having first ascertained that Debbie wasn't ready for another coffee. Debbie watched her as she waited. She really was a remarkably attractive woman for her age – how old would she be? Probably in her mid-sixties. She'd taken off her coat, revealing a slim body which she held erect, clad in the sort of up-to-date clothes that wouldn't be scorned by a much younger woman. *I really must start making more effort with my appearance*, Debbie thought.

'I don't often come in here,' Margaret said as she sat down. 'In fact, the last time I was here it was to rescue Gordy from Charles Pettifer.'

'Rescue? What had happened?'

'Well, out of the blue Gordy had a phone call from Pettifer suggesting they meet for a coffee. Gordy hadn't heard from him for years. He never liked the fellow, but he agreed to go because he wanted to ask him why he retired so suddenly.'

'Did Charles tell him?'

'No. He lost his temper when Gordy asked him. In fact, he was objectionable all through their meeting, and Gordy sneaked into the loo to text me to ask me to rescue him. I was in town, so I called in and made out there was some family crisis.'

'Doesn't Gordon have any idea why he suddenly retired?'

'Oh, he has some suspicions. But never mind Pettifer. Let's get to know each other, shall we? Tell me a bit about yourself, Debbie.'

What was there to tell? She gave a brief resume of her early life, how she'd been born of quite well-off parents in the south of England, how she'd met Keith at Sheffield University before dropping out at the end of her first year, but had stayed in Sheffield where she married Keith soon after he'd graduated.

'Keith was a teacher, didn't he? What career did you have?'

Debbie laughed. 'Career? I didn't really have one. I had various office jobs, then the kids came along. Keith spent most of his time working, evenings and weekends, so it was left to me to run the house and bring up Sam and David.' After saying this, Debbie hoped the resentment she still felt hadn't been apparent in her voice. 'What about you, Margaret?'

'Oh, call me Margy, please. Everybody does. I didn't have a career either. I wasn't bright enough to go to university. I just had a series of dead-end jobs in Luton, my home town. I was content enough, I suppose, but I didn't really know what happiness was until Gordy came along. His first job was in the Luton planning office and we met in a disco, of all places. Are there still discos, or are they called something else now? Anyway, after two years we got married, and like you, we soon had kids. I loved being a mum, and now we've got grandchildren to keep us young – they stop over with us quite a bit. Have you got grandchildren, Debbie?'

Had that been anyone else giving this account of her life, Debbie would have thought it rather smug. But it was impossible not to like Margy; happiness and goodwill shone from her. However, it didn't prevent Debbie from being envious.

'Yes, I've got grandchildren. We don't see much of them though; their parents live in Bristol.' She refrained from saying that they only visited at Christmas because David's wife Susie obviously disliked Keith.

'That's a shame. So what d'you do with your spare time, Debbie? You've lived here a long time; you must have made lots of friends.'

Margaret had asked the question that Debbie had been anticipating and dreading. She'd rehearsed answers to it, but none of them would sound convincing. *Must change the subject; what to say? Ah yes –*

'Margy, I've been meaning to ask you. When we met at the film theatre, you, or was it Gordon? mentioned Gillian, Charles Pettifer's secretary.'

'Oh, back to Pettifer is it? Seems there's no getting away from him. It was Gordon who mentioned Gillian Tebbit.'

'He said she seemed fond of him. Was it any more than that?'

'Why do you ask?'

'It's just that I think I may have seen her on several occasions. She used to visit Charles sometimes. Did Gordon think they were having an affair?'

Margy grinned. 'Well, if they were, Gillian was certainly putting it about. At one time Gordy thought she might be carrying on with a county councillor – oh, what was his name? Oh yes, Jarvis. Jeremy Jarvis. He was a Labour councillor. You see, Gordy's job took him all over the county, and on the way home from work in the north one evening he called in to a pub for a quick drink. There in the snug was Gillian with Jarvis. They were so wrapped up with each other they didn't notice Gordy; he stayed at the bar, downed his drink and left.'

'Did Gordon tell anyone in the office?'

'No, he's not one for gossip.'

'Did Charles know?'

'I've no idea. Debbie, I notice you call Pettifer 'Charles'. Were you friendly with him?'

'No. I suppose I call him that because when he first moved next door, we had him and his wife round for a meal. It was Christian names then, so I suppose it stuck.'

'You met his wife?'

'Celia, yes.'

'What was she like?'

'Like a mouse. Very plain, dressed badly, and hardly said a word all evening. She seemed a most unlikely partner for him. He was most dismissive of her on the rare occasions she opened her mouth.'

'Sounds as though it was a fun evening.'

'Not really.'

Then a thought occurred to Debbie, prompted by her memory of what had happened in her kitchen that night.

'Margy, you said when we last met that Cha … Pettifer came on to you at a staff Christmas party, and 'not very nicely' was the way you put it. What happened? Tell me if I'm being out of order.'

'No, it's ok. It wasn't anything outrageous. It was just that when I agreed to dance with him he held me too close and his hand wandered too far down my back. He'd already annoyed me that evening with his life-and-soul-of-the-party act and his risqué jokes, so I broke away from him and asked Gordy to take me home. Why do you ask?'

'It's just that he behaved like that with me the evening he came to dinner, when we were alone together in the kitchen. He was freer with his hand than he was with you. And he made suggestions.'

'Good heavens! What did you do?'

'I told him to take the coffees into the lounge and to leave as soon as he and Celia had finished theirs.'

'Well, we seem to have something in common in our pasts, don't we?'

Should I, wondered Debbie, tell Margy that just for a moment I was turned on by Charles's touch? No, it was too early in their friendship to engage in intimate revelations. Not only that, it might give a hint that even all those years ago things were not all well in her marriage. There would come a time, she hoped, when their friendship would be deep enough for her to confide in Margy. God knows, she needed a confidante.

'Fancy another coffee?' said Margy. 'I can stay for another half hour if you can.'

The remainder of their time in the café was spent talking, and giggling, about their respective childhoods and adolescence. On parting, they agreed it would be great to meet again soon.

As she walked to the bus stop, Debbie wondered if she should tell Keith about what she'd learned about Gillian Tebbit. But then she remembered she hadn't told him that she was meeting Margy. For some reason she found hard to analyse, she felt almost as though she were starting an adulterous relationship.

Chapter 18

When Margaret returned, Gordon was busy inserting photographs of the Christmas celebrations into the family album. He was assiduous in keeping a photographic record of their life. There was a shelf full of albums in the bookcase, and he would soon run out of space to store any more. Hilary had said to him, 'Dad, why don't you get an iPad? You can store hundreds of photos on it and could carry it about to show friends and family, so you wouldn't have the hassle of having to lug heavy albums around.' But Gordon got satisfaction from the unhurried process of leafing through the pages; somehow, zapping though photos by means of a touch on a screen detracted from the feeling of nostalgia that he always enjoyed. He didn't care for being at the mercy of technology. He'd felt the same when trying to read a novel on the Kindle that Hilary had bought him; he felt under pressure to press on to the next screen and found he wasn't concentrating on appreciating the prose. And you couldn't leaf back easily as you could with a book, something he had to do more frequently these days to remind himself who the characters were and what had happened to them.

He closed the album and got up to kiss Margaret.

'Well, how did your meeting go?'

'Very well. Debbie's a nice lady. But there's something a bit sad about her.'

'Really? In what way?'

'I think she's lonely. When I asked her about how she spent her time and who her friends were, she looked uncomfortable and changed the subject. And she obviously doesn't see as much of her family as she'd like to. And another thing – she hardly mentioned her husband. She didn't say anything, but I get the feeling all's not well with that marriage.'

'Well, I must say I didn't take to the fellow when we met them at the film theatre. I can't stand people who use foul language on first acquaintance. So if you didn't discuss her social life or her marriage, what did you talk about?'

'What do you think?'

'Let me guess. Charles Pettifer.'

'Right in one! She told me something interesting, though it didn't surprise me. When Pettifer and his wife moved in next door to Debbie, she and Keith invited them round for a meal. And when Debbie and Pettifer were alone in the kitchen, he groped her!'

'You're right. That's no surprise. D'you fancy a coffee?'

'I'm awash with coffee, Gordy. I need to drink some water. And I must get out of these clothes. It's time I did some hoovering.'

'Okay. I'll just finish inserting these last photos, then I'd better go and check my emails.'

Margaret went into the kitchen but was back within a few seconds.

'Gordy, there's something I forgot to tell you. Debbie asked me outright if Pettifer was having an affair with Gillian Tebbit.'

'What did you say?'

'I told her it was unlikely because she was might be having an affair with that Jarvis fellow.'

'Did you need to tell her that, Margy?'

'Oh, come on, it doesn't matter after all these years, does it? Gillian left the planning office soon after Pettifer retired, didn't she? And Jarvis hasn't been a councillor for ages. It's all ancient history now.'

'I suppose so.'

Gordon went upstairs to the room he called his study which contained his desktop computer. It used to be Paul's bedroom, but Gordon had commandeered it to do his work after Paul had left home. It remained his space after he retired, a place where he could immerse himself in nostalgia. The walls were covered, not with photographs, but with long-playing record sleeves. All the Beatles albums were there, from *Please Please Me* to *Let It Be.* He could remember clearly the shops in which he'd bought them and the parties where he'd danced to them with Margy. The sleeves all contained the records, scratched and probably unplayable, not that he had a record player any longer – he'd replaced the albums with CDs long ago. The sleeves were grubby, but the beer- and coffee-stains on them, impregnated with cigarette ash, were a further reminder of his youth. Gordon had never been a raver or a hippie, had never even smoked a joint, but the Beatles had had universal appeal – even his mother had liked them.

Apparently, vinyl was making a comeback, but it was probably a preserve of the middle-aged and elderly. Youngsters went in for streaming music, not that Gordon really knew what that involved. They didn't know what they were missing – the sense of anticipation as you went to the record shop, the pleasure in holding the sleeve and gazing at its cover, more anticipation as you hurried back home or to your digs, the glorious moment when the stylus dropped onto the record, and the hiss before the music began.

Stop living in the past, he told himself as he sat down in front of his computer. He checked his emails daily, if only to bin all the junk mail. Occasionally there were emails from old friends, those who lived miles away and whom he rarely saw, and he enjoyed chatting to them. Modern technology did have its benefits. He logged on, went into g-mail and found one message in his inbox. It was from a Jeanette Bennett.

Was this spam? He didn't know a Jeanette Bennett. Could it possibly

be Jeanette Beasley? He'd given up ever hearing from her. It was nearly two months since he'd written his message on her Christmas card, and he'd assumed that his mention of Pettifer had evoked bad memories of a time she no doubt wished to forget. He risked opening the email and scan-read it.

What he read caused him to jump up and go to the

study door.

'Margy!' he shouted down the stairs. 'Have you got a minute?'

'What for?' was shouted back.

'Come up here! I've got something interesting to show you.'

'Hang on. With you in a sec.'

When Margaret entered. Gordon gave her his seat in front of the computer. 'Read that,' he said.

Hello Gordon. Sorry to take so long to reply to the message on your Christmas card, but life got in the way. You'll have noticed my name's now Bennett. Yes, I'm married, and I have a son. He's 21.

I was fascinated to hear you met Pettifer after all these years, but I'm sure you appreciate he's somebody I want to forget.

But I've decided I'd like to visit Staffridge again if only to lay old ghosts, and to see you, of course. Andy, my husband, is away at a conference next week, so I'm free to come up. I've checked and there's a Premier Inn in Staffridge where I could stay for a couple of nights. Can I meet up with you? If so, let me know where.

Do you remember Jeremy Jarvis, the Labour councillor? Is he still around? Could you possibly find his address or phone number for me? We were near neighbours and were quite friendly. I'd like to see him again.

I'll save all my news till we meet. Looking forward to seeing you again.

Jeanette

'Incredible!' said Margaret. 'I'd completely forgotten about Jeremy Jarvis until my meeting with Debbie yesterday, and now he's cropped up again. Did people in your office know that Jeanette was, well, friendly with him?'

'No, they didn't. Remember, Jeanette was an area officer in the north of the county and only came to head office for the monthly meetings. In any case, she wouldn't have divulged it; if Pettifer had got to know about it, he'd have hit the roof – he made it quite clear he loathed Jarvis.'

'Why?'

'Because Jarvis was a Labour councillor. He represented everything that Pettifer despised.'

'D'you reckon anything was going on between Jeanette and Jarvis?'

'I don't think so. Jeanette was a serious young woman. In any case, she ...'

'Go on. She what?'

'Well, I hate to be sexist but ... well, let's say she wasn't the most attractive of women. If Jarvis was having it away with Gillian Tebbit I don't think he'd have been interested in Jeanette.'

'D'you think Jeanette knew about Jarvis and Gillian?'

'Most unlikely. Jarvis wouldn't have told her, I'm sure, and Gillian hardly ever spoke to the area officers. She saw herself as the chief's right-hand woman and treated them with disdain.'

'Gordy, are you going to meet Jeanette when she comes up here?'

'I think so. You don't mind, would you, Margy?'

Margaret grinned. 'Not if she's as unattractive as you made out.'

'There's no competition, darling!' As Gordon leaned across her to turn off the computer, he kissed her cheek.

'When you meet her, are you going to tell her about Jarvis and Gillian?'

'Not directly. But who knows what might emerge in our conversation?'

'And are you going to track down Jarvis?'

'Probably.'

Chapter 19

Charles had made it downstairs to the kitchen, albeit with great difficulty. He'd woken later than usual; it was light outside and it was still only February, but then he remembered it was at the end of this month that one became aware that the days were drawing out. And when he'd pulled back the curtains – thank God for the pulley cords, he couldn't have managed to do it without them – he'd found that the sky was clear and the sun rising.

Perhaps it was this that was making him feel slightly better. It was strange how he had the occasional good day. He'd heard someone once say that the process of aging wasn't a gradually accelerating decline, but a series of plateaux separated by sudden sharp steps downward. There'd not been mention of occasional steps upward, but he'd experienced them, although they'd usually been followed by the briefest of plateaux and then a precipitous downward lurch

As he shuffled around, mishandling the cornflake packet, fumbling to insert the bread into the toaster and spilling the milk when he poured it into his tea, his thoughts were of Katia, who was due to visit him that afternoon. He'd promised to think about her suggestion that he have care workers to visit him. He had indeed given the matter much thought – there was little to occupy him apart from thinking – and had decided to go along with it. The struggle to manage the simplest of daily tasks was becoming profoundly depressing. He was finding it difficult to have a shower: it was hard to stand up in it, and he kept dropping the soap which, of course, he was then unable to pick up. As for his stash of paracetamol, well, he'd keep them locked in his bedside cabinet when the carers came.

Of course, care workers were likely to be youngish females, and their assisting him with dressing and undressing, let alone helping him in and out of the shower, would involve a degree of intimate contact that would once have embarrassed him. But one of the few benefits of growing old was that one lost the capacity to be embarrassed. And he knew he'd welcome the physical contact. He was starved of touch. Annie had made him conscious of this, but it had really hit home when Debbie had held his hand and embraced him when she visited him just after Christmas. Why had he rejected her offer of further visits? Pride, he supposed. *Silly old fool.*

Katia's impending visit was another reason for it being one of his better days. Last time she was here, he'd derived great enjoyment from telling her about his time at university: it was refreshing to have an audience that listened and asked pertinent questions. Thank God he hadn't revealed what happened at the end-of-the-world party: had he done so, he doubted he could have looked her in the face again. He wanted her respect, not her pity. He was determined that she shouldn't see him as just a pathetic old man, which was why today he'd made an effort with his appearance. He'd shaved, cast aside his usual crumpled sweater, and had on a shirt with a collar and tie.

Immersed in his thoughts of Katia, he was startled by the sound of the front door closing and the shout of, 'Anyone in? It's Annie!'

Of course, it was Annie's day to clean! That was why he'd asked Katia to come after two o'clock; they couldn't have an intelligent conversation to the accompaniment of the swishing of mops and the hoovering of carpets, let alone the pop music which Annie now no longer turned off when he was nearby.

'I'm in the kitchen, Annie!'

She entered. 'You're up, are yer? Yer must be feelin' better. Last time I was 'ere I had to help yer out of bed, didn't I?'

This was said without her usual smile. And she hadn't called him 'dear'.

'Indeed you did, Annie, and I was very grateful. I

didn't get a chance to thank you because you left so early. I was expecting you to come up and say goodbye.'

'The van came early, didn't it? Anyway, that nurse said she 'adn't finished with yer upstairs.'

'Oh, well, you see ...' He didn't finish the sentence because she'd left to collect her cleaning equipment from the hall. When she returned with it, she peered at him. There was still no smile, and there was an expression on her face which was hard to evaluate. It was almost one of suspicion.

'You're all dolled up,' she said. 'Expecting visitors, are yer?'

'Visitors? No, I just thought I'd make an effort given I'm feeling a bit better.'

'I'll make a start in the lounge then.' She picked up the hoover and bustled out, almost slamming the kitchen door behind her.

What had got into her? Had he offended her in some way when she was last here? Or maybe she was upset about something else; perhaps she'd had some bad news. He decided to wait until she had her coffee break before asking her.

Well, at least that gave him time to think about and finalise the list of names he'd been compiling. There was an important matter he wished to discuss with Katia. He'd decided to seek her advice and assistance before calling in a solicitor. This would also be an ideal strategy to prevent her from starting another counselling session. Although he'd been happy to talk about his student days, he didn't relish the prospect of her asking about the next phase of his life, his time as a junior planning officer when he'd met Celia and married her. And in particular, Celia's reason for leaving him.

'I'm done in there and in the dining room.'

Charles started. He'd been so engaged in thinking about who should be on his list that he'd forgotten about Annie. Her sudden presence in the kitchen reminded him there was something he needed to tell her.

'Oh, hello Annie. Are you ready for your coffee?'

'Yes, I'll make it now. Yer can go in the lounge while I drink it in 'ere.'

'But don't you want us to have coffee together? We always do, don't we?'

She shrugged.

'Is something troubling you, Annie? You don't seem your usual self. Have I offended you in any way?'

'Think I ought to spend a bit more time cleaning. I ain't really got the time to sit chatting. Last week I only did 'alf the rooms.' While saying this, she stood staring resolutely out of the kitchen window.

Charles decided not to pursue the matter. No doubt she'd tell him what was troubling her in her own good time.

'Very well, I'll leave you to get your coffee. But before I go, there's something I need to tell you.'

'What's that, then?'

'You see, I've decided I need to have the services of care workers and – '

'Care workers? What for?'

'To get me up in the morning and help me wash and dress and get my breakfast. Then another visit later to get my lunch. Then again in the evening to help me get to bed.'

She turned to face him; her eyes narrowed.

'What's that got to do with me?'

'I think we'll need to reorganise your shifts. Instead of coming three hours once a week, maybe come one hour three times a week, timed so you're not here at the same time as the carers. You'll get in each other's way, otherwise.'

'I can't do that!' This was almost screamed. 'The company only lets us do three-hour shifts! The van won't bring me 'ere just for an hour, it ain't worth their while! They 'ave other cleaners to ferry about, don't they?'

'Oh dear, I hadn't thought of that. Well, maybe we could – '

'Yer always said you'd never 'ave care workers in. Why 'ave yer changed yer mind? Wanna get rid of me, do yer?'

'Of course not, Annie. It's just that Katia, my nurse, said I'd feel a lot better if – '

'That bloody woman! I might o' known it! The cow!'

'What on Earth have you got against Katia? She's a highly professional – '

'She's snotty-nosed stuck up bitch! When she was 'ere last week she treated me like shit!'

Charles stared at her. Not only was her face red, but her lower lip was trembling. God, the last thing he wanted was for her to start blubbing.

'Annie, I'm sure she wouldn't have done that. Maybe you misunderstood something she said.'

'Yer mean I'm not clever enough to understand 'er? Is that why yer like her, cos you can talk to her about fancy things? And she's young, ain't she? I reckon yer fancy her, don't yer?'

Charles felt the affection he'd developed for Annie beginning to drain away. Who the hell did she think she was, talking to him like that?

'Mrs Williams, it's not your place to – '

'And she's a nigger! Those bloody coons are getting too high and mighty, takin' over jobs what white folks should be doin'. My Bert says they should all be sent 'ome, and I reckon he's right.'

'Mrs Williams!' It was Charles's turn to shout. 'I will not have racist language used in this house! And for your information, Katia was born in this country.'

'So what? Just goes to show they breed like rabbits. They're takin' over the country. And they like to have it off with white folks. Fancy yer chances there, do yer? Hopin' to get yer leg over, are yer?'

Charles struggled to his feet and stood facing her. 'That's enough, Mrs Williams. I'd like you to leave now. You can wait for the van outside. And I'll be telling your company that your services here are no longer required.'

'No need! I wouldn't come back 'ere for a thousand quid an hour!'

She barged her way out of the kitchen and after a few seconds he heard the front door slam. He sank back down on his chair. He felt ill. In the space of ten minutes, the aging process had accelerated: he'd slipped down a massive step to a very narrow plateau.

It wasn't just the altercation with Mrs Williams that had upset him. He was only too aware that she'd expressed views that had been similar to his until he'd met Katia. He felt not only ill but stricken by guilt.

He reached for the piece of paper on which he'd written the list of names. Without hesitating, he scored through the name Annie Williams. It was atonement of a sort, he supposed.

He was still sitting at the kitchen table when Katia arrived. He hadn't had any lunch. He looked up and greeted her and she immediately said, 'Charles, are you all right? You don't look at all well. Are you in pain? Have you been taking your medication?'

'I'm not in pain. Actually, earlier this morning I felt better than I have for ages. I'm just upset. I've had a major disagreement – no, a blazing row – with Mrs Williams. In fact, I've told her not to come back again.'

'I'm sorry to hear that – about the row, I mean. What was it about?'

'I told her I was going to have carers in, and – '

'Oh, are you? I'm so glad you've taken my advice. You won't regret it. I assume Mrs Williams didn't like the idea?'

'That's putting it mildly. The idea of having someone else looking after me really put her nose out of joint. She said some horrible things. Katia, can I ask you, have you had some sort of disagreement with her?'

'Let me sit down and I'll tell you: no, first I'll make us a cup of tea. Have you had anything to eat?'

'Not since breakfast.'

'Carers will make sure you eat regularly.'

Katia busied herself making tea and putting a frozen meal in the oven. Then she sat down opposite him.

'Right, Charles, let me tell you about your Mrs Williams. I'm not surprised she didn't like the idea of your having carers. I got the distinct impression she objects to *my* presence.'

Charles was immediately concerned that Katia might have been subject to racist comments. 'She wasn't rude to you, I hope?'

'Just offhand. But I had to put her right at one point. She asked me the nature of your illness and had the temerity to ask how long you'd got. I reminded her in no uncertain terms about patient confidentiality and about my professional code. She didn't take too kindly to that.'

'I bet she didn't.' Charles could imagine the tone of voice in which Katia had delivered her lecture.

''Anyway, Charles. I know rows can be upsetting, but you'll get over it. Quite frankly, I think you're well rid of the woman.'

'I've already come to that conclusion, Katia.'

'Can I ask if Mrs Williams didn't like me because I'm black?'

'No. It was because you're what she calls posh.'

'Well, I've no objection to being called that. Now, shall we discuss other matters? Your carers regime perhaps? Or would you like to tell me more of your life story? I'm being serious. It does one good to talk to others about one's past rather than sitting alone mulling over it. Doing that can lead to regrets, sadness and depression. Besides, I enjoy listening to you. You have a gift for narration; have you ever considered writing your life history?' Charles was treated to one of her exquisite smiles.

'That sort of writing was never my forte. Look, Katia, there's something else I'd like to talk about, if you don't mind.'

'Go on.'

'I know what I'm going to ask isn't part of your duties. It's just that I've got to know you better than I do anyone else. You see, I'm going to change my will. My current one was written years ago, just after Celia left me. Things have changed since then, especially over the last six months. So, what I'd like to ask is – would you consider being my executor?'

Katia stared at him, then took a swallow of her tea before answering.

'Well, I'm flattered, Charles. But wouldn't it be better to approach somebody official, like your bank manager perhaps?'

'I'd considered that, but I'd sooner have somebody I knew personally. Besides, there are a few other things I'd like you to do for me. You'll be a beneficiary, of course.'

'Oh, but Charles, I'm not sure that's allowed.'

'Yes, it's perfectly permissible for an executor to be a beneficiary.'

'Yes, I know. But I think to be a beneficiary might conflict with my professional code of conduct. I'll have to ask my manager about that. But Charles, it's sweet of you to think of me. You didn't need to; I've only been doing my duty.' She leaned over and touched his hand.

'If only you knew. You've been doing far more than that.'

'You said there were some other things you'd like me to do?'

'Yes, it's about my funeral – oh, don't worry, I'm not going to ask you to organise that. But when I go, and I know it won't be long, I'd be so grateful if you could contact people who know me, or used to know me, to tell them and invite them to my funeral. I'm making a list of them.'

'Yes, Charles, I could certainly do that.'

'And also to invite them back here for a wake. But it'll be a bit more than that. I'm going to ask my solicitor to be present and read out my will.'

'Are you sure that's a good idea? It might cause a

bit of resentment, unless of course you intend leaving the same amount to everyone.'

'I haven't got round to finalising how the spoils will be divided. But I'll think about what you've said, Katia.'

Katia stood up. 'Right, that's enough about your funeral arrangements. You've got a good few months left yet. Let's make them as comfortable as possible. I want to review your medication and see if it requires any adjustments.'

After Katia left, Charles considered what she'd said about possible resentments amongst those who'd benefit less than others from his bequests. That hadn't occurred to him before. He was seized by an idea. He reached for his list of names and reinstated Annie Williams.

Chapter 20

Gordon was on his way to the Café Rouge in Staffridge to meet Jeanette. He'd asked Margaret if she'd like to come with him, but she'd said that he and Jeanette would want to talk about their time in planning and that she, Margaret, didn't want to be a fly on the wall. In any case she was sure their conversation would be mainly about Charles Pettifer.

Gordon was sorry that Margaret wasn't with him, because he was uncertain how much he'd have to say to Jeanette, or her to him. Although he'd liked her, they used only to meet in planning meetings and had never been close friends. Also, she was about 15 years his junior, and talking about the past should take place only between consenting contemporaries, though the age difference was probably of less significance now he was an old man and she was late-middle aged.

Jeanette had said in her email that she didn't wish to be reminded of Charles Pettifer, but it was inevitable that he'd be discussed at some point. In any case, Gordon was still intrigued by what might have taken place at her final meeting with Pettifer, and he hoped she'd feel able to tell him.

He entered the café. He'd chosen it because it was quiet, often only half full, and with an elderly clientele. If Jeanette was still the serious woman she'd once been, she'd probably not appreciate the near-rowdiness found in most of the coffee houses in the town. He was fifteen minutes early. He ordered a coffee and sat by the window.

His coffee was brought over, and it was, as usual, excellent. Not too strong, and with a small jug of milk which one could add to suit one's taste. He sat sipping it, all the while looking out of the window so he'd be forewarned of her arrival. There was something else he hoped to discover – the nature of her friendship with Jeremy Jarvis. Gordon had done what she'd asked, had found Jarvis's address - he still lived in the north of the county – and emailed it to her. Gordon was sure that there'd been, to use the phrase he remembered being coined by Profumo, no impropriety in their relationship. Jarvis had been a married man, and Jeanette was straight-laced - but he wondered what their matters of mutual interest had been.

'Hello? Gordon?'

Gordon looked up. Standing in front of him was a tall, slim woman, with strong but attractive features and dark hair falling to her shoulders. *Who on Earth...?*

'Gordon! It *is* you!'

My God, it's her! Gordon had noticed this woman approaching the coffee bar, but had dismissed her. He got to his feet. 'Jeanette!' he exclaimed and extended his hand. She didn't accept it, but moved close to him, put her hand on his shoulder and kissed him on the cheek.

Gordon was unable to speak. Not only was this woman totally unrecognisable from the Jeanette he'd once known, but their acquaintanceship had never been such that involved kissing, even pecks on the cheek. He still couldn't quite believe that this attractive woman was her.

'Say something, Gordon!'

'Jeanette, it's great to see you. You look wonderful. I didn't recognise you.'

She laughed. 'That's a back-handed compliment if ever I heard one. You haven't changed much, Gordon, still got all your hair.'

'White hair, though.'

'It suits you.'

'And I've put on weight.'

'Well, you always were cuddly.'

'Sit down, Jeanette. I'll get you a coffee. What sort would you like?'

'A cappuccino, please.'

'Anything to eat? They have a good selection of cakes, here, or maybe you'd like – '

'No, nothing to eat, not yet, anyway.'

Gordon went to the service desk, still reeling from their encounter. He couldn't get his head round the woman Jeanette had become. If you discounted the faint wrinkles round her eyes and mouth she looked younger than she had when she was in her thirties. And just from their brief exchange it was evident that she was comfortable in her own skin and had become effusive. He was reminded of something an old friend had said at a school reunion he'd attended several years ago. He'd commented that many of the girls who'd been 'lookers' at school now weren't up to much, whereas the ones who'd been unattractive were now quite fanciable. Gordon had replied by asking the fellow, who'd been a handsome lad, whether he imagined the women present thought the same about the men.

He placed the order and hurried back to Jeanette.

'Your coffee will be here soon. Well now, what do you think of Staffridge after all these years?'

'It's changed a lot, of course, like most places. More traffic, more supermarkets outside the ring road and lots of empty shops in the town centre. And there never used to be beggars on every corner. But come on, Gordon, tell me about yourself. How's your wife? Any grandchildren?'

'No, you go first.'

There followed accounts of their respective life histories, each frequently interrupting the other with questions and comments. The conversation became animated and accompanied by bursts of laughter. Gordon was enjoying her company, but all the while was wondering how to ask the questions that she might not want to answer, and whether his asking might offend her. He didn't want their meeting to end in discord.

Eventually, there was a pause in their conversation and Gordon decided to grasp the nettle.

'Jeanette, tell me to mind my own business if you want, but there's something I've always wanted to ask you.'

'Go on.'

'It involves Charles Pettifer, and I know you don't want to think about him; you said so in your email.'

She looked at him, and her gaze was serious. 'It's okay, Gordon. I came up here yesterday and ... well, something occurred, and I don't mind talking about Pettifer now, so what is it you want to know?'

'The last time I saw you was in that meeting when Pettifer behaved outrageously towards you about that planning application for a development in Little Drayton. He asked you, no, ordered you, to see him in his office the following week. I'm just fascinated to know what happened then.'

'He demanded that I change my recommendation that the planning application be rejected. He said that if I didn't, he'd overrule my recommendation, but he didn't want any evidence of discord in the planning department to leak out. Then he said he knew that I was friendly with Jeremy Jarvis and tried to make out the friendship was ... well, improper.'

'The bastard! What did you say?'

'I got ready to walk out, but then he suddenly turned on the charm. He actually said he would make it worth my while to go along with what he wanted.'

'In what way?'

'He didn't say, and I had no intention of asking. I just wanted to get out of his office. So I asked him to give me a week to think about it. I knew that if I didn't change my mind, he'd probably find some reason to sack me. I was desperate, Gordon. There was only one person I could confide in. So I arranged to meet Jeremy Jarvis.'

This gave Gordon the opportunity to put to her the other question he'd been itching to ask.

'Jeanette, were you close friends with Jarvis?'

'Not that close. I met him when he was canvassing for his seat on the council. It turned out we were near neighbours, so we used to meet occasionally for coffee to discuss politics – I was a Labour supporter, so we had a lot in common, but we never used to discuss local issues. Not until my last meeting with him, and then I told him what Pettifer had said to me.'

'What was his reaction to that?'

'He was obviously interested but didn't seem too surprised. I asked him what he was going to do, but he said he hadn't made up his mind, but I wasn't to worry: whatever he did he'd be sure to keep my name out of it.'

'So what happened next?'

'Nothing happened for a few months: then, as you know, Pettifer suddenly retired, and I was lucky enough to get the job I'd applied for in Havant.'

'So you never found out what Jarvis did, if anything?'

'Not at the time. But I know now.'

'How come?'

'Because I met up with Jeremy yesterday.'

'Did you, by God?'

'Yes. Oh, thanks for letting me know his address, by the way. Anyway, he told me everything I wanted to know.'

'And are you going to tell *me*, Jeanette?'

'Of course. But let's get another coffee first.'

***

When Jeanette phoned Jeremy to say she was coming to Staffridge and could they meet, in a pub maybe, he replied that it would be best to come to his house because he'd recently broken his ankle.

She hadn't known what to expect and was prepared to see a different Jeremy from the good-looking slim young man she'd known all those years ago. But the man who'd opened the door to her was remarkably unchanged; his hair was greying but his face was only slightly lined, and the coal-black eyes were still beguiling. His voice was still deep, and his smile was as warm as it had always been. However, he was leaning on a walking stick: his broken ankle, she'd supposed. He'd greeted her effusively, and she'd thought he was going to kiss her, but he hadn't.

Now, sitting in the lounge waiting for him to enter with the promised cup of coffee, she was wondering whether she should ask him about his wife. There was no evidence of female occupation in the house. Was his wife dead, perhaps, or might they be divorced?

He entered, pushing a trolley on which were two cups of coffee and an ashtray. Jeanette had been assailed by the smell of cigarette smoke as soon as she'd entered the house.

'D'you mind if I sit down? This bloody ankle's debilitating. Then perhaps you could pass me a cup? Doesn't matter which one, neither of us took sugar, and I assume you still don't.'

Jeanette obliged. 'How did you come to break your ankle?' she asked.

'Playing tennis. That's what comes of trying to keep fit.'

'It seems to be working. You do look remarkably youthful.'

'Thanks. And if I may say so, Jeanette, you look fantastic. I always thought when you were working up here, that under that severe exterior there was an attractive, sexy woman waiting to get out.'

Jeanette was tempted to ask him why he hadn't told her that at the time, but remembered she was here to pump him for information, and that to engage in flirtation would divert her from the serious purpose of her visit.

'Oh, to save you the embarrassment of asking, Maureen and I split up shortly after you left the area. Looking back, I don't blame her. I spent all my time on council business and working for the Labour party. I didn't give her the kids she longed for. But enough about me; what about you?'

Jeanette gave a brief resume of her life, career, and marriage.

'Well, I'm really glad that things turned out well for you.'

'Are you still an active member of the Labour party, Jeremy?'

'A member, yes, but I'm not active. I don't like the way the party's going under Corbyn.'

'I feel exactly the same way.'

'Could you take my cup, please?' Relieved of it, he settled back in his chair. 'Now, shall we cut to the chase? You said on the phone you had some things to ask me. I think I can guess what they are. You want to know whether I was involved in securing that bastard Pettifer's hasty retirement, don't you?'

'Right in one. After our last meeting, you said you'd contact me again, but you never did. Why was that?'

'Too risky. If you'd been seen with me, you'd have been in trouble, and it might have compromised the action I was taking.'

'That's all in the distant past. There's no reason why you can't tell me now, is there?'

'None at all. But before I start, would you mind very much if I have a fag? I started smoking again when I retired.'

Jeanette hated smoking and disapproved of smokers, but he was in his own house, wasn't he?

'Carry on,' she said.

He pulled a packet of cigarettes and a lighter from his shirt pocket.

'Could you pass me the ashtray, please? I'll have it on my lap.'

She obliged. He lit a cigarette and inhaled deeply, then turned his head so the exhalation was directed away from her. Jeanette was struck by the way society had changed since her youth, when almost everyone smoked. It was long time since she'd been in the company of someone who relished the ritual of nicotine inhalation, although vaping in the street was becoming a common sight.

'Right. Where shall I start? At the beginning, I suppose. No doubt you remember Counsellor Dobson, the

Tory chairman of the planning committee? Well, I was told by a friend that Dobson was very pally with Christopher Deveraux, the property developer; they were often in cahoots at the local Rotary club. Not only that; Pettifer was often with them. I'd never met Pettifer, not being on the planning committee myself, but when Deveraux applied for planning permission for the large development in Little Drayton I started to take an interest.'

'Were we meeting for coffee by this time?'

'Yes, we'd just started. I didn't want to involve you; we'd agreed not to discuss local politics, hadn't we? And I have to tell you something more to tell you: I was also meeting someone else.'

'So?'

'It was a young woman. I met her in a pub where I used to gather with some Party members. She was by herself but got chatting to me when I went to the bar. She made it pretty clear she was up for it, and I was flattered. My marriage was already failing.'

'What's all this got to do with the planning application?'

'I'm coming to that. After I'd met her a few times we … well, started going to bed. It had to be in hotels; she was married, and of course I couldn't bring her back here. Then after a while, she began to change. She became less flirtatious and more serious. Then she started asking me questions about my role as a councillor and where I stood on planning issues.'

'Where's all this going, Jeremy?' Jeanette felt betrayed, but at the same time was starting to get impatient.

He stubbed out his cigarette and looked searchingly at her.

'Her name was Gillian, Gillian Tebbit.'

'What? *What*? There was nothing more that Jeanette could say. She was shocked, of course, but felt even more betrayed because he'd never told her about it at the time

'Jeanette, you must understand that I didn't know who she was. She told me she worked in a solicitor's office in Congleton. Don't forget I wasn't on the planning committee and I'd never been to the planning office. I hadn't even met Pettifer.'

He lit another cigarette.

Jeanette wished she could take refuge in a similar distraction activity. She stood up. 'I need to visit the toilet. It's upstairs, I suppose?'

'There's one across the hall. I can't manage the stairs.'

In the toilet, Jeanette found herself shaking. Her distress came not just from what Jeremy had told her, but from the nature of the telling. He'd been dispassionate, matter-of fact, seemingly uncaring about the effect on her of his revelation. Part of her wanted to leave now, but she knew she needed to hear the full story.

'Jeanette, I'm sorry if I've upset you,' he said as she re-entered the lounge, 'but there was no way I could break it to you gently. Do sit down, I've more to tell.'

'Go on, then.'

'Although I had no idea that Gillian was Pettifer's secretary, my suspicions about her had been raised by her interest in planning matters. I decided to keep on seeing her to see if I could discover what her game was.'

'So that meant you carried on sleeping with her, I suppose?'

He had the grace to look embarrassed. 'Yes, I had to. It would have looked strange if I'd suddenly broken it off. And it was a good job I did, because a few weeks later something happened which brought home to me what might be going on.'

He stubbed out his cigarette, only half smoked. Perhaps, Jeanette wondered, he was not so relaxed as he seemed?

'We were in a pub together. I saw this woman looking at us, and she came over and said, "Gilly? It is Gilly isn't it? Gilly Deveraux! We were at school together!" Gillian looked embarrassed. The woman kept talking to her, and while she was, I realised the significance of Gillian's maiden name.'

'You mean she was Christopher Deveraux's daughter?'

'That's what I assumed. As soon as the woman left us, I asked Gillian if she was. She said she wasn't, but I kept pressing her. I said it was an unusual name, so she must know who Christopher Deveraux was. She finally admitted to being his niece.'

'Bloody hell.' It was rare for Jeanette to swear.

'It was then I broke it off with her. I assumed she was trying to discover what the Labour Party's policy towards Deveraux's planning application might be. So I started doing more research, and it was then I discovered Gillian was Pettifer's secretary. It was shortly after that when you came to tell me about how Pettifer was trying to get you to withdraw your recommendation that Deveraux's application be rejected.'

'And even *then* you didn't tell me you'd been seeing Gillian Tebbit!'

'I didn't want to involve you, Jeanette. You had enough on your plate.'

'So what happened next?'

'Well, it seemed to me that there might be some dodgy dealing going on. I mean, Pettifer, Gillian, Dobson, Deveraux, probably all in it together. But I had no way of proving it. So I decided to confront Dobson. It may surprise you to know that even though he was a Tory, I got on quite well with Dobson, politics aside. We used to exchange jokes about our fellow councillors after council meetings had finished. It's strange how one often develops an affinity with political opponents. It happens quite a lot in Parliament apparently. I went to one of Michael Portillo's lectures recently, and he said that even when he was cabinet minister the person he got on best with in the Commons was David Blunkett; you know, the former Labour MP.'

'Yes, Jeremy, I know who David Blunkett is.'

Jeremy laughed. 'That's the Jeanette I remember! Okay, nearly finished now. I met up with Dobson in a pub and told him everything I'd learned. I didn't make any accusations, I just said it would be embarrassing for him if my Labour colleagues who were on the planning committee got to know about the Pettifer-Gillian-Deveraux connection because they'd undoubtedly raise the matter when the planning application went to the committee. And of course, that might be leaked to the local press.'

'And what was his reaction to that?'

'He was silent for a while. Then he said to leave it with him; he'd get his colleagues on board and the planning application would be rejected, and that in any case he'd always had reservations about it. He then said, "Between you and me, Jarvis, that Pettifer fellow is a ghastly little man. I've been thinking for some time that the Council could well do without his services." Then he winked at me.'

'So you reckon Pettifer's early retirement was forced on him?'

'Looks very much like it. I reckon that there *were* back-handers flying about and it was Pettifer who was the beneficiary – and Gillian Tebbit as well, no doubt. I don't think Dobson was involved, he was a man of principle, despite being a Tory. That's about it, Jeanette. Now you know everything that I do. Would you like another cup of coffee?'

'Yes please, but let me get it.' Jeanette wanted a few minutes to herself to digest what she'd been told.

'Thanks. The coffee and milk are on the draining board.'

When she returned to the lounge, Jeremy was smoking again.

'Thanks,' he said. 'There's one more thing I have to tell you.'

'Another revelation? Not sure I can take any more.'

'It's something you ought to know. When Dobson hinted that Pettifer's time was limited, I told him about the way he tried to bully you into changing your planning recommendation. I said that you were thinking of applying for a deputy's post down south, and that I reckoned Pettifer was such a shit that he'd probably write you a bad reference. Dobson said he'd take care of that; he'd insist that Pettifer handed over any requests for references to him. That's what happened.'

'But Dobson never really knew me.'

'That's why he handed the reference request to me. I wrote the reference, he signed it.'

***

'That's some story, Jeanette,' said Gordon. 'I suppose the only thing we don't know about is what happened to Gillian Tebbit.'

'Jeremy said she resigned from her post even before Pettifer left. He hasn't heard anything about her since.'

'I can tell you something about her. Margy's become friendly with Pettifer's next-door neighbour, and she called round on Pettifer before Christmas to see if he was okay – he lives alone. While she was in there, she found a Christmas card. It was signed 'love Gillian' with three kisses, and the message said she'd like to visit him again.'

'My God, the old ram! Still at it at his age!'

'I doubt that very much, Jeanette. He's apparently very ill, housebound. Jeanette, d'you think you'll be seeing Jarvis again?'

'No. What's past is past. I doubt I'll be coming up here again.'

Chapter 21

Come on, can't you, Charles muttered to himself. The fellow was ten minutes late. Charles had given him a precise time to arrive, 2.30pm, by which time Sally, his lunch-time carer, would have left. As requested, she'd left tea, coffee, milk and cups out on the kitchen table so Charles could offer hospitality without having to struggle to get the items out from cupboards and the fridge. She'd even filled the kettle so all he'd have to do would be to plug it in and turn it on. She was a thoughtful young lady, was Sally, and very pretty. It was a pity she only called at lunchtime; Charles would have welcomed her attentions when getting up and having a shower. The morning and evening carers were efficient, but were middle-aged and overweight and didn't show the sort of kindly affection for him that Sally did.

Charles was standing, leaning against his walking frame. He hadn't sat down because he wanted to get to the front door quickly when the doorbell rang. His knees were beginning to tremble. Why wasn't the bastard on time? It didn't say much for the efficiency of the firm, but he hadn't had dealings with it for nearly 30 years. He had it in mind to tell the fellow what he thought about that, but perhaps it would be unwise to alienate him before their discussion began.

When the doorbell rang, Charles jumped. Why was it that he was so often startled by an event that he'd been anticipating? Had it always been like that, or was it yet another symptom of old age? As he shuffled slowly to the door he struggled to remember his visitor's name – he'd only said it once during their phone conversation. What the hell was it? Ah, yes: Sobers. *Think about the cricketer,* he told himself.

He opened the door to find a young man dressed in a formal black suit standing there.

'Mr Pettifer? Good afternoon. I'm Mr Sobers from

Hassle Legal Services.' This was said unsmilingly.

'Come in, Mr Sobers. Go through to the kitchen and take a seat. I'll be with you in a minute.'

When Charles got back in the kitchen, he found that documents were spread over the table and Sobers was leafing through them.

'Can I offer you a coffee? Or would you prefer tea?'

'Perhaps later, Mr Pettifer, when our business is concluded.' He pulled another document from his briefcase and placed it on the table. 'I was informed by my colleague to whom you spoke on the phone that you wish to make amendments to your will. That is, I assume, correct.'

Charles was struck by the man's formal speech which verged on the pompous. It seemed out of place coming from the mouth of such a young fellow. He assumed young people no longer spoke like that, but his accent was that of a 1950s BBC newsreader. Perhaps it was a requirement of his profession, or maybe he'd been to public school?

'If you don't mind, I'm going to make myself a cup of coffee before we start.'

In response to that, Sobers looked pointedly at his watch.

Bugger him, thought Charles, and deliberately took longer to make his coffee than was necessary. He'd barely settled in his chair before Sobers started speaking.

'I have here a copy of the will that you made in 1995. It was a straightforward will, and I'm assuming that you wish to make only minor amendments to it. If that is the case – '

'Old Simon Fletcher ran your company back in 95, when it was called Fletcher Legal Practice. I suppose he died years ago. Who's in charge now?'

'I'm not sure I see the relevance of your question to the matter in hand, Mr Pettifer, but I assume Fletcher's company was one of those acquired by Hassle Legal

Services. We have a chain of offices in the Midlands, and I assure you that we're noted for our expertise and our efficiency. Now, if we can return to the matter of your will.'

Evidently this was not going to be the informal chat that Charles had been anticipating.

Sobers pointed to the will. 'Would you please give me a brief summary of the changes you wish to make to this. I will return to the office to make the necessary amendments, and then email you a copy of the new will for your approval. I assume you use email?'

Charles's was irritated. Was this what the young bugger meant by efficiency? He decided to give as good as he was getting.

'Yes, Mr Sobers, I do use email. But I don't wish to proceed as you suggest. I don't want to make minor amendments to the will. I want major changes, a completely new will, in fact. No, let me finish. I have here a list of the names of those whom I wish to be beneficiaries. I also have a draft of how I'd like the will to be expressed, and your role will simply be to ensure that what I've written conforms to legal requirements. And when you've done that, I'd like the completed will to be posted to me, not emailed, so I can check it at my leisure. When I've done so, you can come out here again to witness my signature. *No*, I still haven't finished. I'm not sure of the size of my estate because I don't know the current value of my house. I've therefore expressed the sizes of the bequests in terms of the percentage of the total estate. I assume this is acceptable.'

This was the longest and most formal speech that Charles had delivered since his time as chief planning officer. It left him drained, but satisfied as a result of the open-mouthed expression on Sobers's face.

'*Is* that acceptable, Mr Sobers?'

'Er, yes, I suppose so.'

'Good. Now, there's something else. I have an executor who will see to the arrangements after my funeral. All those named in my will be invited, and then to come back to this house, where I want my will to be read out. Is the reading of a will in those circumstances a service that Hassle Legal Services can provide?'

'I think so, but I'll have to check with my superiors.'

'Oh, you have superiors, do you, Mr Sobers? I assumed you'd already climbed to the top of the greasy pole. Now, as our business seems to be complete, perhaps you'd like the cup of tea or coffee I offered?'

'No, I must get back to the office.' He stood up.

'Don't forget to take my draft of the will; I've got it here. You can see yourself out; I've left the front door unlocked. Goodbye, Mr Sobers.'

Sobers scrabbled to collect his papers and left the kitchen without a goodbye. Charles slumped back in his chair.

After half an hour had passed, Charles managed to hobble into the lounge where he sank onto the settee. He would have liked to have gone to bed but was condemned to remain where he was until his evening carer came to help him upstairs.

It was a long time since Charles had had the opportunity to demolish a person such as Sobers. Although he'd enjoyed it at the time, he now felt slightly remorseful; perhaps the fellow's pompous attitude stemmed from insecurity? It occurred to him that he was starting to consider other people's feelings, something he'd always regarded as a weakness. That belief had stood him in good stead when he'd been a boss, and had been useful even in his retirement.

It was, he knew, down to Katia that his change had come about. She was the only woman in his adulthood whom he'd felt able to treat as an equal; their conversations were intellectually stimulating as well as entertaining. But she'd done something more. Getting him to talk about his youth had forced him to acknowledge the problem that had undermined him all his life, though he hadn't admitted it to her. Celia had tried to counsel him about it, but she wasn't forceful enough – that was why he'd married her. The problem was of no consequence now, of course.

But at least he now had his will sorted – well, so long as Sobers delivered the goods. Once that was done, he'd be able to do what he'd been planning to do for months. It couldn't happen too soon.

Chapter 22

Katia let herself in. Now that she had a key, it was a relief not to have to watch him struggle painfully from the front door into the kitchen. She found it hard to be dispassionate about his accelerating decline, despite her training which had emphasised the need not to become emotionally involved with patients.

He was in the lounge: his lunchtime carer Sally, whom Katia had met, made sure he was settled there after he'd had his lunch. He was usually slumped semi-prone on the settee, but today was sitting upright in the armchair. It was evidently one of his better days; he still had them, but increasingly infrequently. Katia thought it was only a matter of a month or so before he'd need to go into a care home. She was not relishing the prospect of having to tell him this.

'Hello Katia! Good to see you. How are you today?'

Katia was surprised by his greeting. Though always scrupulously polite and friendly, this was the first time he'd enquired about her welfare. Few of her patients did; they were too concerned about their own health to consider that *she* might have off days.

'I'm very well, thank you, Charles. How are you? I must say you're looking quite sprightly.'

'Sprightly! I wish! Those were the days. Sit down, Katia. I want to tell you something, and it's not about my symptoms. They're under control – well, as much as they'll ever be.'

She sat on the settee opposite him.

'Well, it's done at last! My solicitor came yesterday with my will. I've signed it, and he and his colleague witnessed it. That's a relief, I can tell you.'

'I imagine it must be.'

'Now, I want you to see it. You'll need to see it eventually as my executor, and who knows, I could go tomorrow. So I'd like you to read it now just in case you have any questions. It's here.' He pointed to a large envelope on the coffee table in front of him.

She went over to him and picked it up.

'Before you read it, Katia, just let me explain something. I don't know the precise value of my estate because I'm not sure how much this house is worth, but I reckon in total I must be worth something approaching £900,000. So what I've done is to bequeath percentages of my estate to some of the beneficiaries, but not to all of them. To some of them I've left specific items. Okay, you can read it now.'

She extracted the will from the envelope. It comprised several pages. She started to read it carefully but was so taken aback by its content that she then scan-read the remainder in order to have some idea of his overall intentions. She was a beneficiary.

'Charles, you've been far too generous to me. I told you I wasn't sure I should benefit at all.'

'Yes, but you checked and found it doesn't conflict with your professional code of conduct, didn't you? You deserve every penny, so let's hear no more of it.'

In fact, the research Katia had undertaken about a possible conflict of interest had been inconclusive, and she hadn't yet referred the matter to her superiors. But she knew that to argue further might annoy him.

'Can I just read through it again carefully?'

'Of course.'

It took her several minutes to fully digest the contents. There were parts of it that didn't read like a will at all. She put it down and looked at him. He was smiling.

'Well?'

'Charles, are you sure that this is … well, a legal document?'

'Yes, it is. I've checked with my solicitor.'

'It's just the way it reads. Some people might be upset by it.'

'Isn't that often the case with wills?'

She supposed it was, but didn't answer. She was shocked by the malevolence behind some of the bequests. She put the document back in its envelope.

'Right, now to the next thing. My funeral. I've been in contact with the local funeral directors and it's all sorted. It'll be at Staffridge crematorium and will be a humanist ceremony, although ceremony's the wrong word. No music, no eulogies, just the celebrant saying the usual things when a coffin descends.'

He spoke as though he were talking about someone else's funeral; there was no trace of emotion in his voice. Katia wondered if he'd rehearsed what he'd just said. Most of her patients never mentioned their forthcoming funerals, but of course most of them had relatives with whom the matter had probably been discussed. It heightened her awareness of Charles' isolation.

'But before I'm consigned to the flames, I want you to invite all those attending to come back here for the wake. I call it a wake, and maybe you could arrange for a company to serve drinks and eats, but the purpose of the gathering will be for the guests to hear the will read out.'

'You mean it's going to be read out in public? But Charles, do you really want some people to be humiliated in front of the others?'

'Maybe some of them deserve to be. Anyway, enough of that. You very kindly agreed to let people know when I've gone and invite them to the funeral. Are you still okay with that?'

'Yes, of course,' said Katia, but she was no longer so sure that she was.

'I've finalised the list. It's here.' He indicated a second document on the coffee table. 'There's an address and telephone number against each name. I asked the cleaning company for Mrs Williams's address, but they wouldn't divulge it for some reason. When I explained why I wanted it, they agreed to forward the invitation when you send it to them.'

'Okay.'

'There's another address I don't know. It's for a woman called Jeanette Beasley. Last I heard she was working in a county planning office down south, but she may well have retired now. I was never told which Authority she was working for, but I think Gordon Tagg – he's on the list of contacts – might know. If he does, and assuming he tells you, could I trouble you to contact that Authority and see if they'll give you her current address? I'm sure they will if you explain you're my executor.'

'I'll do my best, Charles.'

'Thanks so much, Katia. I'm indebted to you. Just one more thing.'

'What's that?'

'Would you mind making me a cup of tea? And one for yourself, of course.'

By herself in the kitchen, Katia tried to come to terms with all that Charles had said. She knew that patients nearing the end of life sometimes exhibited changes in their personality, but Charles had revealed a side to him that had shocked her. She didn't know quite what she'd say to him when back in the lounge. Perhaps it would be best to revert to cool medical professionalism, but no: that would be cruel. After all, they'd almost become friends, and he was obviously fond of her. He wouldn't have bequeathed her all that money otherwise, would he?

***

Three hours later, Charles was still in the lounge, awaiting the arrival of Beryl, his evening carer. He was wondering what reason he could give for not wanting the snack she always prepared for him before getting him to bed. She was inclined to be bossy, was Beryl, and said it was part of her duties to ensure that he ate properly. Maybe he could say he felt sick? But that would only result in more extended ministrations, and he wanted to be rid of her as soon as possible. He'd just have to be firm; maybe say that he'd eaten too much at lunchtime. It was essential that he ate nothing before retiring because food would diminish the effect of the whisky he was going to drink once he was in bed. The bottle was locked in his bedside cabinet, along with three packets of paracetamol.

He was surprised how calm he was feeling. He had no concerns about the final outcome, just apprehension about the process of getting there. Would it be like drifting off to sleep? Even if it were, descent into sleep was sometimes interrupted by flashes of wakefulness when one suddenly thought of something important that one should, or shouldn't, have done that day. Even worse, he might be gripped by panic on suddenly realising, too late, that he was making a mistake.

Or maybe his entire life would flash before him, like it was supposed to for a drowning man? Would he be haunted by regrets? He had some regrets, now. Talking to Katia, and even to Annie Williams, had evoked memories of things he'd done that maybe would have been better left undone, things which at the time had seemed perfectly reasonable. Although a convinced atheist, part of him wished for a very brief afterlife so he could look down and witness the attitudes of those attending his funeral and their reactions on hearing his will. Then he'd really know what they'd all thought of him.

He had one major regret, and it was a very recent one. Perhaps because of what he'd told her, his final conversation with Katia was not as congenial as most previous ones had been. But it was also because he'd not been relaxed: how could he have been when he knew it was the last time he'd see her? There was so much he would like to have told her; how much she'd come to mean to him, how after each of her visits he'd counted the days till her return, how intelligent she was, and how beautiful. But he couldn't tell her; such an outpouring might have alerted her to his intentions.

I love her. I love her. He said this out loud. It was the first time he'd ever said it, the first time he'd even thought that way about a woman. It saddened him, but at the same time brought comfort, for he now knew what he would do if his descent into oblivion were to be interrupted by flashes of dreadful consciousness. He'd think of Katia. In his mind's eye he'd summon up images of her, her beauty, her radiant smile. And she always used a delicate, fresh perfume. He was suddenly struck by the fact that though he'd be able to conjure images of how she looked, and the things she'd said to him, it would be impossible to summon up her smell. One had a mind's eye and a mind's ear; why was one deprived of a mind's nose? Was that perhaps why, when suddenly encountering a familiar smell, it was so evocative of the past?

'Hello Charles! Ready for your evening snack, are you?'

It was Beryl, the evening carer.

Chapter 23

Debbie woke up alone in the visitors' bedroom. Visitors' bedroom! When was the last time they had visitors to stay, apart from the children? What was the point of their having such a large house now there was only her and Keith to rattle around in it?

She'd thought for some time that it wouldn't be long before she and Keith came to sleep apart. It wasn't just his snoring and farting, but his ever increasing need to get up for a pee, always waking her by his loud complaints about having to do so. He'd even said he was considering having a chamber pot under the bed. Debbie had been aghast at the prospect. He'd asked why: it had been good enough for his father as it had for most working-class blokes, and in any case his parents' bog had been outside, something he knew Debbie wouldn't understand having had a fuckin' posh upbringing.

Debbie had decided to occupy the spare bedroom the previous evening after an afternoon spent bickering, the disagreements culminating in a ferocious row during which he'd raised his fist to her. She'd been in tears when she got into bed, despairing of the sort of man that Keith had become since he'd retired. She'd fallen into a restless sleep sometime after four o'clock. Now, fully awake at six, she knew the time had come to face the fact that her marriage was on the rocks, and resolved that from now on she and Keith would permanently occupy separate bedrooms. Marital intimacies were in any case a thing of the distant past. She'd tried to persuade herself that this was an inevitable consequence of aging, but having met Margy and Gordon, a couple who obviously still doted on each other, she knew she'd been fooling herself. She resolved to tell Margy about her unhappiness; she'd been keeping it to herself for too long. She was in urgent need of a counsellor - no, not a counsellor, but a friend on whose shoulder she could cry.

She lay in bed for a further hour, thinking about her marriage. When had it started to go wrong? When they'd met at Sheffield University, she'd immediately been intrigued by him. Although most of her fellow students were northerners, Keith was the first one she really got to know. They'd soon begun sleeping together, and started sharing a flat when Keith started his post-graduate Certificate in Education.

It was time, she'd decided, that Keith should meet her parents. Her mother was obviously unimpressed by his Yorkshire accent and responded with her Lady Bracknell impersonation. But her dad was okay; he showed interest in what Keith had to say, and they soon started talking politics.

It was down to her dad, Debbie supposed, that her mother had eventually became resigned to their engagement and the marriage which followed soon after. The reception after the wedding had been like a Monty Python sketch, the respective families eyeing each other suspiciously and straining to find something in common about which they could converse.

It was after Keith obtained his first job teaching at a comprehensive school when he'd begun to change. He was obsessed by career advancement and spent all his time when not at school marking and preparing lessons. He'd eventually became head of the History Department, which involved even more work, and he began to moderate his northern accent. 'Seems you have to talk like a bloody southerner if you want to get anywhere,' he'd said. It evidently worked, for he became deputy headmaster.

But he failed to get the headmastership when it became vacant. He'd become embittered, resentful that the new headmaster was a Londoner. It was then he started exaggerating his Yorkshire accent and began using foul language. After he retired all he seemed interested in was his garden and politics. When Jeremy Corbyn became Labour leader, Keith joined the Party and was spending an increasing amount of time at its meetings. Debbie found she had little in common with him; their conversations became restricted to the division of household duties.

The previous evening's blistering row had been prompted by Debbie reminding him how it was due to her parents' bequest that they were able to live in a lovely house in such a pleasant area. He'd turned on her, saying he was ashamed to be … what were the words he'd used? Ah yes, *the beneficiary of those patronising bastards.* Debbie had replied that he'd been quick enough to grab the money when it came, whereupon he'd begun hurling abuse at her. Enraged, she'd given as good as she'd got, though without using his bad language. It was that which resulted in him raising his fist and her running, weeping, into the spare bedroom.

It was beginning to get light. She looked at her watch; it was nearly seven. There was no point in laying here any longer. As she got out of bed, it occurred to her that she'd need her own bedside clock and radio in what was now her bedroom. And her wardrobe and chest of drawers would have to be moved in here. What other adjustments would have to be made to accommodate the separate needs of two people who were no longer a couple?

She had to go into the other bedroom, Keith's bedroom, she supposed she'd have to learn to call it, to collect her dressing gown and some clothes to change into. She hoped to God he was still asleep. Yes, from the landing she could hear his snores through the door. She tip-toed into the room and carefully removed items of clothing from the wardrobe and chest of drawers. As she did, Keith began snuffling between his snores, and his body moved. Just as she made it to the door, he farted.

At least I'll no longer have to put up with that, she thought as she went back to her bedroom to dress. She'd wash and take a shower after Keith had left the house: he had a meeting arranged that morning with one of his Labour Party friends. He seemed to be seeing a lot of that fellow. At least, Debbie assumed it was a fellow.

Washed, showered and dressed, Debbie had taken her belated breakfast through to the lounge and was still sitting there, gazing out at the crescent. The sun was streaming through the windows, the sky was cloudless, and it was possible to believe that spring had arrived. But it was only late March, the clocks had only just gone forward, and she knew that cold and damp would return as it always did, though the weather was more unpredictable these days. Some said this was a consequence of global warming, but Debbie hadn't got her head round the science behind that.

Keith hadn't spoken to her this morning. He'd waited in his bedroom until she visited the bathroom and hadn't acknowledged her when she returned to the kitchen where he was finishing his breakfast. She'd said 'Good morning', but he'd ignored the greeting, and after ten minutes he'd put on his coat and left the house, slamming the kitchen door behind him. Even after he'd gone, the kitchen had seemed tainted by his malevolent presence, which was why she'd taken her breakfast into the lounge.

She was eager to phone Margy to arrange a meeting, but it was perhaps too early to do that – it might show her desperation. She tried to relax by watching the morning comings-and-goings on the crescent; it was surprising how many of her neighbours still had a milk delivery. Charles next door did, of course. She wondered how he was. He must be deteriorating rapidly because he now had visits three times a day from women whom she assumed must be carers. The black nurse still visited him once a week, but Debbie hadn't seen his cleaner for weeks.

Then she noticed the morning carer's car draw up outside his house. Debbie had timed her visits to him; she always stayed for exactly twenty minutes, her allotted time, Debbie assumed. It didn't give her much time to chat to the poor old devil, but engagement with her clients probably didn't form part of her duties. Debbie wished that Charles hadn't rejected her offer of further visits and admitted to herself that she needed the company as much as he.

What on earth ...? The carer was running back down the drive to her car. She opened the door and extracted what looked like an intercom – yes, she was talking into it. Then she ran back to the house. Something was obviously wrong. It had to be Charles. Debbie got up and stood by the window, the better to see what would happen next.

She heard the siren long before the ambulance pulled up. Two paramedics jumped out and ran up Charles's drive. Ten minutes passed before one of them returned to the ambulance and then emerged carrying what must be a folded stretcher. Debbie couldn't tear herself away from the window and felt guilty about being voyeuristic. At the same time, she felt a growing sense of sorrow. Was this the end for Charles? To her shame, she found she was thinking not of the old man whom she'd visited recently, but of the beguiling fellow who'd propositioned her in her kitchen all those years ago. Might things have been better for both of them if she'd gone along with his implicit invitation? Then even deeper shame overtook her; she'd completely forgotten he'd been married to Celia.

The inevitable happened. The two paramedics walked back down the drive, one at each end of the stretcher on which lay what could only be Charles. As they manoeuvred the stretcher into the ambulance Debbie caught a glimpse of an ashen face; at least it wasn't covered, but there were no signs of resuscitation, no face mask, no equipment attached to the body.

The rear doors of the ambulance were shut, and it immediately set off, siren wailing. Debbie needed to know *now* how Charles was, whether there was hope for him. She ran to the front door, then down her drive and took up position outside Charles's house. The carer would come out soon, wouldn't she?

She did.

'Oh, please forgive me for asking, but is Charles ill? You see, we've been neighbours for over thirty years. My name's Deborah Barker.'

The woman's bottom lip was quivering. 'Yes, he's very ill. I found him unconscious and he didn't seem to be breathing. So I called the ambulance. The paramedics took his pulse and did other checks.' She swallowed. 'I asked them if he was dead, but they wouldn't say yes or no to that. They just said they had to get him to A and E immediately.'

'But … well, you must have come across this sort of thing before in your line of business, surely? What do *you* think his chances are?'

'I think he's already gone. Now, I'm sorry, but I've got to get back and report to the care company.'

Debbie walked slowly back to her house. At least she now had a valid reason for phoning Margy Tagg so early.

Chapter 24

Gordon and Margaret were about to set out on their weekly visit to Waitrose. It was a ten-mile journey to the nearest branch – Staffridge wasn't sufficiently up-market to have one – but shopping in the store was always a pleasant experience, and the coffee and snacks in its café were excellent. Just as Gordon was locking the front door, they heard their phone ringing inside.

'Oh, let it ring, Margy. It's probably only a junk call at this time of day; that's all we get on the landline these days.'

They climbed into the car and set off. They'd only driven a few hundred yards when Margaret's mobile chirruped. She fished it out from her handbag.

'It's a text. Oh, it's from Debbie.'

'You two seem to have a lot to say to each other recently.'

'Well, I think she's ... oh, hang on. Bloody hell!'

'What's happened?

Margaret read it aloud. *Margy, I think Charles Pettifer is very ill, or even worse. An ambulance has just taken him away. Is it convenient to phone you?*

'Well, I suppose it had to happen sooner or later, Margy.'

Margaret was already texting; *Yes, phone me.*

The phone rang immediately. Margaret held it close to her ear: Gordon didn't like distractions while he was driving.

'Yes, Debbie. Okay to talk. What happened exactly?'

Only Margaret was party to Debbie's long rambling explanation on the phone, to which her only interjections were, 'But you knew he was very ill, didn't you?' followed some minutes later by, 'Yes, of course. We're going shopping, but Gordy will drop me off at your place. See you in about ten minutes.'

184

She switched off her phone and returned it to her handbag.

'Is there some problem?' asked Gordon as he carefully manoeuvred round a roundabout. 'Apart from Pettifer, I mean? Why have you got to go to her place?'

'She sounded very upset, Gordy; in tears some of the time. She seemed desperate to see me.'

'Well, if Pettifer's gone, it's sad, of course, but why the tears? It wasn't as if they were friends, despite being neighbours for all those years.'

'I think it's about more than Pettifer. She implied she'd had a major bust-up with Keith. I reckon it's that she wants to talk about. Apparently he's out all morning, and he's taken the car, of course. Would you mind taking me to her house, Gordy?'

'Of course I will. Good job Littleton Parva's not far out of our way. I assume you'd like me to do the shopping?'

'Yes please, darling. I've got the shopping list here, so – '

'No, give it to me when I've stopped the car. Will you need picking up when I'm on my way back?'

'I don't know how long I'll be there. I'll give you a ring.'

'I won't be able to answer the phone if I'm driving, Margy.'

'Oh, no worries. I'll get a taxi.'

'Just one thing. If Keith gets back while you're still there, don't get involved in any dispute. That fellow's bad news, if you ask me.'

Margaret was waiting for Debbie to bring refreshments in from the kitchen. She was sitting on a settee in the lounge and was struck by how shabby the furniture was, totally out of keeping with a large house located in an affluent neighbourhood. And Debbie, when she'd opened the door to her, had looked similarly down-at-heel. Margaret had been further taken aback by being hugged while she was still on the doorstep: okay, they were becoming friendly, but hadn't yet reached a stage in their relationship where embraces were exchanged on meeting or parting. When she'd been released, she noticed that Debbie had obviously been crying. The offer of a cup of tea or coffee had been made, and Margaret had been shown into the lounge.

Her cup of tea was brought in on a tray. It was already milked, and Debbie hadn't asked if she took sugar.

'Here you are, Margy.'

'Aren't you having any, Debbie?'

'Don't feel like it at the moment.'

Margaret sipped the tea. It wasn't sugared, thank God, but it tasted metallic, obviously a cup of instant. Margaret and Gordon abhorred instant tea and always took the trouble to brew theirs in a teapot. The taste evoked the brew served by their parents in the days before teabags had been invented.

Debbie sat down next to Margaret.

'Thanks so much for coming, Margy.'

'Well, you sounded very upset on the phone. I take it you saw what happened next door with Pettifer?'

Debbie gave a hesitant account of all that she'd witnessed, hesitant because she began sniffing and then dabbed at her eyes with a handkerchief. Margaret was certain that her distress wasn't entirely the result of what had happened to Pettifer. When they'd met previously in the Caffé Nero, Debbie had given no indication that she had any feelings for him at all – indeed, hadn't she given him short shrift that time he'd groped her? No, this must be about Keith. Margaret was tempted to ask her a direct question about this, but perhaps it was best to continue the conversation about Pettifer. If Debbie wanted to talk about her marriage, it would have to be when she was ready to.

'... so I don't know whether he's alive or dead,' she was saying. 'And how can I find out? I phoned the A & E department at the hospital, but they wouldn't tell me anything because I'm not related to him.'

'Yes, I'm afraid that's standard procedure.'

'So what on earth can I do? I need to know; it's terrible if you don't know if your neighbour's died.'

'Yes, Debbie, I can understand that. Oh, hang on a minute; didn't you tell me that he had a nurse visiting him regularly? A black woman?'

'Yes.'

'Well, she might not know yet that he's no longer at home. She might be due to make another visit. Why don't you post a letter through the letter box, addressed to her, asking her to call round? Or maybe give her your phone number and email address and ask her to contact you? Explain you've been a neighbour for years and that you're concerned about – '

'Yes! Yes! Why didn't I think of that?' She leapt to her feet. 'I'll write it now. You never know, she might call round this afternoon. Will you help me write the letter?'

This was the first sign of animation on Debbie's part since Margaret's arrival. Without waiting for a response to her question, she hurried out of the room, returning after a few minutes carrying a reporter's pad and a biro. She sat down next to Margaret, pad on her lap, and started sucking the biro. Then she wrote a few words, but immediately crossed them out. More biro-sucking followed, then a few more words were written, only to be vigorously scored through. She threw back her head and howled; there was no other word to describe it.

'What the hell's wrong with me? I can't think what to say!'

Margaret put a hand on her arm. 'You've had a shock, Debbie. Would you like me to write a draft for you?'

'Oh, would you please? Why am I being so bloody useless?'

Margaret took the pen and pad and after a few minutes had completed the draft. It was a simple enough message after all, but it occurred to her it was easy to be dispassionate when writing to someone whom she'd never met and about someone she'd only encountered twice. She handed the pad back to Debbie.

'That's great, Margy. Thanks so much. I'll take it round now, just in case the nurse comes this afternoon.'

'But wouldn't it be better written in your own handwriting? And on proper writing paper? And put it in an envelope – you need to address it; just write *To Mr Pettifer's Nurse*. Oh, and you need to add your phone number in case she'd prefer not to call round on you.'

'Of course, of course. Oh, why can't I think straight?' She jumped up, crossed the room and began rummaging in a dilapidated bureau, evidently searching for writing paper. But she didn't extract any: she stopped and put her head in her hands.

'Debbie, what's wrong?'

'It's pointless! Pointless! The nurse called on him yesterday! I saw her leaving! So she won't be back till next week!' She started crying; great, heaving sobs.

Margaret got up, put an arm round her shoulder and led her back to the settee. The sobs continued; Margaret kept her arm round her. When at last the sobs subsided, Margaret withdrew her arm, but grasped her hand. It was time, she decided, to broach the issue that she was sure was the real reason for Debbie's distress.

'Debbie, this isn't just about Pettifer, is it? You hinted when you phoned me that things weren't good between you and Keith. Would it help if you talked about it?'

'Yes, I've no one else to talk to.'

She began an account, punctuated by sobs and sniffles, of what had happened the previous day. But she didn't stop there: she went on to describe all that had been going wrong with the marriage right back to the time when Keith had started work as a teacher. Margaret didn't interrupt her, not even to ask questions, not that she had the opportunity. It was a continuous outpouring of resentment and grief.

At last she finished. She seemed calmer but looking

at her, Margaret saw a hint of the old woman she would soon become.

'Debbie, I'm not going to presume to give you advice, not now anyway. But I'd like to say a few things which might help. But first, I need to visit your toilet.'

'It's first right at the top of the stairs. Would you like another cup of tea?'

'I'd prefer a coffee if you don't mind.'

Margaret took her time in the toilet, trying to think of a way in which she could comfort Debbie. Margaret knew she wasn't qualified to give marriage guidance counselling, but in any case there seemed to be no future for their relationship because if all that Debbie had told her was true, Keith was an out-and-out bastard. Perhaps she should talk about marriage in general; quite a few of her friends had had difficulties. It might comfort Debbie to learn she wasn't the only one.

As she'd climbed the stairs to the antiquated bathroom – it must be at least thirty years old – she'd had a sense that something was missing in the house. Now, on her descent, she realised what it was. The walls were bare; no paintings, no photographs. Margaret's staircase walls were lined with family photographs – her wedding, the kids as children, the kids' weddings, the grandchildren. There was no indication of Debbie's attachment to her family. Was the absence of photographs Keith's doing, she wondered?

When she entered the lounge Debbie was back on the settee. She looked more composed. Two cups of coffee were on the occasional table.

'Thanks, Debbie: just what the doctor ordered.' She took a sip: it was instant, of course.

'Margy, thanks so much for listening to me. I'm so sorry I rambled on.'

'It obviously did you good to talk, Debbie. You look all the better for it.'

'You must have found it hard to understand, you having such a happy marriage.'

'Well, yes, but all marriages have their problems from time to time.'

'Yes, but not yours, surely? Your Gordon is such a nice, gentle, man! He obviously dotes on you.'

'Yes, but he can be too nice, sometimes.' As soon as she said this, Margaret wished she hadn't.

'What do you mean? How can someone be too nice?'

What shall I say? thought Margaret. She didn't want to voice the niggling irritations that sometimes came from living with Gordon. When they occurred, she buried them by engaging in strenuous activity, lest she start thinking about them too much. To answer Debbie's question would be to articulate the very thoughts she dare not to admit to having. But Debbie was looking at her quizzically. Her question needed to be answered; perhaps she could do so by just giving vague generalisations?

'He's a bit too much the gentleman, too polite. I think he used to let people walk all over him when he was at work. And sometimes he doesn't even challenge our friends when they say things I know he disagrees with.'

'Well, that's better than someone who's always rude to people, isn't it?'

'I suppose so, but I wish he'd be more direct sometimes, speak his mind.'

Margaret knew she was dissembling, but too late, because in her mind now were all the irritations she felt as a consequence of Gordon's niceness. The way he always kissed her on greeting or parting, the way he always insisted on holding her hand whenever they walked as though they were a pair of teenagers; sometimes she saw people staring at them, no doubt thinking *silly old fools*. But even when they *were* teenagers, Gordon had always been scrupulously polite and had behaved decorously towards her. She had secretly envied her friends who told tales of fighting off the amorous advances made by their boyfriends. But theirs was a courtship that proceeded at a snail's pace, even though they were joyous participants in the youth culture of the time – Gordon came alive when dancing to Beatles and Stones records. Margaret came to love him. It was nice to be worshipped, and he made her feel safe. But now, having acquired the sort of security that comes with late-middle age, she wished he'd sometimes act out of character and do something to surprise her. Even the odd argument, followed by a loving making-up, might bring a spark to their marriage: all they had were mild disagreements, at the end of which he usually conceded that she'd been right.

Her thoughts were interrupted by the sound of gravel being scrunched by car tyres. Debbie leapt up and went to the window.

'Oh God, it's Keith. He's back early. What shall I do, Margy?'

'Just do whatever you usually do whenever he comes home,' said Margaret, only too aware that what she was suggesting might result in a variety of different scenarios, some unpleasant, given the nature of their parting.

The front door slammed. Debbie ran into the hall. 'You're early,' Margaret heard her say. 'Would you like a cup of tea?'

'Tea? *Tea?* Is that all you have to fuckin' offer, woman? How about an apology for last night?'

Margaret decided it was time she left. She'd phone for a taxi once she was outside the house, but she needed to say goodbye to Debbie first. She picked up her bag and went into the hall, which had fallen silent. Debbie and Keith were standing facing each other. Keith was glowering; the expression on Debbie's face was hard to read.

Keith didn't look at Margaret, but it was evident he'd registered her presence. 'What's *she* doing here?' he demanded. 'Giving you advice on how to humiliate me, is she?'

'Can't I even have a friend call round for a cup of tea now?' Debbie's voice showed more determination and assertiveness than Margaret thought possible given the emotional state she'd been in for the past hour.

'Debbie, I'll have to go now. It's been lovely seeing you. Give me a call or text whenever you want.'

'But how will you get home, Margy?'

'I'll phone for a taxi when I'm outside and wait for it down the road.'

'No need for that. I'll give you a lift home.'

'Oh, will you?' said Keith. 'And what makes you think I'm going to let you have my car?'

'It's *our* car!' Debbie shrieked. She turned and grabbed a set of keys hanging from a hook by the front door. 'Come on, Margy, let's go.'

Margaret hurried after her. 'Fuckin' bitches!' Keith shouted after them.

Margaret wondered if Debbie was in a fit state to drive, but once they'd left the estate where she lived she showed a degree of competence, though perhaps driving too fast. Neither of them spoke. Margaret thought it was best to let her concentrate, and in any case the only topic of conversation would have to be the recent altercation with Keith, something that Debbie probably wouldn't welcome.

Margaret sank back in her seat and gave an inner sigh of relief. She was looking forward to getting home, to the peace and comfort that dear old boring Gordy would provide.

Chapter 25

Katia was one of three Macmillan nurses based at the Wedgwood Hospice in Staffridge. Her time was divided equally between ministering to those in the hospice and those who were still able to manage at home. Of the two duties, she preferred the latter. Even though her clients there had received their final sentence, it was possible to lighten conversations with them by chatting about their surroundings. Family photographs often provided a means of getting them to talk about their happier pasts, and she could also involve members of their families who were often present during her visits. It was much harder to engage with those in the hospice who were usually nearing the final curtain and often so drugged that they were unable to communicate. Saddest of all were those who had no relatives to visit them; it was akin to solitary confinement. She could well understand Charles Pettifer's reluctance to leave his house.

She was returning from a visit to a client who had only just received her prognosis. Those initial meetings were always difficult. Sometimes the clients were in denial and it was hard to establish any sort of relationship with them. That had been the case with the woman she'd seen today. It was best at these first visits to remain coolly professional, but she found the process exhausting.

On her way to the office she shared with her two colleagues, she had to pass the matron's office, whose door was always open. 'Oh, Katia,' Mrs Hemmings called, 'can you come in for a minute?'

Katia entered.

'Katia, I'm afraid I have some bad news. I've had a call from the hospital. Mr Pettifer was rushed to A & E this morning. He was pronounced dead on arrival.' Mrs Hemming's voice was cool, matter-of-fact. She often had to impart such news.

'Oh, I'm sorry to hear that. I only saw him

yesterday, and he seemed, well, not exactly cheerful, but more alert than he'd been for some time.' Katia managed to match Mrs Hemmings's detached delivery, but it was news she'd been dreading. Her suspicions were confirmed by Mrs Hemmings's next remarks.

'There'll have to be an autopsy, of course, but it looks as though he took his own life. The paramedics found an empty whisky bottle and paracetamol packets by his bed. Did he give any indication that he was intending to do that?'

'Not in so many words.' Katia didn't feel up to divulging what took place at her last visit; she was feeling more upset than she thought possible.

'This has obviously come as a shock, Katia. I suspected you were close to him when you asked me if it was acceptable for you to be executor for his will. If you remember, I did warn you at the time that you might be getting too involved with him. It's always inadvisable to put yourself in a situation which might lead to your becoming emotionally involved with a client. However, what's done is done. I will, of course, keep you informed about the autopsy.'

She looked down at her desk and began rifling through papers. The discussion was obviously over. Katia gratefully escaped.

Fortunately, neither of Katia's colleagues were in the pokey room they called their office. Katia wanted some time to herself. It wasn't time to go home, and in any case she didn't want to return to an empty house. David, her partner, was away at a conference. The office was a suitable place to try and concentrate on all the things she was now faced with. If she were at home, she knew she'd sink into an armchair and start blaming herself for not doing more to stop Charles doing what she'd suspected he had in mind.

She reached for her writing pad and began to make a list of what she had to do, and in what order. First would be to inform all the people on Charles's list about his death. But she couldn't give them details of his funeral because that would have to wait until after the autopsy – no, wait, there'd probably have to be an inquest. Would that be before or after the autopsy? Whichever was the case, it could be well over a month before the funeral could be held.

What next? Oh, yes, go to Charles's solicitor and apply for probate. But no, she couldn't do that until after the inquest had been held and a death certificate issued. And she'd need to have probate before the will could be signed off, and that needed to be done before the funeral. So the date of the funeral might have to be put back even further, because it was just after the funeral that Charles wanted his will read out. Oh God, it could be May before Charles was laid to rest.

But wait – she would need to see the solicitor to get Charles's estate valued. That could be done immediately, couldn't it? No: before that could be done, she'd have to get an estate agent to value his house. And might the estate be liable for inheritance tax?

All she'd written on her list were the words *Inform people he's dead. Autopsy? Inquest? Date of funeral? Value estate? Inheritance tax?* She was no further forward. She'd have to see the solicitor tomorrow to get some answers, always assuming she could get an appointment.

In her job, she'd often been told by the bereaved that the volume of work resulting from a loved one's death was such that they didn't have time to mourn the departed until after the funeral was over. She could understand that now. But Charles hadn't been a loved one, had he? So she couldn't be mourning, but she could think of no other word to describe the way she was feeling.

She must snap out of this somehow. She'd have to take a day's leave tomorrow, providing she could get an appointment with the solicitor, and in any case, she'd have to make a start contacting people on Charles' list. Then the thought occurred to her: as Charles's executor, might she be responsible for the upkeep of his vacant house?

Something else to ask the solicitor.

She had an uncanny feeling of detachment as she walked up the drive to Charles's house, probably the result of her having spent an hour that morning in the company of Mr Sobers, his solicitor. He was a very pompous young man who'd patronised her until she'd interrupted him and told him, in no uncertain terms, that she'd come for advice on specific issues, not for a long lecture on the duties of an executor. She'd got satisfaction from his resulting discomfiture: it was something that still happened, even in 2019, when people were evidently surprised that a black person, and a woman at that, gave articulate responses using words of four syllables in what used to be called a BBC accent, something that was rarely heard on the radio these days.

But at least he'd told her about her responsibilities regarding Charles's house. Once probate had been granted, the house could be put on the market, but until it was sold the company that insured it would require someone to visit it regularly to check that all was in order; otherwise the insurance cover would lapse. As executor, she would be responsible for this. Sobers said someone would need to go through all the documents in the house to discover the name of the insurance company: did she know of anyone who might have access to the house?

'I do,' Katia had said. 'I was his nurse, and he gave me a key. I still have it.'

Sobers had conceded that as the named executor it would be acceptable for her to visit the property before probate was granted.

This was why Katia was now standing at the front door, about to let herself in.

Katia was a rational woman and had no qualms about entering the house of someone who'd died there, no thoughts that Charles's ghostly presence might haunt it. But it was discomforting to be in a place where she'd had regular contact with him and where only two days ago, in this very lounge, they'd had a lengthy discussion. The place was rather less clean and tidy than it had been when Mrs Williams had been his cleaner. She went to check the kitchen; it also bore hallmarks of neglect, but of greater interest was an envelope on the table with her name on it. She ripped it open; it had to be a final message from Charles. It was, but just further instructions regarding what she should say at the end of his cremation. Katia sighed. Her duties were becoming ever more burdensome.

She returned to the lounge. She knew where Charles probably kept such documents as the house insurance policy; he'd once told her that his horizons had shrunk so much that it was possible to keep all records pertaining to his life in the drawers of the desk on which sat his computer.

She took the seat in front of the desk, and for the first time felt as though she were an intruder. Who knew what personal items might be contained in the drawers, private things which Charles might have wished not to be seen by anyone? But this was probably the case for everyone; Katia had items relating to her past secreted away lest David catch sight of them.

She opened the top left-hand drawer. In it was a pile of folders of varying colours. The one on the top of the pile was neatly labelled *Current Account Bank Statements*. She pulled all the folders out from the drawer and spread them on the desktop. They were each carefully labelled in neat handwriting – *Credit Card Statements. Deposit Account. Premium Bonds. ISAs. Direct Saver*.

Katia was relieved to find that Charles had been such an assiduous record-keeper; it would make her duty as an executor much easier. She flipped through the folders in the other drawers and found, in the drawer devoted to insurance, one labelled *House and Contents Insurance*. She pulled it out and was about to open it when she thought she may as well check through the remainder of the drawers to see if there were any other items likely to be of relevance to an executor.

The bottom right-hand drawer did not contain folders. In it was something that looked like a photo album. She extracted it. Although it was a thick volume, it seemed surprisingly light. Should she open it? To do so wouldn't really form part of her executor's duties; photographs were usually personal. Would Charles have wanted her to see them? He'd revealed little of his personal life other than his time at university, and even then had stopped short of telling her how his relationship with that girl Jenny had progressed.

Katia battled with her conscience. No, she told herself, it wasn't just prurient curiosity that was tempting her. As she'd come to know more of Charles, she'd realised there was material in his persona that might contribute to the dissertation she hoped to write. She wasn't content just to have an M.Sc. in Health Psychology, she wanted a Doctorate and a career in academia. Being a Macmillan nurse no longer satisfied her.

She opened the album and began leafing through it. The first few pages were blank but had obviously once contained photographs which had been pulled out. A few pages further on was a small monochrome snapshot underneath which was the handwritten legend *With Bonzo Barnes, 5th Form 1959.* She peered at it, wishing she had a magnifying glass. Yes, the very short boy had to be Charles. He had a full head of hair, of course, but his 16-year-old features were still recognisable. The fellow standing next to him was much taller, strikingly handsome, and with black hair combed back in a quiff. Then she remembered: a Rodney Barnes was one of those on the list of people she had to contact.

She turned the page, hoping to find more evidence of Charles's time at school. But there was none, just more pages from which photographs had obviously been extracted. She leafed impatiently through the blank pages until she encountered the next photograph, a larger one but still monochrome. Underneath it was written *With Ken Gubbins, Armley, Leeds, November 1961.* Charles was

Chapter 26

It had been a long time coming. Nearly five weeks had elapsed since Gordon and Margaret had received a letter from a Ms Katia Whittaker informing them of Charles Pettifer's death and stating they'd be informed of the date of the funeral as soon as it became available.

Last week they'd received another letter from Ms Whittaker which told them. It was worded rather strangely, saying that it had been Charles Pettifer's specific request that they both attend the cremation and then join fellow mourners at his house for a short wake, at which refreshments would be provided. Gordon had commented to Margaret that he didn't know of anyone who would mourn Pettifer's death, and that perhaps 'attendees' would have been a better word. Margaret had replied that she couldn't understand why she'd been invited: she'd only met the man once – no, twice if you counted the recent brief encounter in Caffé Nero. Gordon had said it was probably to make up the numbers; he imagined the number attending would be embarrassingly small.

The day had arrived. It was a sunny morning as Gordon drove into the grounds of Staffridge crematorium, the trees newly clad in the fresh green leaves of early spring. The thought occurred to Gordon as he parked the car that attending funerals would now be something that would occur with increasing frequency. It was selfish of him, he knew, but he hoped to God that Margy would have to attend his rather than the other way round.

They walked, hand in hand of course, towards the entrance to the crematorium. It was an imposing building. Standing outside the entrance, they spotted Debbie and Keith Barker. That was no surprise: Debbie had informed Margy that they'd be attending. Margy had said to Gordon that she couldn't understand why Keith had been invited, given what Debbie had told her about his and Pettifer's mutual antipathy. Gordon had replied that the same could equally be applied to himself.

Standing next to the Barkers was a tall, strikingly attractive black woman, smartly dressed in clothes of the same colour. Was she the celebrant, Gordon wondered? As they neared her, she approached them.

'Good morning,' she said. 'I'm Katia Whittaker, Mr Pettifer's executor. May I ask who you are?'

Gordon told her. She referred to a piece of paper she was holding and marked it with a pen. Ticking off our names, probably, thought Gordon, wondering why it was so important that she knew who was present.

They went to talk to the Barkers. Gordon noticed that Debbie had obviously made an effort with her appearance. She was more smartly dressed than he'd seen before and was wearing make-up. Keith, however, was clad in a casual jacket and – could it be? Good God, yes, he was wearing jeans.

'Good morning,' said Gordon, but Barker just nodded at him and then turned away, a surly expression on his face. From what Margy had told Gordon about the Barker's marriage, he wondered how Debbie had managed to persuade him to attend. His attire was no doubt designed to make his attitude to Pettifer clear.

Margy was talking with Debbie. Gordon was obviously going to be ignored by Keith. It was only ten minutes before the ceremony was due to start; surely there'd be more people attending than this? He glanced towards the car park. A woman was getting out of her car and began walking towards the entrance.

There was something familiar about the way she walked. As she got nearer to Gordon, he began to wonder – could that really be …? He heard Katia Whittaker introduce herself and ask the woman her name. 'Gillian Tebbit,' she replied.

Gordon was taken aback, not so much by Gillian's attendance, but by the sight of the woman she'd become. How old would she be – in her mid- 50s maybe? Most of the women Gordon had known for some time had put on weight with age - even Margy was a bit plumper round the waist – but Gillian, once possessed of a shapely figure - and how she used to flaunt it - was now skinny, almost emaciated. Her face was scored with lines and her once blonde hair was now grey.

Gordon had never really liked Gillian and was sure the feeling had been reciprocated, but the sight of someone from his past who'd once been so attractive and who now looked so old and wizened filled him with pity. He approached her.

'Gillian?'

She stared at him; maybe he also had aged beyond recognition?

'Gillian, it's me, Gordon Tagg.'

Her eyes widened. 'Gordon! Oh Gordon, how lovely to see you. I thought there'd be nobody here I'd know.' She came up to him, flung her arms round him and hugged him. She didn't release him, so he felt obliged to embrace her. Christ, there was nothing of her; it was like holding a skeleton.

When she eventually stepped back he saw her eyes were filling. 'Oh, Gordon,' she said, 'Isn't it sad? I was so fond of Chas. After he retired, I used to visit him sometimes, but when he became ill, he wouldn't let me. He said he didn't want me to see him as an old man.'

'And how are you, Gillian?'

'Nice of you to ask, Gordon, but I'm sure you must realise I'm not too well – no, don't ask, I don't want to talk about it. I hate having to look at myself in the mirror every day. Gordon, I suppose you're going to the wake?'

'Yes, of course.'

'Will you do me a favour, please? When we're there, come and talk to me now and again. Otherwise I'll feel like a spare part.'

'Yes, I will, Gillian.'

'Thanks. I'll let you go now. There must be others here you want to talk to.'

Gordon was reeling from his encounter with

Gillian, and it took him a few minutes to adjust to his surroundings. Two more people had arrived. One was an obese women, plastered with make-up, and dragging furiously on a cigarette. The other was a smartly dressed slim woman who had features that would never distinguish her in a crowd, making her instantly forgettable. Not being close to the Katia woman when they arrived, he'd had no opportunity to overhear these women's names.

The hearse drew up. Two young men made short work of pulling the coffin from it onto a trolley which they wheeled into the crematorium. A man stood at the open doors, announced himself as the Celebrant, and invited them to follow the coffin.

Before Gordon turned to do his bidding, he caught sight of a woman running from the car park. It was Jeanette. His surprise at seeing her at Pettifer's funeral was almost as great as that which he'd experienced when being cuddled by Gillian Tebbit.

What a pathetic little gathering, thought Gordon. Just nine people standing facing the coffin mounted on the podium, and of the nine, the Katia woman was there in a formal capacity. The scene was made bleaker by their being dwarfed by the vast interior of the crematorium, which was seemingly designed to seat up to a hundred. Sitting on one side of him was Gillian, and her occasional snuffles echoed in the oppressive silence. Gordon was dreading whatever ceremony might follow, and hoped there'd be no hypocritical eulogy, though he could think of nobody present who'd want to deliver it, except perhaps Gillian, and she was in no state to do so.

The celebrant was standing at a lectern to one side of the podium. He wore a no doubt long-practiced sympathetic smile, tinged with gravitas.

'I'd like to welcome you to Staffridge crematorium,' he said, 'to join in celebrating the life of Charles Pettifer, whom I am told was your friend or colleague.' As he said the words *Charles Pettifer* he turned and bowed slightly in the direction of the coffin.

'This will be a very short ceremony,' he continued. 'It was the wish of the deceased that there should be no address from me or from anyone here present. I am told that you all received specific invitations to attend, and the reason for his inviting you will be explained after the committal by his executor, Ms Whittaker. It was also the wish of the deceased that there should be no readings or music. It therefore falls to me simply to say the committal. Today and always may long memories bring you peace, comfort and strength.'

Was this, Gordon wondered, addressed to the departed or to the mourners? He rather liked the absence of certainty in humanist ceremonial.

The celebrant pressed something on the lectern, and the red curtains in front of the coffin juddered closed.

'There will now be a minute's silence during which you will no doubt wish to think of all the happy times you had in the company of Charles, and of course, those of you who hold religious beliefs may wish to pray.'

Gordon couldn't help but smile to himself. If the celebrant had known of his experiences in the company of Pettifer, he wouldn't have suggested he think of them. No doubt Jeanette was feeling the same way. But Gillian obviously had different memories; he heard her start to quietly sob.

He detected a collective sigh of relief when the minute's silence was over, and Katia Whittaker left her position to stand facing them.

'I just have one thing to add,' she said. 'You all know that it was Mr Pettifer's wish that you now come to his house where refreshments are available. On your way out, you will find on the bench on the left, some papers on which I've given directions to his house. As Mr Pettifer's executor, it is my duty to inform you that this will be the occasion when his will is to be read. Mr Pettifer made it clear that I should emphasise the importance of everybody attending. In the event of any absence, the reading of the will and the execution of its provisions will be delayed until such time as all are present.'

What an articulate and self-confident young woman, thought Gordon. Then he wondered where the hell all this was leading to.

Chapter 27

Annie Williams lit a cigarette as soon as she got outside the crematorium and walked to the car park where her son Kevin's van was parked.

'Bloody hell, Mum,' he said as she climbed in, 'that didn't take long.'

'Good job too. Can't stand funerals, even when there are folk there what I like.'

'Right then. Where to?'

'I've got directions 'ere. But there ain't no rush. Don't want to spend more time with that crowd than I 'ave to. Let me finish this fag first.'

'Dunno why you wanted to go anyway. That Pettifer bloke won't have left you anything, will he?'

'Course he won't 'ave. I just want to 'ave a look round the 'ouse.'

'I'll have a fag too.'

As they sat nursing their addiction, Annie saw Katia Whittaker walking to her car.

'Hey Kev, look. There's that bloody nurse I told yer about, the black bitch. She acted like she was in charge in the crem. Better let her go ahead. She's probably got the keys to the 'ouse anyway.'

'She's a real looker, isn't she? I wouldn't say no to a bit of that.'

Annie chose to ignore his comment. Some of Kevin's employees were black, and he seemed to like them. She hoped to God he'd never bring a black woman home. Bert wouldn't let them into the house if he did.

Cigarettes finished and the stubs thrown out of the window, they set off. It was only a ten-minute drive to the house. Kevin pulled up outside.

'Okay, ma. Give me bell a few minutes before you want me to collect you. Have you got your mobile?'

'Course I 'ave. Seeya, Kev.'

She got out and walked up the drive. It was strange;

she'd thought she'd never be here again after her last encounter with Charlie. The front door was ajar. She pushed it open. Standing in the hall was that bloody Whittaker woman.

'Ah, Mrs Williams. You're the first to arrive. Please go into the lounge. Refreshments will be served after the will has been read. Now if you'll forgive me, I'm going out to the drive to welcome the other arrivals.'

She didn't wait for a reply, not that Annie was going to give her one. Annie didn't go to the lounge. She now had a chance to look round the house to see what had changed since she no longer cleaned here.

'Who was that woman you were talking to?' Margaret asked Gordon as they walked to the car.

'That, believe it or not, was Gillian Tebbit.'

'Gillian Tebbit? You always said she was attractive, but she looked, well, emaciated. I can't imagine Pettifer fancying her.'

'She told me she's ill, Margy. But she didn't say what was wrong with her.'

'You always said you didn't get on with her, but she greeted you like an old friend. You had quite a cuddle, didn't you?'

Gordon unlocked the car and they climbed in. 'Isn't it often the case, Margy, that when you run into someone from your past, you find the memories you have in common outweigh any disagreements you may have had?'

'That wasn't the case when you met Pettifer in Staffridge last year, was it?'

'I didn't know he was ill then. And even if I had, I doubt we'd have cuddled each other.'

He started the engine. As he drove off, Margaret was giggling.

Gillian had been dreading the funeral, and the wake at the house even more so. But she felt more relaxed now that she'd spoken to Gordon. She didn't know why she'd embraced him – she'd started doing that to people recently – and it was so comforting that he'd embraced her in return. There was no one else at the ceremony whom she'd recognised, so maybe she could cope with the wake: there'd be nobody else there who'd be taken aback by her appearance.

She parked her car outside the house. The black woman standing in the drive welcomed her. What was she to Charles, she wondered? She was very attractive. Trust Charles to choose a sexy woman to be his executor.

She entered the lounge and was relieved to see that the only others present were Gordon and a woman she presumed to be his wife. She went over to them.

'Ah, Gillian,' said Gordon. 'I don't believe you've met my wife. This is Margy. Margy, this is Gillian.'

'Hello, Gillian. No, we haven't met, but I used to hear a lot about you from Gordy.'

Gillian was on the verge of saying that Margy had probably heard nothing good about her, but stopped in time. The cuddle with Gordon had brought about a reconciliation between them and it would be stupid to resurrect their past. But wasn't it one of the purposes of funerals, to talk about the past? She would like to speak to Gordon alone, to talk about Charles, but she couldn't do that with a third-party present.

'Not all bad, I hope.' she contented herself by saying.

What else could they talk about? Gordon was evidently struggling with a similar inhibition. 'There've been a lot of changes in Staffridge since our time in the planning office, haven't there?' he said.

They resorted to discussing how Staffridge was not the place it used to be.

Keith opened his car door and was halfway out when Debbie said, 'Hang on, Keith.'

'What?'

'Before we go in, will you promise me you'll

behave?'

'What d'you mean?'

'You know very well what I mean. Can't you for once try to be polite to people? We'll only be here a short while.'

'For Christ's sake, what the fuck are we doing here at all? I didn't like Pettifer, and he didn't like me. Why in hell's name were we invited to his funeral anyway? And why should we be interested in his will? It's not as though we're likely to benefit from it.'

'We've been through all this before. His executor specifically requested our presence. Look, all I'm asking is that you chat to anyone who wants to talk, and just smile occasionally, can't you? Oh, look, the executor's standing at the front gate. We'd better go in.'

Debbie got out of the car and approached the front gate, Keith trailing behind her.

When they entered the lounge Debbie was relieved to see Margy there, with Gordon of course, and a woman she didn't know.

'Oh Debbie, hello again,' said Margaret. 'Can I Introduce Gillian Tebbit? Gillian, this is Debbie Barker. She's ...she was Charles's next door neighbour. And this is Keith, her husband.'

'Are you the woman who used to visit Pettifer?' said Keith, 'the one who claimed to be his personal assistant?

'Well, I *was* his P.A.,' said Gillian.

'Well, you don't look anything like her now.'

Debbie cringed. Was there no limit to his oafish behaviour?

Celia hadn't been sure how she'd feel, visiting the house that had been her home for so many years. But she felt strangely detached as she walked up the drive because the front garden was unrecognisable. All her careful planting was hidden, if indeed it was still there, by couch grass and overgrown shrubs. She'd been, if not happy, then reasonably content here for the first few years before she'd come to realise there was no future for her marriage. She'd done the right thing to leave Charles, though she'd been stricken with conscience for the first few years afterwards. But her sister, who'd had the courage to leave their strict parents and marry a man of whom they disapproved, had taken her in, given her counsel and then helped build up her confidence by advising her on what to wear, how to apply make-up, how to walk assertively. Now, even in her sixties, she no longer felt the need to avoid mirrors.

She was greeted by the executor and invited to go into the lounge. On opening the door, she was taken aback. All the furniture was new except for the bookcase, and there was a large-screen television in the corner. Had Charles perhaps refurnished the place so as to expunge all memories of her? But he'd continued sending her Christmas cards, and to her surprise, the last Christmas card she'd received had been signed with love.

There were five people in the room standing together and conversing. She didn't recognise any of them but … hang on, wasn't that Debbie Tagg, her erstwhile neighbour? Yes, the fellow with her was her husband – what was his name? Yes, Keith.

She walked over to them and stood at the edge of their circle, waiting for a break in the conversation. When it came, she turned to Debbie.

'Hello, Debbie. It's been a long time.'

Debbie stared at her blankly. Then recognition obviously began to dawn.

'Celia?'

'Yes, Debbie, it's me.'

'Celia, you look so young! I mean …'

'Thanks, Debbie. Yes, I hope I'm no longer the woman you remember.'

'Keith, it's Celia!'

Keith turned to her. 'Well, I must say you're the last person I expected to see here after the way that bastard treated you.'

Celia was taken aback: what a crass remark to make about Charles at his funeral! She was tempted to say as much, but it would probably be for the best to ignore it. She noticed that Debbie was looking horrified, and the other couple present were staring at Keith disbelievingly.

Celia was grateful to Debbie for rescuing the situation by introducing her to the couple, Gordon and Margy. Debbie then turned to the other woman present, a very thin elderly lady, and was obviously about to effect another introduction when the woman stepped towards Celia, saying 'Celia! Oh, Celia! How good to see you!'

The face and figure were unrecognisable, but her voice hadn't changed.

'Gillian! Oh, Gillian!' The two flung their arms around each other and exchanged kisses. When the embrace was over, Celia noticed that Gordon was staring at them with a look of total amazement. Well, he would, wouldn't he?

Jeanette hadn't wanted to come to the funeral nor to the wake. She was sure the only person there whom she'd know would be Gordon, and she'd said all she had to say to him when they last met in Staffridge. She liked Gordon, but he was part of the past, a past that included Jeremy Jarvis, and which she'd now put to bed. It had been with relief that she'd returned south to the life she'd made with her family. But the summons from the executor to attend the funeral was couched in such terms that implied that her absence would cause disruption to the proceedings.

She entered the lounge. There was no one there she recognised, apart from Gordon, of course, and he was talking to the woman whom he'd been standing next to at the crematorium; his wife, probably. Jeanette stood alone, feeling a bit of a spare part.

Her attention was drawn to two women, standing close together, and talking with such animation that their voices were clearly audible. One of them looked much older than the rest of the assembled company.

Then she heard the younger of the two women say, 'Oh Gillian, I'd completely forgotten that.'

Gillian? *Gillian?* Was that painfully thin, wizened old woman really Gillian Tebbit? The one person, apart from Charles Pettifer, whom she'd hoped never to see again? Then she heard her speak: yes, the voice was definitely Gillian's. Jeanette moved to the far side of the room to distance herself from her.

Then it occurred to her. If she couldn't recognise Gillian Tebbit, then she herself would probably be unrecognisable, for her appearance had also changed since last they'd met. *But at least mine has changed for the better.* On thinking that, she was almost tempted to make herself known just to see the look on Gillian's face.

At last, they're all here, thought Katia. It was nearly two o'clock, the time that Sobers was due to arrive. She entered the lounge. All the guests were standing; some of them were talking, others were standing alone.

She cleared her throat. 'Ladies and gentlemen, can I ask you all to take a seat? The solicitor is about to arrive, and we all need – '

The doorbell rang, and Katia hurried back to the hall to let him in.

'Good afternoon, Ms Whittaker. I'm on time. Are all the beneficiaries present?'

Katia thought he seemed rather less self-assured that he'd been at their last encounter. Perhaps he was one of those men who needed to be behind a desk to assert his authority. Or maybe he, like her, was apprehensive about what was to follow?

'Yes, they're all here, Mr Sobers. Come into the lounge.'

She led him in.

'May I introduce Mr Sobers, Mr Pettifer's solicitor. Please take a seat, Mr Sobers.'

'I'd prefer to remain standing.'

Katia hadn't considered that he might wish to adopt

a formal position rather than sit in an easy chair along with all the others. She glanced round at the assembly – *oh my God, where's Mrs Williams?*

'If you'll excuse me, Mr Sobers, one of our number isn't present. I'll go and find her.'

Why, wondered Katia as she entered the hall, had that damn woman chosen the very time of Sobers's arrival to visit the toilet? But the door to the downstairs toilet was ajar. Had she gone to the upstairs loo, maybe, and if so, why? She ran up the stairs. The door to the toilet was closed. She rapped on the door. 'Mrs Williams, are you in there? The solicitor's arrived.' No response.

Then, standing bemused on the landing, she heard, coming from what used to be Charles's bedroom, a sound like a drawer being tugged open. She charged into the room. Mrs Williams was in there. Drawers to the bedside cabinet were open, and she was kneeling, rooking about in one of them.

'Mrs Williams! What the hell are you doing in here?'

She turned and stared at Katia. There was not a trace of guilt in her expression. 'What d'yer mean? I've got as much right to be in 'ere as you 'ave.'

'You have no right at all! And certainly no right to be searching though the deceased's belongings.'

Mrs Williams rose slowly to her feet. She had to clutch the cabinet while doing so.

'You snotty-nosed bitch! I were lookin' to see if there's anything what I mighta left 'ere when I was Charlie's cleaner.'

Stay calm, Katia told herself, *don't descend to her level*. 'We don't have time to discuss this now. The solicitor is in the lounge, ready to read Mr Pettifer's will. He can't begin until everyone's present. So will you please go downstairs, Mrs Williams. I'll follow you.'

Mrs Williams lumbered along the landing and slowly descended the stairs.

Katia found she was now dreading the reading of

the will, and regretting that she'd agreed to be Charles's executor.

Chapter 28

Katia followed Annie Williams into the lounge. The occupants were sitting in silence and the tension in the room was palpable. Maxwell Sobers was standing in front of the chair provided for him, in the same pose he'd adopted before Katia had left to search for Annie. It struck Katia how youthful he looked in comparison to everyone else.

'I'm sorry for the delay, Mr Sobers, but it seems we're all ready, at last.' She said this with a glance at Annie, who had subsided onto one of the settees and was panting slightly. Katia took the only remaining available seat, next to Keith Barker.

'Thank you, Ms Whittaker.' Sobers reached down and pulled some sheets of paper from his briefcase, then cleared his throat.

'You will all be aware that it was the deceased's wish that his last will and testament be read out loud to the beneficiaries. I have to say that this is a most unusual way to proceed. I must therefore ask for your co-operation by not interrupting me, and that you refrain from making any comments while I am reading. In addition, as soon as I have completed the reading, I shall leave immediately, as I do not wish to be party to any discussion you may have once I have finished.'

Katia heard Keith mutter 'pompous git,' but if Sobers heard him he chose to ignore it.

'There are two other matters about which I have to inform you before

I commence the reading. Firstly, one of the beneficiaries, Mr Rodney Barnes, is unable to attend as a result of illness. He has, however, agreed to his legacy being read out at this meeting.'

He cleared his throat again before resuming.

'The second matter is of greater importance. When the deceased wrote his will, this house had not been valued. He therefore made bequests to beneficiaries in terms of percentages of the total estate. However, this house has now been valued, and I can inform you that the total estate amounts to something in the region of £950,000.'

There were intakes of breath at this revelation. Katia heard Keith mutter, 'Fuckin' hell!'

Sobers held up his palm in a gesture that requested total silence.

'However, I am obliged to read out the will as signed by the deceased, so shall refer to the percentages of the estate bequeathed to each beneficiary. Those of you who are adept at mental arithmetic will no doubt be able to calculate the monetary value of each bequest.'

He smiled as he uttered the last sentence, then hesitated, as though he were waiting for his wit to be acknowledged by laughter. He waited in vain.

'Finally,' he said, 'there are those amongst you who have not received a financial bequest, but have been left specific items, doubtless of sentimental value. Assuming I have made everything clear, I shall now proceed to read out the will.'

People shuffled in their seats as they prepared for the last act. Katia noticed that Annie Williams was groping in her pocket, and – *oh heavens, surely not?* – she produced a packet of cigarettes.

'Before yer start, mister, are there any ashtrays in 'ere?'

Katia intervened. 'Mrs Williams, I'm sure I speak for everybody when I say it would be most inappropriate to smoke at this time, and in any case, you should consider the comfort of those of us here who are non-smokers.'

Mrs Williams scowled, but replaced the cigarette packet in her pocket, as she did so, muttering 'Charlie let me smoke, didn't 'e? And 'e 'ad a fag with me quite often.'

'Please proceed, Mr Sobers,' said Katia.

Sobers looked uneasy as he shuffled the papers in

his hand.

'Very well.' He referred to one of the papers and began reading.

'I, Charles Pettifer of 58 Stannet Crescent, Littleton Parva, revoke all former wills and testamentary dispositions and declare this to be my last will and testament. I appoint Katia Whittaker to be sole executor of this will. I set my hand to this will on 26 February 2019. Signed Charles Pettifer in the presence of Maxwell Sobers and Arthur Bailey, both of Hassle Legal Services.'

He cleared his throat again before continuing to read.

'The percentages in these bequests refer in each case to the percentage of my total estate. To Rodney Baines, I bequeath ten per cent, in gratitude for his friendship which made my schooldays tolerable. To Gordon and Margaret Tagg, I bequeath ten per cent, to be divided between them as they think fit, in recognition of Mr Tagg's forbearance when working for me, and of Mrs Tagg's delightful presence at an office Christmas party.'

Katia observed the Taggs raising their eyebrows at each other.

'To Katia Whittaker, I bequeath ten per cent in gratitude for the care and companionship she provided during my illness, and for her skill in enabling me to come to terms with at least some of my past.'

Katia was relieved that Charles had been less effusive than in the draft of the will that he'd shown her.

'To Deborah Barker, my next-door neighbour, I bequeath five per cent in gratitude for her recent visit where she provided the comfort I so badly needed, and with apologies that I rejected her kind offer of further visits.'

At this, Keith Barker half rose to his feet and turned to his wife, before subsiding back in his chair, glowering at her.

'To Gillian Tebbit, my devoted personal assistant for many years, I bequeath twenty-five per cent in

gratitude for her support which went far beyond the call of duty. To Celia Pettifer, still my wife after years of separation, I bequeath thirty per cent in gratitude for the love and support she tried to give me, despite my failure to accept or even acknowledge it.'

Sobers paused as if to allow the company to digest what they had heard. People were shifting in their seats. Katia noticed that Gillian Tebbit and Celia, sitting next to each other, were holding hands, and Deborah Barker seemed to be in tears.

'The remaining bequests,' said Sobers, 'are not monetary. The deceased has left items which were in his possession to the following beneficiaries.' He reached in his briefcase and extracted an envelope and a brown paper parcel.

'To Jeanette Bennett nee Beasley I bequeath the reference that I would have written for her when she applied for a post in Havant, had I been in a position to do so.'

'Mrs Bennett?' Sobers surveyed the gathering. 'This envelope contains your bequest.' Jeanette rose, took the envelope from him and sat down. She didn't open it. Her expression was inscrutable.

'To Mrs Ann Williams, formerly my weekly cleaner, I bequeath the cleaning equipment she left behind when she suddenly left my employment without notice. The items are to be found in the cabinet under the sink in the kitchen.'

Mrs Williams heaved herself from her chair, advanced on Katia and screamed at her. 'Yer a fuckin' bitch! It were you what put Charlie up to that, I bet!'

'Mrs Williams, I can assure you that – '

''Oh, piss off!' With that she turned, waddled out of the room and slammed the door behind her.

The inevitable stunned silence that followed this outburst seemed to be never-ending. Katia, despite her anger at Annie's outburst, noticed Sobers take a handkerchief from his pocket and mop his brow. He had somehow become a diminished figure, no longer in total charge of the proceedings. Eventually, he cleared his throat yet again.

'I shall conclude the reading of the will,' he said in a voice that trembled slightly.

'To Keith Barker, also my next-door neighbour, I bequeath two books I recently purchased with him in mind, with regret that I did not recommend them to him when he was a younger man.'

'Mr Barker? This parcel contains your bequest.'

Keith rose and snatched the parcel from Sobers. He tore it open, glanced at the books and hurled them across the room. He turned to Debbie, shouted, 'I'm going. And I won't be back tonight,' and strode from the room. In the silence that followed, the slamming of the front door made everyone jump.

Sobers picked up his briefcase. 'My business here is concluded. I bid you all good day.'

Katia stood up. 'Thank you, Mr Sobers,' she said, but he had already left. 'Well, ladies and gentlemen, refreshments are available in the kitchen. Please help yourselves.'

She waited until everyone had shuffled out before retrieving the books that Keith had thrown across the room. One was titled *Work on Your Accent*, the other *How to Win Friends and Influence People*. She stowed them away in the bookcase. As she walked into the kitchen, the thought occurred to her that Charles would have benefited from reading the second book himself.

It was a subdued gathering in the kitchen. Nobody was eating, though Gordon and Margaret were sipping coffee and exchanging the odd muted remark. Celia was pouring coffee from the urn into two cups, one of which she then handed to Gillian, touching her shoulder as she did so. Debbie was standing alone, red-eyed and silent, not looking at the array of nibbles on the table in front of her. Jeanette was also standing by herself, not even facing the table. She was grasping the envelope she'd been given, her face screwed into a mask of grim determination.

Katia was accustomed to attending wakes, those held after the funerals of her clients whom she'd nursed and counselled. They were invariably cheerful affairs. Friends and relatives of the deceased were always relieved when the solemnities of the funeral ceremonies were over, because the words 'happy release', used so often to apply to those who'd died after long illnesses, were even more apt for those who'd faced the strain of watching their loved ones decline. It didn't take long before conversations became animated and then laughter began to be heard, at first muted, then hearty. Of course, at most wakes alcohol was available. Katia was now regretting having told the catering company that only beverages and soft drinks were required. But after the scenes enacted in the lounge, she doubted that even booze would have lightened the atmosphere.

The almost whispered conversation between Gordon and Margaret was interrupted by Jeanette marching up to them.

'Here,' she said to Gordon, 'You can take this.' She thrust the brown envelope at him.

'Oh, Jeanette, this is Margy. I don't think you've been introduced. Margy, this is – '

'I'm going to leave now, Gordon. I don't feel like eating, and anyway I've got a long journey ahead of me. I don't want to see whatever Pettifer's written about me, but I know I'll be tempted to read it if I take it with me. So you have it, and promise me you'll tear it up without reading it.'

'If that's what you want, Jeanette, I'll do that.'

'Thanks. I'll be off, then. Nice to see you again.'

'I hope you'll come and see us sometime, Jeanette.'

'No. I won't be doing that. Nothing against you Gordon, but I never want to visit Staffridge again.'

She turned and walked to the door.

'Well!' said Margaret, 'How impolite! I thought

you always said you got on with her. She didn't strike me as being very likeable.'

'I think she's upset, Margy.'

Gillian drained her coffee.

'Thank God that Beasley woman's gone,' she said to Celia. 'I was dreading having to talk to her. I imagine she still dislikes me as much as I do her.'

'Well, Charles used to tell me how you two never got on.'

'I must say she looks a lot better than she used to, though. When she was in the planning office she dressed like an old-fashioned school-marm. She never wore make-up either. And she wore thick horn-rimmed glasses and had frizzy hair. But she's still got her big nose.'

'D'you have any idea what Charles might have written; you know, the reference he would have written had he been allowed to?'

'Nothing good, I bet. She was very disloyal to Charles. Didn't he tell you about it? Look, Celia, I'm awfully sorry, but I'm going to have to go. I'm looking after my grandson, and I need to be home by five.'

'I never knew you had a grandson!'

'Yes, just the one grandchild. I don't see much of him or his mum since Arthur left me.'

'Arthur left you?'

'Yes, years ago, soon after I had to give up work. We've got a lot of catching up to do, haven't we? And I'd like to be relaxed when we do it. This afternoon's been a bit of a strain.'

'Shall we meet up sometime soon then? I can come up to Staffridge any time.'

'Oh, that would be lovely! Let's make it very soon. It's been so nice seeing you again.'

They hugged. 'I've not even thanked you for all you did for Charles,' said Celia. 'And you know I don't just mean at work. Come on, I'll walk to the front door with you.'

After another embrace at the front door, Celia returned to the kitchen. There were so few people left that it was embarrassing. Nobody appeared to have eaten anything. The only person whom Celia knew was Debbie Barker, still standing by herself, still looking tearful.

'Are you alright, Debbie?' asked Celia, and then realised what a stupid question that was.

'Oh, thank God you're still here. I thought you might have left with that Gillian woman, the one who was Pettifer's secretary. And, no, I'm not all right. Charles's funeral was upsetting enough, then bloody Keith ... ' She sniffed.

'Is there anything I can do to help?'

Debbie reached for a handkerchief and dabbed her eyes.

'Yes, there is. I can't stand it in here any longer. I'm going to go home. I only live next door – oh, you know that don't you? You and Charles came to dinner, just the once. And you came and spoke to me just before you left him.'

'I remember both those occasions very clearly, Debbie.'

'What I was going to ask was ... would you mind coming home with me for a bit? I'm not sure I can face being in an empty house. I'd like to talk to you, if you've got the time.'

'Of course I'll come with you. Shall we go now?'

'Yes, let's.'

Before following Debbie out, Celia approached Katia, who was standing with the only two people remaining. 'Thank you for all you've done today. I'm sorry things didn't turn out too well.'

Katia, Gordon and Margaret stood in awkward silence. There was nothing left to say. The table in front of them, laden with food that hadn't been touched, was testimony to the calamitous afternoon.

Eventually, Gordon spoke. 'Well, Ms Whittaker,

I'm sorry, but there seems little point in our remaining here. I can only repeat what Mrs Pettifer said and thank you for all your efforts in organising everything. Before we go, is there anything we can do to help, maybe by clearing this table?'

'Thank you for the offer, Mr Tagg, but it's better left to the catering company. I'll need to stay here until they arrive.'

'If you're sure about that, then we'll say goodbye. And thanks again for everything you've done.'

After they'd left, Katia poured herself a cup of coffee – the urn was full, so the coffee was still warm – and sank back onto a kitchen chair. What an unmitigated disaster! Why the hell hadn't she told Charles that she could not be party to his will being read aloud? Why had she agreed to be his executor? Many of the mourners – well, those who could be called mourners – probably blamed her for what had transpired. Charles Pettifer had taken advantage of her friendship. She should never have counselled him; she should just have performed her medical duties.

And yet ... he'd left her a large sum of money, always assuming she'd be permitted to have it. Perhaps she was wrong to think he'd just taken advantage of her? And he'd referred to her kindly in his will, hadn't he?

She knew what was bugging her. He'd died before she'd had a chance to get him to talk more about his history, in particular his childhood, and his marriage. She hadn't nearly enough material on which to base a dissertation for a Ph.D. But she'd already started thinking about an alternative course of study, and today's events had heightened her interest in that.

Chapter 29

Debbie led Celia into the lounge.

'Oh, what a relief to be out of that house! What a terrible afternoon – sorry, Celia, it must have been much worse for you. I know this must sound strange, but I kept forgetting you were Charles's widow.'

'I'm not surprised, Debbie. Once I got settled with my sister in Leamington, I almost forgot I was his wife.'

'Sit down, won't you? Don't know about you, but I'm dying for a cup of tea, and I'm suddenly peckish. I've got some cake if you fancy some.'

'Tea would be great, and yes, so would some cake.'

'Be back with you in a second. Make yourself at home.'

Celia sat back on the settee and stared round the room. She hadn't noticed when she'd entered, but the room was almost as it had been when she was last in here, decades ago, though the furniture was now shabby and the carpet threadbare. Yet somehow it didn't seem lived-in. There were no ornaments, no pictures on the walls, just a large bookcase containing paperbacks.

She was facing the door and was taken back to the time when Debbie's children had come through it to be introduced to her and Charles, and how dismissive of them Charles had been. That had been a stressful evening for her; Charles had focused his attention on Debbie when he wasn't lecturing Keith, and she felt, as she often did when in his company, that he would have preferred her not to be there. And after the meal was over, Debbie had seemed eager for them to leave. That was after Charles had followed her into the kitchen, and Celia had wondered – had he perhaps tried his old tricks in there?

Debbie came in bearing a tray, and she placed a teapot, cups and a plate containing slices of cake on the table in front of her.

'Help yourself to cake, Celia. Do you take sugar? I

bet you don't; you're still marvellously slim.'

Celia laughed. 'I was always as skinny as a rake, don't you remember? In fact I've put on a bit of weight since you last saw me.'

'Well, it suits you. You look marvellous, and I love that outfit you're wearing. It's very smart.'

'Makes a change from the sort of gear I used to wear when I was living with Charles, eh?'

She took a bite of cake. It was obviously shop-bought. Debbie hadn't responded to her question – she was probably embarrassed.

'Anyway, enough about me. How are *you*?'

Debbie's face crumpled. 'Not good. You saw how Keith behaved back there, and what he said to me when he left. He's impossible, Celia. He's rude to what few friends I have and beastly to me. It's been like that for years.'

'Oh, I am sorry. Would it help if you told me more about it?'

'Not really. I've accepted the fact that the marriage is over. I'm steeling myself to tell him that. No, what I need now is some distraction. I've got so many questions I'd like to ask you.'

I bet you have, thought Celia. And now that Charles was dead, there'd probably be no harm in telling her what she obviously wanted to know.

'Fire away, Debbie.'

'You and that Gillian Tebbit. I didn't know you'd even met her, but you behaved like you were old friends.'

'It didn't start out that way, but I came to depend on Gillian as much as Charles did. You see, she was able to provide him with the comfort that I wasn't able to.'

'Comfort? You don't mean …?

Celia smiled. 'Not exactly. But you need to know more about Charles before you'll understand. Do you remember the day I called to tell you I was leaving Charles? I think I told you not to think too badly of him, because he had problems. Well, Gillian was able to help him with those.'

Debbie continued to look puzzled. 'I'm still not sure I understand.'

'I think I'd better start from the beginning. Could I have another cup of tea, please?'

While Debbie was pouring the tea Celia was wondering just how explicit she should be. But there was no point in hiding the truth, and she had nothing to be ashamed of. She took a sip of tea.

'I met Charles when we were both 23. He was in lodgings in the house next door to where I lived with my parents. He'd just started his first job as a junior in the local planning office. I was a teacher at the local primary school. We both caught the same bus into work, and we started chatting. He used to chat to my father as well – they met in the local shop.'

She hesitated and took another sip of tea.

'I should tell you that my parents were members of a very strict Baptist church. I had a very strict upbringing. They didn't let me do any of the things young people were doing at the time, and I wasn't allowed to dress like them. It was still like that even when I was 19. Can you imagine it – 1966, miniskirts and rock music, and I'd have been thrown out of the house if my skirts had been less than two inches below the knee!'

'Weren't you allowed to go out with other young people, then?'

'Only those who were members of our chapel, and that meant no discos, no dances, no pubs, and no way could I be by myself with a young man.'

'Weren't you ever tempted to rebel?'

'No. My sister did, though. She's six years older than me and started misbehaving when she was thirteen. When she was sixteen she met a boy and started seeing him, with his parents' approval. There was an almighty row and my parents threw her out. She went to live with the boy's parents, and, to cut a long story short, ended up marrying the boy. She was lucky – he's not only very nice, but very rich. Anyway, after she left home, my parents were even stricter with me.'

'How awful for you.'

'Well, yes, but you see I took on board all my parents' beliefs and prejudices, and that included sex. Sex was for procreation only, and it was made quite clear that we, especially women, weren't supposed to enjoy it.'

'Bloody hell.'

'Anyway, back to Charles. My father got friendly with him. He said he was an upright, sensible young man even though he wasn't a Baptist. It was probably because he dressed as though it was still the early 1950s and was always polite. Daddy invited him round for a meal, and Mummy liked him as well. They thought he was a suitable young man for me, and after a while, they let me go out with him.'

'Did you fancy him, Celia?'

Celia laughed. 'I didn't know what "fancy" meant! It felt like just having a friend, and God knows I needed one. We went for walks, and occasionally to the cinema, so long as the film was a U certificate. Charles never made any advances. It was at least six months before we started holding hands.'

Celia paused. There was so much more she could tell about their courtship, if such it could be called, but she wasn't here to tell Debbie her entire life history. She knew that what Debbie really wanted to hear about was Gillian.

'To cut a long story short, we got married, with my parents' approval of course. All through our courtship we'd never touched each other intimately. Charles made no approaches at all, and I was grateful for that. So, as you can imagine, our wedding night was a complete disaster. I just lay there, terrified, and Charles ... well, after getting no response from me, he gave up, turned over and went to sleep. We never talked about it afterwards. We never made love, ever.'

Debbie made no comment about that, just stared at her with a look of disbelief.

'Our marriage became a bit like sharing a house

with a friend, no, an acquaintance, really. Charles started to become more distant; all he talked about was his job and how he wanted to advance his career.'

'I can sympathise with you there.'

'But things began to change for me, Debbie. I found I wanted children, even though that would have meant having sex, something I was still terrified of. I told Charles I wanted them, and that was when he first lost his temper with me. He told me that raising a child would get in the way of his career, and then said that he wanted me to give up my job so I could devote time to running the house. It was just after that when he got his job here in Staffridge, and a few years later we moved next door to you.'

'Why on earth did you stay with him, Celia?'

'Where would I have gone? My parents wouldn't have had me back; they always said it was a sin to leave your spouse. The thought of setting up on my own frightened me, even if I could have afforded it. I had no alternative but to stay with him. Debbie, I'm sorry, but I need to use your toilet, please.'

'It's the door opposite you when you get to the top of the stairs.'

Debbie was finding it all hard to take in. Celia's story was so far removed from anything she'd heard before. True, some women she'd known had had marital problems, but nothing like Celia's. A lifetime without sex! At least that was something she and Keith hadn't experienced, not until recently, anyway. From what Debbie had heard from Gordon and Margy about Charles's philandering, let alone the fact that he'd once come on to her in her kitchen, she found it hard to comprehend that he could have tolerated a celibate marriage, but then perhaps that was the reason why he behaved as he did? It then occurred to her that in one respect Pettifer and Keith were similar, but after he'd retired Keith had at least found a new interest, the Labour party. What had filled Charles's days in retirement, living alone as he did? Of course, it might have been Gillian Tebbit. Debbie began to feel impatient with Celia for the way she seemed to be holding out on telling her about Gillian.

'Would you like another cup of tea?' she asked as Celia entered.

'No thanks, Debbie.' She sat down. 'Now, where was I?'

'You'd just arrived in Staffridge, and I assume that's when Gillian Tebbit came on the scene.'

'Well, almost. She didn't become his PA until he became chief planning officer of course, but even before that he'd mentioned her a few times. When he was promoted, he started talking about her a lot. He praised her to the skies for her efficiency and the support she gave him. I first met her when she came round on a Saturday to deliver some office stuff.'

'So, she came round to your house while you were there?'

'Yes. And she started coming quite frequently. I noticed how fond of Charles she seemed, and it looked like he felt the same way about her. But she was very friendly towards me as well, and … I got to like her. One day she came round when Charles was out, and … and we started talking about him. You won't believe this Debbie, but I, well … I confided in her about our marital problems. I was so lonely, you see, and I desperately needed to talk to someone.'

'I can understand that, Celia.' Debbie noticed that Celia's speech was becoming more hesitant. She'd been very articulate up until now.

'A few months after that conversation, Gillian phoned me. Charles was away at a conference at the time. She asked if she could come and see me as she had something to tell me that I ought to know. All sorts of things went through my head, but I wasn't prepared for what she told me.'

She started to breathe deeply, and was no longer looking Debbie in the face.

'Take your time, Celia.'

'She ... told me she was sorry, but I ought to know that Charles had started taking her out, for lunchtime drinks start with, but more recently in the evenings.'

'Good heavens! What did you think about that?'

'I knew all about it. Charles had told me. I didn't mind. It had taken the pressure off me, because Charles was more relaxed and friendly than he'd been for ages.'

She took a few more deep breaths.

'Then she told me she'd always fancied Charles even though he had the reputation in the department of being a bit of a toucher. When they got to know each other better, she told him that we'd spoken and that she knew all about the problems in our marriage.'

Debbie was aghast. She wondered how she'd feel if she discovered that Keith was confiding in another woman. Maybe he was?

'How on earth could you carry on talking to the woman knowing she'd broken a confidence?'

'I'd got to the stage where nothing could shock me. And I still liked her, despite everything. Anyway, after she'd told him about our marriage, he asked her to meet him at a hotel one evening. He'd booked a room there for the night. She went. After a few drinks in the bar she said ... she said she might be able to help him, and maybe they should go up to the bedroom.'

She stopped talking. Debbie had the strange sensation that she was watching the start of a porn movie. After taking another deep breath, Celia resumed.

'She said that when they got up to bedroom they sat on the bed and she started cuddling him. She said she expected him to respond, but he didn't. He looked almost tearful, and he told her the problems in our marriage weren't all down to me. Then he said he valued her friendship and that he was going to tell her something in complete confidence, and that she wasn't to tell anyone.'

'But I assume she told you?'

'Yes. It was something I'd sometimes suspected,

but I thought it was all my fault. He told her … he confessed he was impotent and always had been. He'd never in his life had sex with anyone.'

Epilogue

Gordon and Margaret were sitting in the garden, making the most of the September sunshine. It had been a strange summer, weather-wise; days of hot sunshine, interrupted by torrential downpours. The grass was still as green as it had been in spring, and the leaves showed no sign of turning.

'Well, Gordy, after a morning doing nothing, your back must be better now, surely?'

'Yes, it is. But the trouble with sitting out here is that I keep noticing what a mess the garden's in.'

'Maybe it's time you thought about getting a gardener in? For the heavy work, at least.'

'I've been dreading the day you'd say that, Margy. It means you must think I'm getting old. No, I'll wait and see how I feel next spring.'

He levered himself out of the deckchair, managing as he did so to prevent himself from wincing. 'There's life in the old dog yet. I'll go and get us some lunch.'

'So you'll be okay to go to the Candelabra tonight, will you?'

'Try and stop me! I'm looking forward to seeing Paul chatting up Debbie.'

'Just cheese and biscuits for me, Gordy,' Margaret shouted as he walked towards the house.

Left to herself, Margaret's thoughts turned to Debbie, who'd changed remarkably over the summer. Apparently, Celia came to stay with her occasionally, and it was probably down to her that the change had come. At first, it had just been her appearance: she now dressed smartly, had a short hairstyle which suited her, and her make-up was carefully applied. And recently she seemed to have grown in confidence, as evidenced by her upright stance and assertive walk. A fortnight ago, Margaret and Gordon had persuaded her to join them and their friends at their usual meeting-place, the Candelabra, where a band played, quietly, songs from the 1960s to an appreciative audience. Debbie had been reluctant to attend, but once there, and after a few numbers had been played, she'd seemed to shed years and began to sing along. Gordon's old friend Paul Morgan, a widower, had joined her in the singing. Then he'd started to chat to her, and the pair began to laugh heartily; something, Margaret had realised, she'd never seen Debbie do before. She had taken little persuading to come to the Candelabra tonight. Like Gordon, Margaret was wondering if something might come from her second meeting with Paul.

Gordon emerged from the kitchen carrying a tray.

'Cheese and biscuits as ordered, madam, and a cup of tea.' He put the tray on the ground in front of her deckchair.

'Aren't you having anything?'

'I had a banana while I was waiting for the kettle to boil. I really must lose some weight. The grub that's served at the Candelabra is very inviting, and I know I'll be tempted.'

He eased himself back into his deckchair.

'I've been thinking about Debbie,' said Margaret. 'I know we've said this before, but I still find it strange that she's never once mentioned Keith since the day he left her, not even to slag him off. It's almost as though she's forgotten him.'

'Don't you reckon that's the best thing she could do?'

'And how come she's still living in the marital home? And it seems Keith didn't take the car.'

'Maybe the bastard's got a bit of a conscience after all. He's shacked up with that woman in the Labour Party; maybe he feels guilty about that?'

'But surely he'll want his share of the house? What will Debbie do then? She didn't inherit all that much from you-know-who, did she? She won't be able to afford to buy Keith out. And that's somebody else she never mentions. You-know-who.'

'But we never mention him either, do we? What's gone's forgotten. Anyway, Margy, she might be on to a good thing with Paul. He's quite well off.'

'It'll be interesting to see how they get on tonight. He's obviously taken with her.'

'Isn't it a relief not to have to go through all that again?'

'Through all what?'

'Oh, you know, chatting up, courtship, first time sex. I found that hard enough when I was young. Heaven knows how old folk manage to summon up the energy. Thank God I've still got you, Margy.'

Gordon reached for Margaret's hand and held it until she pulled it away to reach for her cup of tea.

***

'We'll have to face up to it, Dad,' said Kevin as they entered the ward, 'Mum hasn't got long. I spoke to the consultant yesterday, he said it was a massive stroke, and even if she pulls through, she'll be disabled.'

'Best if she don't then,' said Bert.

Curtains were drawn around Annie's bed. Kevin pushed them aside. A nurse, a black woman, was sitting by the bedside, holding Annie's hand. She'd been there yesterday when Kevin had visited. Knowing his dad's attitude to black people, Kevin wished he'd warned him about this.

'How is she?' he asked.

'She's comfortable, Mr Williams, not in any pain.'

'Does she know what's going on?'

'It's always hard to say with stroke victims. Sometimes she gets a bit agitated, but she calms down when I hold her hand.'

''Well I can 'old 'er 'and now, can't I?' said Bert. 'No need for you to stay 'ere.'

'Of course, Mr Williams.' The nurse got up and offered Bert her seat, then pushed through the curtains.

Kevin followed her.

'Just a minute, nurse. I'm sorry if my father sounded rude. He's very upset.'

'Oh, don't worry about that, I quite understand.'

'Has Mum ever spoken to you? When I was in here yesterday, she had her eyes open and I think she knew who I was, but she didn't say anything when I spoke to her.'

'It's always hard to know how aware people are when they're in your mother's condition. But yes, she has spoken to me. Could I ask, does she know anyone called Katia?'

'Katia? No, don't think so. Why?'

'Yesterday after you left I went in to see how she was. When she opened her eyes and saw me she said, "Katia!" and grabbed my hand. She keeps calling me Katia. And this morning she said, "I'm sorry, Katia". Any idea what that might be about?'

'No, sorry, no idea. Can you tell me how long she's got?'

'She could go any time, I'm afraid.'

'When we leave, will you go back to sit with her? Don't like to think of her by herself.'

'Well, I do have other duties Mr Williams, but when I'm not with her the other nurses on duty in the ward will go in as often as possible to see how she is.'

'If ... if she seems to be on the way out and someone else is with her, could they call you so *you* could be with her?'

'If I'm on duty and there's no other emergency, well, yes, I'll do my best. Now if you'll excuse me, I have another patient to see to.'

'Thanks very much, nurse.'

Kevin went back through the curtains. Bert was sitting by the bed, holding Annie's hand.

'Has she said anything, Dad?'

Bert turned towards him. Could those be tears in his eyes? Kevin had rarely seen his father express any emotion, and certainly not sorrow.

236

'Yeah, she's said something alright. But she ain't spoken to me, 'as she? She keeps asking for bloody Katia.'

'Yes, the nurse told me she keeps doing that. D'you know who Katia is?'

'You mean yer don't remember? Yer never did take much notice of what yer mum talked about, did yer? Katia was that bitch who did Annie out of the money what Charlie Pettifer was gunna leave her. Why the fuck does she keep asking for her?'

***

Jeanette was in bed, laying on her back, eyes wide open. Sleep wouldn't come. She assumed Andrew was dozing, but he suddenly turned towards her and grasped her hand.

'Jeanette, won't you please tell me what's troubling you?' he said. 'You've not been yourself for several weeks. Why won't you talk to me?'

'I'm sorry, Andy. I don't know what's wrong with me. I'm depressed, and I don't know why. I'm sure I'll shake out of it soon.'

'Would a cuddle help?'

'Just a cuddle, darling. I'm not in the mood for anything else at the moment. Maybe in the morning, when I've had some sleep.'

'Come here, then.'

He turned onto his back and pulled her towards him. She rested her head against his chest. 'I love you, Andy.'

'And I love you, darling'. He caressed the back of her neck. 'You're all tense. Try to relax.'

It was good to be comforted, but she was unable to relax. They lay cuddling for some time, then she became aware that although his hand was still on her neck, it was no longer stroking her. His breathing began to deepen and then his hand slipped away from her. He'd fallen asleep.

She eased her head from his chest and slowly moved back into her former position, on her back, eyes open. She was now feeling guilty because she hadn't been honest with him. She knew why she was depressed. Staffridge had come back to taunt her.

On returning home after Charles Pettifer's funeral, she'd felt only relief to be away from the discord that had resulted from the reading of his will. She'd settled back into her comfortable domestic routine; she and Andy visited their son and grandson frequently, and after a while she hardly gave Pettifer's funeral any thought.

Then suddenly, about a fortnight ago, for some reason she couldn't understand, she began thinking about Pettifer's bequest to her, the reference he said he would have written for her had he been in a position to do so. She'd thought she'd done the right thing in handing the unopened envelope to Gordon Tagg, but it began to seem like an act of cowardice, an admission that despite the confidence she'd gained since working in Havant, she still wasn't up to facing whatever vitriol Pettifer had written.

Then, no doubt as a result of thinking about Gordon, she'd begun to mull over her visit to Staffridge and her reunion with Gordon and Jeremy Jarvis. The sense of betrayal that she'd felt on learning about Jeremy having slept with Gillian Tagg had begun to re-emerge. Although Jeremy had insisted he'd just been using Gillian, why hadn't he told her about it at the time? Even the fact that Jeremy had written a reference for her was now something for which she felt no gratitude. Somehow, she felt she'd been patronised.

It was a lunch-time gathering with some of her friends just over a week ago that had been the tipping-point. They were all women of about her own age, and the conversation had turned to the way they thought about their younger days. Her companions had all agreed that being in their thirties had been the age they'd enjoyed the most – still young enough to misbehave on occasions, yet sufficiently self-confident not to care what others thought of them, nor to be assailed by the guilt-tinged uncertainties they'd had when in their teens and early twenties.

Jeanette had left without finishing her lunch. She couldn't participate because she could remember few joyous occasions in her thirties. She'd never really become reconciled to her appearance in her teens and twenties, and had compensated for it by immersing herself in her studies, then in pursuing a career. She'd been full of hope when she moved to Staffridge to take up a senior post – this was when she'd assumed she'd gain the sort of confidence of which her lunch-time companions had spoken. But she hadn't.

Now, laying wide awake next to a sleeping Andy, she felt overcome by grief. She didn't want to wake him by weeping, so carefully eased herself out of bed, pulled on her dressing gown and went downstairs to the lounge. She left the lights turned off: darkness was appropriate to her mood. Wasn't it at times like these that people sought comfort in alcohol? But she'd never acquired a taste for it; had been appalled by the behaviour of her fellow students when they used to return to her hall of residence, shrieking and whooping, after an evening of debauchery.

She sank back into an armchair. *Get a grip, woman. Think how well things have turned out for you.* And they had turned out well, hadn't they, eventually? Successful career after she'd turned forty, a loving husband, a delightful son, a circle of friends, a comfortable house. But she was getting old, and old age wasn't something to look forward to, especially when one had regrets about the past. And the great regret she had, the one that had brought on her sudden depression, was that so much of her youth had been lonely, and that in her thirties, in Staffridgeshire, unhappiness had been piled on top of loneliness. Half her life had been wasted.

And it was all down to one man. She stopped weeping. Her sorrow was being overtaken by anger. That man had bullied her, demeaned her in front of her colleagues, and, she now realised, had, by his corrupt and immoral behaviour, prevented Jeremy Jarvis from becoming more than just a friend. He had robbed her of part of her youth.

Jeanette hated bad language and rarely used it apart from the occasional 'bloody' when something annoyed or frustrated her. But she knew all the words; how could she not, given that these days most people laced every sentence with them? Now, under her breath, she employed them all, directed at Charles Pettifer. In one respect, she regretted he was dead. She wished he was present so she could shout abuse at him.

***

Celia embraced Gillian as soon as she entered the house.

'Lovely to see you again so soon, Gilly. And I'm so glad you managed to come to me.'

'I'm glad I made it. The journey wasn't as bad as I thought, only one change at Birmingham. I must say it makes a pleasant change to get away from home.'

'That's good to hear. You can stay as long as you want. Barbara and Eddie will be away for a fortnight. Now the kids have left home they always go on holiday in September; everywhere's so less crowded at this time of year. Anyway, come in, I've prepared a light lunch. First let me take your case up to the bedroom.'

Gillian followed her up the stairs.

'What a beautiful spacious bedroom, Celia! It's a huge house, isn't it?'

'Eddie's a top-notch solicitor, just coming up to retirement, and he had money anyway, left him by his grandfather. I count myself lucky that their house is so big. It meant that he and Barbara could take me in when I left Charles. Do you want to freshen up before lunch? The bathroom's en-suite, just through there.'

'Yes, I will. I'll only be a few minutes.'

'I'll be in the dining room.'

As Celia waited for Gillian to join her, she was hoping that the surprise she'd had when she'd come into the house hadn't been too obvious. Gillian looked so much better than when Celia had last seen her; still thin but no longer emaciated, still wrinkled but not wizened, and her hair was no longer grey.

'Lovely en-suite,' said Gillian as she entered. 'Better equipped than my one bathroom.'

'Sit down, Gilly, and help yourself. It's only a snack, but I thought we might go out for a meal this evening. We've got some good eating places in Leamington. Would that be okay by you, or do you want an early night?'

'No, eating out's fine by me,' said Gillian as she helped herself to some brie. 'I don't get to eat out much; it's no fun being by yourself in a restaurant.'

Celia watched as Gillian tucked into her brie-coated crackers. She certainly seemed to have an appetite. That probably accounted for her weight gain.

'Gilly, I hope you don't mind my saying, but you look so much better than when I last saw you.'

Gillian spluttered over her cracker, then laughed. 'I was wondering when you'd comment on that! Well, I do feel much better. I have Charles to thank for that.'

'Charles? How come?'

'All that money he left me! First thing I did when I got hold of it was to go for private medical treatment. I've spent years battling with the NHS, being shuttled from one consultant to another, waiting months for appointments. But I'm sorted now, well, as sorted as I'll ever be.'

'What exactly is your problem, if you don't mind telling me?'

'I'll spare you the gory details, but I've got chronic gut problems. Had them for years. I've had cameras shoved up every orifice I've got. It won't ever get better, but my symptoms are now under control, and I can live my life again. I used to spend half my time in bed. I was getting very depressed. But now I can get out and about again, I feel like a new woman, and I've started paying more attention to how I look.'

'All down to Charles, eh?'

'Yes, but never mind that. There's something I want to ask you.'

'Go ahead. Oh, would you like a coffee?'

'Yes please.'

'Well, go through to the lounge, and I'll bring it in.'

Once in the lounge, seated together on one of the four double-seater settees with coffee cups in hand, Celia said, 'Well? What was it you wanted to ask me?'

'I wondered if you see any of the other women who were at Charles's funeral? I'm not interested in that Beasley woman; I was thinking more of Debbie Barker. I felt so sorry for her when her husband behaved like a lout when Charles's will was read out. I just wondered what's happened to her. I know you see Margaret Tagg sometimes, and I gather she's quite friendly with Debbie.'

'Well, I was going to tell you about that. You know I go and visit Debbie quite often? I've got quite close to her. Anyway, Keith left her. It had been on the cards for ages. He's got another woman, and Debbie was dreading that when the divorce came through the bastard would get half the house. Anyway, I had a phone call from Margy only yesterday and it seems Debbie may have found herself a fella, an old friend of Gordon's.'

'Does that mean she's going to shack up with him? If I was her, I'd want to get out of that house. It must have horrible associations for her, what with Charles having been her neighbour – oh, sorry, Celia! I'd completely forgotten that you'd been her neighbour as well.'

'I think the relationship's in too early a stage for her to think about moving in with him. In any case, she doesn't need to now.'

'How come? Charles didn't leave her that much.'

'No, and I've always felt guilty about that. So I've given her enough money for her to buy Keith out. She insists on calling it a loan, but thanks to Charles, I don't need the money, do I?'

Gillian couldn't think of a response to that because it had occurred to her that now she herself was well off, she also ought to consider deserving cases whom she could help.

Celia put down her cup on the coffee table and turned towards her. Gillian noticed that she looked serious, and several seconds passed before she spoke.

'Gilly, I've got some questions I'd like to ask you.'

'Sounds ominous. What do you want to know?'

'First of all, do you like living in Staffridge?'

'Well, it's my home-town. But to tell the truth, I've not felt at home there, not since … well, you know. Too many people there know about my history. I haven't really made any new friends there since I've lived alone, and my illness didn't help. Why do you ask?'

'Have you ever thought about moving away?'

'Where would I go?'

'How about Leamington?'

'What are you getting at, Celia?'

'Look, Gilly. Barbara and Eddie are thinking of downsizing. This place is far too big for them since the kids left. So I'll be looking for a place of my own. We're both quite wealthy women now, aren't we? And we've got a shared history. Would you consider … I mean, what would you think of us buying a house here so we can live together?'

'You mean …?'

Celia laughed. 'Oh, the look on your face! I haven't become one of *those* women! I'm just suggesting we share a house. I've reached the age where it'll soon be no fun living alone. And Leamington's a nice place. I've made quite a few friends here, and I'm sure you'll like them. You can start a new life, leave the past behind.'

Gillian was speechless. Leaving Staffridge was something that had never crossed her mind. And to live with a woman! Yes, she was very fond of Celia, and she was right about them having a shared past. But how would they get on, being together every day? Might it end disastrously? Would she then be left alone in a strange town?

'Don't worry, Gilly. You don't need to give me an answer now. I've got another suggestion.'

'What's that?'

'Winter will soon be with us, and I find the long nights depressing, don't you? What would you think about us going on a sea cruise, to somewhere where it's warm and sunny? We can well afford it. We could go for three weeks, and that would give us a chance to really get to know each other, wouldn't it? Then you can decide whether you'd like to share a house with me. What do you think?'

Gillian didn't have to think. 'That's a great idea! I'd really like to do that. Where would we go? I've always liked the idea of visiting the West Indies.'

'Oh, I'm so pleased! Pity we're only drinking coffee; I think a toast is called for.'

'What shall we drink to?
Celia picked up her cup.
'To Charles, of course!'
Gillian picked up hers.
'To Charles!'

***

Katia walked out of the care home for the final time. She had no regrets about having handed in her resignation soon after Charles Pettifer's funeral, but working out her month's notice had been fraught. Mrs Hemmings had made it obvious that she thought Katia was being unprofessional, abandoning her duties for the sake of financial gain. Consequently, there had been no final goodbye ceremony today. Even her two colleagues had been cool towards her, no doubt envious of her good fortune.

At least David's been at home and will be cooking dinner tonight she thought as she got in her car. His job – he was a journalist - permitted him to take the odd day off, though for Katia the downside of his profession was his frequent lengthy absences attending newsworthy events all over the country. She needed him to be at home and in a relaxed mood this evening; she had something important to tell him.

The traffic on her journey home was stop-start. No doubt yet again the M6 had been closed and the northbound traffic diverted through Staffridge. Katia didn't mind. It was giving her time to think.

She'd been certain for some time that she no longer wanted to be a Macmillan nurse. Quite apart from the workload, it was depressing having to spend most of her days with people who'd received a death sentence. She'd always found it hard to balance the requirement on the one hand to be dispassionate and efficient in discharging her duties, while on the other trying to succour those clients who wanted only comfort and affection. Just occasionally she had a client who was her intellectual equal and with whom she could engage in meaningful conversation, which was of benefit both to the client and to her. Charles Pettifer had been one of those. They'd struck up an accord and Katia had grown to like him, though his will had shown an entirely different side to his personality. And she still felt a lingering resentment that he'd chosen to commit suicide before she'd gleaned enough information about his upbringing and his psyche to form the basis of a Ph.D. dissertation.

But contact with Pettifer and with those who'd attended his funeral had awakened her to a new possibility. She had encountered people from all social classes in the course of her duties. Visiting them in their homes had made her aware of the disparities of wealth and education that still existed in society, and the varying attitudes and prejudices resulting from it. There were all social classes in the care home, but the only opportunity for them to mix was in the communal lounge, and she'd noticed that most of the middle-class residents chose not to go there.

So she'd been fascinated by the varied collection of people who'd attended the Pettifer funeral, and by the way they interacted, or failed to interact, with each other. Mr and Mrs Tagg – obviously comfortably off, southerners, solidly middle-class, but benign and polite to everyone they encountered. Mr Sobers – he had all the haughtiness of his profession and an accent that spoke of a public school education. Mr Barker - he was a conundrum. Apparently he'd been a deputy headmaster, but he had the broadest Yorkshire accent that Katia had ever heard, was dressed as if he were down the pub, and had behaved like a yob. How come his wife was so polite and genteel? Then there was that old, ill-looking woman, Mrs Tebbit, was it? She had a slight north Staffridgeshire accent, but she and Mrs Pettifer, who was as genteel as Mrs Barker, acted as though they were old friends. Then, of course, there was Mrs Williams - aggressively working-class and racist. It had been a long time since Katia had encountered such overt racism.

It had been witnessing the interactions between the so-called mourners that had given Katia the idea of a possible alternative career. She'd done some research into this but hadn't told David. All he knew was that she'd had enough of her job and had handed in her notice. Now she was unemployed, it was time to tell him her intentions. This didn't worry her too much; he was a very supportive partner.

The dinner was already in the oven when she got home, and David was laying the table.

'Well, how was your last day?' he asked after they'd kissed.

'Not good. I could do with a drink.'

'Glass of wine?'

'No, I need a stiff G & T.'

'Think I'll join you. Dinner will be a while yet. Shall we go through to the lounge?'

'Not yet. Before I can relax I need to tell you something.'

'Sounds serious.'

He poured the drinks and they sat at the kitchen

table.

'Go on then, Kat. What's all this about?'

Katia decided to cut straight to the chase.

'I've made up my mind what I'm going to do. You know how I became fascinated by the different social backgrounds of my clients? And by the way people from varying backgrounds interacted at Charles Pettifer's funeral?'

'Yes, Kat. There've been times recently when you've spoken of little else.'

'Well, I've decided to study for a degree in sociology.'

'Sociology? What on earth for? And what sort of career do you think you'd be able to take up afterwards?'

His amazed reaction was what Katia had been expecting.

'Sociology because it analyses many of things I've become interested in – differing cultures in society, inequalities and injustices, the role of the family. As for a career, well there are so many options that I haven't decided yet.'

'But you're going to commit yourself to a three-year course?'

'No. I'm not going to do an undergraduate course; I don't want to commit to three years full-time study. But I could do a part-time two-year course leading to an M.A., and I could get a part-time job while I'm studying.'

'Well, you've certainly given it some thought. Why haven't you told me about it before?'

'I didn't want to bother you until I'd made up my mind.'

'Just one thing, Kat. Most of your education and training so far has been in the sciences. Would you be accepted for a course leading to an M.A.?'

'Oh, these days universities take people from all sorts of educational backgrounds onto M.A. courses. I knew a guy who spent half his life teaching geology, then got accepted to do an M.A. in creative writing, of all things.'

'Well, you know you'll have my full support. And you'll have the money to do it, and with some to spare, so why not? While we've got booze in our hands, let's raise a glass to your new endeavours. Here's to you!'

They clinked their glasses.

'And to Charles Pettifer,' said Katia. 'If I hadn't known him, and without his bequest, I wouldn't even have considered it.'

'You got quite fond of him, didn't you?'

'David, you know very well that I never developed emotional attachments to my clients.'

Lightning Source UK Ltd.
Milton Keynes UK
UKHW040629070220
358338UK00001B/310